THE
BLACK MAST MURDER

A Driftwood Pirate Adventure

ALEX P. BERG

BATDOG PRESS
KNOXVILLE, TN

Batdog Press
www.batdogpress.com

Cover Art: Damon Za
Book Layout: ©2013 BookDesignTemplates.com

The Black Mast Murder / Alex P. Berg — 1st ed.
ISBN 978-1-942274-11-7

1

A warm Caribbean northeasterly blew in through the open window, licking my bare chest with its balmy tongue and seducing me with humid, airy kisses, but despite the vaporous desires of the wind, my eyes couldn't be drawn away from the subject of my own foremost affection: Gwen.

She sat at the edge of our bed, her loose curls—colored like a European hare's coat—cascading down her back over skin that resembled cream, despite the best efforts of the relentless tropical sun. She faced the wall at an angle, and it was because of this kindness that I was able to gaze upon both the curvature of her breasts, partially concealed under her tumbling locks, and the full of her derrière—a round thing that invoked in me feelings of adoration as well as other baser, more burning desires.

I snaked a hand across the surface of the sheets and pinched her bottom, eliciting a squeak and a slap of my hand in response.

Gwen turned her pale aquamarine eyes on me and narrowed them slightly. "You rogue."

"Your one and only." I readied another pinch and lunged.

Gwen parried my fingers with a swift riposte. "Come now, John," she said, shifting further toward the edge of the bed. "You cannot tell me you're still unsatisfied."

"With the divine offerings you provide?" I raised an eyebrow in what I could only hope was a seductive manner. "Never."

Gwen batted her long lashes at me and puckered her full, pink lips. "Truly? Because I seem to recall a tryst three nights past that supported a different conclusion. Despite no small amount of effort on my part, I couldn't seem to satisfy you *even once.*"

I frowned and leaned back into pillows of down. "Now, why would you bring that up? You know I was tired. And by continuing to harp on it, you threaten to undermine the foundations of my fragile, male psyche."

"Perhaps," said Gwen. "But you must acknowledge how the encounter affected me, as well. Like you have now, I had desires that went unfulfilled. Taken as a whole, the entire experience was extremely...*deflating.*"

Gwen smiled an evil smile. There was no doubt in my mind her word choice had been deliberate.

"You're a cruel woman, my love," I said. "Had I learned of your wicked temperament during our courtship, I'd have never taken you as my bride."

Gwen scoffed. "Liar! Your mind was made as soon as you tasted my *divine offerings,* as you called them. But with a name such as yours, at least I was prepared for such fibs."

She referred, of course, to my surname, which she'd accepted as her own: Malarkey. The moniker was a source of never-ending amusement for others as well as exasperation for myself. New acquaintances naturally assumed I was a master of confusion and misdirection and that I relished in the dissemination of balderdash, and it aggravated me to no end that they were so correct in their assessments. In my own humble opinion, never had a namesake been more well deserved by anyone—at least until Gwen took on my family name. Her irreverent personality was perhaps the most attractive of all her virtues, such as they were—although, I have to admit, I hadn't exactly ignored her physical attributes when judging if I should wed her. I glanced at her buttocks and wondered whether another dig of my fingers into her supple flesh would make her reconsider my advances.

Before I could decide on a course of action, Gwen rose from the bed and reached for her smallclothes. She moved fluidly, like one of the African deer the French called *gazelle*, as she drew a thin petticoat up her slender legs and across her milky thighs.

Grace, which came so easily to her in both motion and speech—when she wished it, of course—was not a trait I was particularly blessed with. Gwen and I, so similar in our sharp tongues and nimble minds, differed in so many other respects, physically not least of which, though at least we were consistent in our differentiation.

In almost every respect, she was the light to my darkness. My hair, the hue of damp soil, made hers seem brilliant by comparison, and her eyes, colored like foot-deep shoals, shone next to my blues picked from the deepest ocean depths. There was, also, the matter of our skin: hers, delicate and flawless, and mine, weather-beaten and resembling a piece of worn leather. Some-times I envied Gwen and her pale complexion. It re-minded me of my own prior to having spent a decade in the West Indies, but she seemed to enjoy my tanned hide, so who was I to regret my appearance? And, of course, there were our hearts, with mine almost cer-tainly blacker than hers—though not nearly as sullied as the hearts of other men I'd once known.

"So," I said with a frown as I watched Gwen slip into a thin shift. "I suppose this means our afternoon esca-pades have come to an end?"

Gwen turned, bent over the bed, and placed a gentle hand against my bearded jaw. She followed the gesture by pressing her mouth against mine, refilling the font of my desire with a passionate kiss. All too soon, she pulled back, leaving me with little more than the taste of her tender lips and the scent of her breath, heavy with the syrupy sweetness of the guava that had served as our dessert after supper.

"And usually I'm the one whose longing is insatia-ble," she said with a twinkle in her eyes. "If you're so desperate for more, I'm sure I'll be able to accommodate you later."

Gwen straightened, draped a peignoir across her shoulders, and approached the bedroom window. The sea responded to her presence, whisking forth a curt breeze that billowed her hair and filled the room with scents of salt and spray. The flute-like song of the thrushes wafted in alongside the breeze, as did the symphony of insect noises that always reached a crescendo in the early evening. With the sun sinking low over the horizon, a shadow stretched across the side of her face, casting a sullen pall over her otherwise dazzling features.

As she stared at the sea and its churning waves, her hand resting on the edge of our dresser made of mahogany, or *caoba* as the Spanish called it, I couldn't help but wonder what tickled the far reaches of her mind, as clearly something did. Based on the stillness of her frame and the placement of her gaze, I could only assume it was the same topic that crossed her thoughts with any frequency following our bodily unions. Though our lovemaking was fervent and impassioned—and thoroughly enjoyable for us both, I might add—I could understand how it might elicit unwelcome emotions in Gwen once the thrill of the act itself faded.

Gwen was barren, the product of a devastating accident that almost claimed her life.

As a child, she'd oft climbed and played make-believe in the boughs of an enormous wych elm near her familial home, one that happened to grow in a graveyard. I suppose it must've been the best tree for climbing, as why else would a young girl visit such a place unless she had a morbid fascination with the dead—which at the time, I doubt she did. She'd test her skills by pushing herself higher and higher into the thin branches that reached toward the heavens. As all children do, she thought herself invincible. But happenstance would show her otherwise.

One day, Gwen slipped from the boughs, and rather than fall on the ground, she hit her hip upon a gravestone near the bottom of her descent, breaking the bone and lacerating her skin. The wound itself was grievous, but worse still, it became infected. Gwen's memories of the injury eluded her, but her father maintained that never in his life had he felt such a fever. Doctors and family alike feared her death was a certainty, but by some miracle, the Creator decided her time hadn't yet come. She recovered...*more or less.* Though the bone healed, her body and mind were forever altered. For one thing, she'd never bear children, unless by divine intervention. And then, there were the other effects...

I sat up, swung my legs over the side of the bed, and fumbled for my breeches. Once I'd stepped into them, I joined Gwen by the window. I wrapped my arm around her side and took a deep breath, enjoying the scent of the sea as it flowed over the bay, into the nooks and crannies between huts in the town of Soledad below before curving off into our bungalow at the foothills of the Isla de Perdición.

Perhaps without my full intent, my arm had slipped. Gwen smiled at me as she shifted my hand north from her rump to her hip, then turned her eyes back to the setting sun.

I kept quiet for a moment, enjoying her embrace, but eventually I spoke. "Are you well, my love?"

Gwen looked up at me again. "Pardon?"

"Your gaze," I said. "You've kept it trained out this window for some time."

Gwen took her time in responding. "Am I truly so easy to read?"

She was, but I tried to ease her emotional fall. "You forget. I was once a constable. The collection and interpretation of evidence is something of a strong suit of mine."

Gwen laughed. "Ah. Of course. Well then, Constable Malarkey, what do your keen deductive skills tell you about me?"

"I'd hazard to guess you're thinking about something."

Gwen rolled her eyes. "An unimpeachable conclusion, my love, though somewhat vague, I must say."

Another of the qualities I appreciated about Gwen was her willingness to enter into open conversation on any subject, even those that might lie close to her heart, and so it was without trepidation that I broached the obvious next question.

"Are you thinking about our hypothetical progeny once again?" I asked. "About who they might resemble?"

"Hmm?" Gwen lifted her brows. "No. Not today. Besides, I've already determined what they'd look like. They'd resemble me in all the best ways, of course, and you in the worst."

"So, what does that entail?" I said. "Fair skin and bright eyes, but with bellies full of lies and thick, scratchy beards?"

"Beards? On children?" said Gwen. "Don't be absurd. Though they'd carry your bushy eyebrows. I can't imagine any child of yours lacking those furry ridges."

I made the brows in question dance, which elicited a laugh from Gwen.

"So then," I said. "What bothers you?"

"Nothing," said Gwen with a flick of her hand.

"Clearly it's something," I said, "At least I hope it is. I'd hate to find out that *nothing* drew you away from my warm, tender embrace."

"*Tender?*" said Gwen.

"Close enough." I prodded her with a finger.

Gwen sighed. "Very well. I've been thinking...about my father."

I blinked twice and shook my head. "Your father?"

"Yes. You know. The man who sired and raised me? I assume you had one."

"How droll," I said. "Yes, of course I know. But I must say, that's a rather *disturbing* person to be thinking about in the aftermath of our lovemaking."

Gwen punched me in the arm, making me flinch. "You're a cad."

"True. And your deeply twisted relationship with your father must be the reason you fell in love with me, I suppose."

Gwen deigned not to respond to that, and she shifted her gaze away from me.

"I meant that in jest, you know," I said, hoping I hadn't crossed a line.

"I know," she replied.

I moved my hand to her shoulder and rubbed at the muscles that resided between her neck and clavicle. "So, what is it? You miss him?"

"Yes," she said, plainly.

I paused a moment and considered the sun that hovered over the edge of the sea. "Well...why don't we go pay him a visit, then?"

"What? Now?" Gwen looked me in the eyes. "Are you sure that's wise?"

"Why not?" I said. "I can't imagine he's up to much of anything at the moment."

Gwen tilted her head and regarded me with both brows raised.

"You know it to be true," I said. "Come now. Let's finished getting dressed and head out before the light fades completely. That is...unless..."

I aimed another pinch at her bottom. Gwen slapped my hand away again, this time with a little more heft in her swing.

"That's what I suspected," I said, rubbing my wrist. "Very well. Another time then. Off we go."

2

The sun had just dipped below the horizon as we reached the crest of the hill above our home, painting the sky's clouds in swaths of deep violet, salmon pink, and cerulean. Tall *jabillo* trees, covered in smooth brown bark interspersed with sharp spines, shaded our path, standing alongside smaller *manzanillas de la muerte*, their boughs hanging low under the weight of hundreds of undisturbed yellow-green fruits. It seemed only fitting that such trees, filled to bursting with caustic sap and vile toxins, would surround the village of Soledad's lone graveyard.

I trailed my hand along the low, moss-covered dry stone wall that served as the cemetery's boundary from the jungle—although to refer to it as dry stone in the humid Caribbean climes was as much of a misnomer here as it had been in the damp misery of my native Ireland. I shifted my hand to avoid touching a *manzanilla* sapling attempting to push its way though the rocks and moved my eyes to the burial ground's interior. Most of the gravestones had been completely overgrown with weeds, and I had to wonder why the isle's settlers had even bothered with a wall. Attempting to stifle the will of the jungle was akin to trying to slow the winds or still the lapping waves of the sea.

Gwen and I entered the graveyard through a gap in the stone wall. According to locals, an elegant wooden gate once stood there, but the jungle had consumed it as thoroughly as it threatened to devour the cemetery itself. We passed a trio of fern-shrouded headstones before reaching one whose surface was mostly free of growth, but only by the toil of Gwen's and my own hands.

Gwen smoothed her dress at her knees—she'd chosen an elegant, bright yellow gown that accentuated her waist—and knelt at the foot of the headstone. With a gentle hand, she reached out and swiped her thumb against the lichens growing in the cavity of the stone's recessed text. As they crumbled and fell to the ground, the words, already familiar to me from numerous visits, became clear:

HERE LIES
PAUL NATHANIEL SNELLING
DEVOTED FATHER AND FRIEND
1640-1681

Gwen dropped her right hand to the damp soil at the stone's base, patting it tenderly, as if the sensation could compensate for the touch she could no longer receive from the man who raised her. She then dusted her hand with a kerchief to free it from dirt, clasped it with her left, and rested the pair in her lap. She closed her eyes, and after a pause, spoke.

"Dear Father," she said. "I can scarcely believe a full four seasons have passed since last we embraced."

Four seasons? Could it truly have been a year already? No wonder Gwen's thoughts had strayed to her father. I was surprised she hadn't mentioned anything earlier in the day, but of course, Gwen had always maintained a quiet stoicism in such regards. Then again, Gwen's father had passed just as twilight had fallen. Perhaps that was why she'd chosen to wait until this moment to approach him.

Gwen continued. "I can only hope that the hereafter continues to treat you well. Have you found any childhood friends, father? Anyone you might've known back in England? Or do you continue to roam the warm Caribbean waters? I know how much you loved it here, though your time on these isles was short."

Gwen's father, Paul, had been a thespian of some repute in London before coming down with a bout of consumption of the lungs. His physicians had informed him his time on God's green earth was limited, but he might extend his years by moving to warmer, more temperate climes. The man had always harbored a fascination with the New World, and with buccaneers in particular, so he traveled to the West Indies with his faithful, loving daughter as his only companion. He knew he couldn't escape death's clutches—merely elude them momentarily. Honestly, the man faced his assured demise with more poise than most, giving me something to aspire to. At least he lived to see his daughter married, though I can't say with certainty that as a father, I'd approve of a man such as myself as a son-in-law.

Thinking of Paul always made me keenly aware of my own mortality. The man had scarcely been a decade my senior at his passing. At least he'd led a full life. Having sired Gwen at such a young age helped in that regard—and it helped me feel less roguish for taking her as my bride. Not that I *wouldn't* have married Gwen if she'd been more than ten years my junior, but keeping the age gap at a mere eight felt more urbane. And Paul had approved of our union, for what it was worth.

Throughout Gwen's soliloquy, mist rolled in from high in the mountains above Soledad. It snaked through the creeping vine tendrils that hung from the branches of the *jabillos*, across the forest floor strewn with damp leaves and rotting wood and the corpses of thousands of gnats and weevils and other insects that buzzed and bit, before ultimately pouring over the low rock fence and intermingling with the graveyard's sentinel headstones. The deepening gloom combined with the shadows of the trees limited my vision, though Gwen and her bright yellow dress still appeared prominently before me.

I felt a chill mere moments before hearing the voice.

"Gwenevere? Is that you?"

I lifted my head. A man in a powdered wig stood at the edge of the mists, wearing a knee-length parti-colored justacorps coat over a waistcoat and breeches. A delicate lace cravat puffed out at his neck, and his stockings and polished black shoes showed no sign of the grime one would've expected of a man who'd traversed through a tropical jungle.

Gwen stood and took a step forward, her eyes now fully open. "Father. Yes. It's me."

I've often heard it said that in a relationship honesty is the best measure, but is it truly? Would I have still married Gwen had I known at the time of our nuptials that in addition to nearly dying during her battle with infection as a child, the brush with death had pierced her soul, thinning around her the veil between the worlds of the living and the dead? Had I known that by committing myself to her I'd forever more be forced to suffer the presence of ghosts at inopportune times, would I have still accepted her? It was a question without an answer. As it stood, I loved Gwen more than life itself—more than I ever knew I possessed a capacity for prior to meeting her. I wouldn't trade her for anything, supernatural quirks and all.

And of course, I couldn't truly blame her for keeping such a secret from me. Despite our openness with one another, there were more than a few secrets I harbored in the deep well of my heart that I hoped Gwen would never discover, either.

Paul blinked and looked around himself. "Gwen, pardon me for the inquiry, but where are we? Is this...a graveyard?"

"Yes, Father," she said. "It is."

"But why are we..." Paul paused as he noticed me for the first time. "Ah, John. So you're here, too. Good to see you. Although I can't say I understand the environs." He spread his hands out to his sides.

Gwen and I had called on Paul a few times since his death, but memories in the departed seemed to be fleeting—at least regarding events that had transpired since their passing. The problem worsened the longer it had been since their deaths, but given that Paul's passage into the netherworld had occurred a short year ago, he remained rather lucid—which wasn't to say he didn't need a bit of prodding to help him understand his situation. Luckily, Gwen knew how to apply the proper metaphorical fingers in the proper places.

"Father," said Gwen. "Do you recall John's and my marriage?"

Paul glanced at his daughter and then at me. "What? Of course, I do. What a grand time, it was. Our feet in the warm sand, the breeze in my hair, the shade of the coconut palms protecting me from the sun. Why do you ask?"

Gwen took another step toward her father. "And do you recall why we rushed the wedding?"

The man scratched his head. "Well, let's see. I suppose it was because of my cough, and..."

Paul paused, blinked, and cocked his head to one side. Gwen began to take another step forward, but he held up a hand to still her approach. The man swept his hand to the side to part the tall weeds before him, which moved languidly under his ghostly touch, and walked to my side. He turned and set his gaze upon the gravestone.

"Ah, yes," he said as he read the text. "I'd almost forgotten. Well...I had a good run, didn't I?"

"Unquestionably, father," said Gwen. "Though I doubt if any of us wouldn't have preferred the run to be longer."

I kept my mouth shut. I'd liked Paul—the man was as accepting of me as I could've ever hoped—but I had to admit, I appreciated the privacy his absence from our bungalow provided us with. Gwen could get loud in the throes of passion.

"What's a man to do," said Paul with a shrug of his shoulders. He reached his hands up and removed his wig, revealing a crop of long, dark blonde hair that he mussed with a thorough scratching. "Blasted wigs. Even in death they bother me. So, what brings you here my dear?"

Gwen moved to her father's side. "I simply wished to see you. It's been a year."

"Already?" Paul's eyes rose in surprise. "My, how time flies among the spirits."

"And also among the living," said Gwen. She stood a foot to his right, her hands clasped before her, and I spotted a hint of moisture beading at the corner of her eyes.

Paul said nothing for a moment as he watched his daughter wrestle with her inner turmoil. Eventually, his lips parted. "My darling...as much as I relish your company, this is unnecessary. You needn't be here. My time has come and gone."

Gwen sniffed back a tear. "That's a sweet sentiment, father, but you're mistaken if you think I visit you solely for your own wellbeing."

Paul raised an arm as if to pull her into a warm embrace, but he stopped himself in mid-motion. "Oh, daughter of mine. You never were particularly adept at letting go."

Gwen raised her hand opposite her father's, extending it toward his own. Though his form appeared as solid as true flesh, when Gwen's fingers met his, Paul's digits faded into the mist, allowing Gwen's hand to pass through. Gwen bit her lip and pulled her hand back, and based on the tension in her cheeks and the creases at the corners of her eyes, I could tell she hoped to touch him once more, though she knew well enough such a thing was impossible.

I heard the snap of a branch and turned my head toward the edge of the jungle. A dozen figures, some of which I recognized from previous visits, stared at us though the thickening fog with varying levels of comprehension and interest.

"Speaking of moving on..." I said.

Gwen spared a glance at the gathering ghosts, surely considering whether or not staying longer with her father would be worth the cost.

Luckily, I didn't have to convince her to leave. The ringing church bell did it for me.

3

We hurried from the graveyard and toward the bell's chimes, but we'd barely made it a hundred paces along the path toward Soledad before I spotted Tall Tom and his distinctive tricorne hat lumbering toward us. The sun's rays had faded completely, but the moon waxed gibbous, a few days shy of full, and its light reflected off the collection of glass bobbles and macaw feathers Tom kept tucked under one of the cocked portions of his hat. I'd asked the man about the odd collection once, and he claimed it was a means to attract women—an addition of brilliant plumage and glitter to a body that was otherwise completely unspectacular, as he put it.

On that front, I was forced to disagree with him. Though his mundane facial features, day-old beard, and close-cropped, thinning hair did nothing to set him apart from others, one quite notable and fairly spectacular aspect of the man presented itself right upon meeting him, a feature that would've made it easy to recognize him on the dark trail even without his distinctive headgear.

Within a few short moments, our descent brought us to Tom. His breaths came in short, ragged bursts following his rapid climb up the hilly path. As we reached him, he paused, bent over, with his hands resting on the brown breeches that stretched over his massive thighs.

"Ho, Tom," I said, clapping the big man on the back. "What's the commotion?"

Tom straightened. Though I stood above average in my height, Tom loomed over me by a good foot, and he made Gwen seem downright minuscule. The well-honed axe he always carried in a belt loop at his side was half her height. He took another breath and straightened his coat before responding.

"Constable Malarkey," he said in his deep, rumbling voice, and then, after snatching his hat from his head and giving a curt bow to my wife, "Milady."

"Confound it, Tom," I said. "How many times do I have to tell you to call me John?"

"And me, Gwen," interjected my better half.

"Sorry, Constable, John, sir," said Tom. "Just a matter of habit, y'understand. And my apologies, milady. But I can't very well call you by your given name. It's a matter of propriety, see."

Gwen rolled her eyes and snorted. She knew Tom's respect for proper behavior only extended as far as the ears of the nearest well-bred maiden. In the company of men, the man cursed and smoke and drank with the best of them.

"No matter," I told Tom. "Now, out with it. What set the church bells to ringing?"

Tom replaced his elaborate hat upon his head. "It's a ship, sir. She sailed into harbor at dusk."

"And?" For a town as small as Soledad, the arrival of a merchant vessel would cause some stir, but not enough for someone to set the church bells a-ringing.

Tom swallowed and wrung his hands. "Well, John. Ain't just any vessel, it is. It's the *Black Mast*."

I felt a cold hand grip my heart. *No. It couldn't be...could it?*

I blinked and tried to recover my voice. "You're...certain, Tom?"

The big man nodded. "Ain't a doubt in my mind, Constable. I saw her as plain as day. Well, not pre-cisely—that's a figure of speech, it is. In all truth, the light was fadin' by the time she rested at anchor, but I saw her well enough. Big billowin' red and white striped sails, square-rigged. Figurehead of a snarlin' four-armed buccaneer at its prow. And of course, its main-mast. Even in the twilight I could see it. Black as night, sir."

I clenched my teeth. *The Black Mast.* One of the most renowned—and reviled—pirate vessels in all the West Indies. She was captained by Raphe Bartholomew Thatch, but most people referred to the man as the Badger, more for his blond hair dyed with streaks of black than for his ferocity—which wasn't to say the man or his crew were kind and compassionate. Far from it. But enough sailors and crewmen escaped from the aftermath of the *Mast's* raids to give me some hope for the people of Soledad. That, and other reasons...

I noticed Gwen glancing at me in the moonlight. She appeared pale, though with her complexion and the muted lighting, it was hard to tell. She'd heard stories of the *Black Mast* as well as I had, which could've explained her pallor, though there was another element to her glance. A more personal concern.

"John," she said. "Is something amiss?"

"You mean other than the fact that we have a gang of bloodthirsty pirates lapping at our sandy beaches?" I shook my head. "No. Tom, have they rowed ashore? Or made any demands?"

Tom shook his head. "No, sir. They dropped anchor and have been sittin' there since. Haven't heard a peep from them. Yet, anyway. And they weren't flyin' their colors when they sailed into the harbor. It was only after they'd anchored they hoisted a Jolly Roger."

I raised an eyebrow. "All black?"

Tom nodded.

"Well for God's sake, man, why didn't you mention that?" I said.

A black flag meant they'd be willing to offer quarter. It would be small recompense for the villagers if the *Mast's* crew took all their belongings and left them to fend for themselves, fighting and scrapping over wild cassava roots and hunting wild *javelinas* in the jungle, but at least they'd have their lives, and us ours. For a while.

Tom shrugged and looked abashed. "Sorry, John. I mentioned it now."

I passed a hand through the tangles of my beard. "Hmm. Still strange they haven't come ashore. I wonder what they want." *Or who,* I left unsaid.

Tom chewed on his lip and hooked his thumbs into his belt, letting his arms hang loosely at his sides. "So, um...what should we do, Constable?"

Given Soledad's size, which fluctuated just north and south of three hundreds souls, I, with my former training as a constable, was as close to a peace-keeping force as the village had. Few enough arguments erupted amongst the citizens that the responsibilities of my unofficial position were minor, and Tom, who'd self-appointed himself as my deputy upon Gwen's and my arrival to the isle, helped calmer heads prevail. His size was a fair deterrent to quarrels. Honestly, Tom's and my largest hurdles regarding conflict resolution usually came as a result of interpretation problems. Most of Soledad's inhabitants were of Spanish descent, and both Tom and I spoke precious little of the tongue.

I cracked my knuckles as I considered our options. As much as part of me revolted against the idea, I knew what course of action the *Black Mast's* arrival precipitated.

"Steel yourself, Tom," I said. "Because if the pirates refuse to come to us, then that necessitates we, in turn, reach out to them."

4

Gwen didn't afford Tom a chance to express his disbelief, as she decided to do it for him. "Are you mad? You can't mean to say you'd willingly set foot on that ship. You've heard the tales!"

"Some of them are exaggerated," I said. "Or...I believe so, I should say. And besides, what would you rather me do? You can't tell me you think the crew of the *Mast* chose to anchor in our harbor simply to cool their heels in the shadow of our isle's bluffs? If we act preemptively, perchance we can avoid unnecessary turmoil."

"But to whom?" said Gwen with a raise of her brows.

I gathered Gwen in my arms and raised her chin so she'd look me in the eyes. Her body pressed against mine, warm and supple, and I had to fight my passions from betraying the more volatile portions of my body.

"Gwen," I said. "You know what sorts of services Tom and I provide to the people, and you know what sort of man I am. This is something I must do. And should I choose not to act, the ultimate consequences might be far worse. But I promise you, I *will* be careful."

Tom scratched his neck and stared at the ground. Public displays of affection were a keen reminder of his own bachelorhood.

Gwen stared into my eyes, her blue-green irises reflecting the bright light of the moon. She leaned in and kissed me. A hint of guava still lingered on her lips. As she pulled away, she sighed.

"Very well," she said. "But I'm coming with you."

This time, Tom's disbelief wasn't hindered by either of us.

"*What, milady?*" he sputtered. "No. I can't allow it. It'll be much too dangerous, it will. You should stay in your bungalow where it'll be safe."

Gwen shook her head. "Honestly, Tom, try to use your head every now and then. John just explained that should you and he fail to evict these pirates from the bay, even the furthest corners of this isle won't be safe. Better I accompany you. At least then, I might be able to invoke my womanly charms in the aid of our cause."

"Careful, now," I said. "I married you for those charms, and I don't expect you to be giving them away for free to cutthroats and thugs."

"Who said it was to be for free?" said Gwen with a grin. "Pirates have gold, do they not?"

I raised an eyebrow. "Ever flippant, I see, even in the face of danger."

Gwen trailed a finger along the edge of my furry jaw. "And do you know why I act in such a fashion?"

"Why?" I asked.

"Because it's better than succumbing to the alternative." She started down the path toward the shore, leaving the giant and I in her wake.

Tom grumbled.

"What was that?" I said.

Tom cleared his throat. "Nothing. I was just thinkin' it's not right for her to be so forthright. Not ladylike at all, I say. You should rein her in, John."

Despite the gravity of the situation, I laughed.

"What?" said Tom with a frown.

"I'm simply amused you think I can," I said. "Come, now. Let's move before she outpaces us."

The fog followed us down the mountain as we walked, rolling over the jungle's dark green canopy as silently as a jaguar stalking its prey. It swirled around trunks and pooled at the bases of the trees, which gradually shifted from the spiked *jabillos* to palms and bobwoods flush with fist-sized green fruits.

The mist filled me with a sense of foreboding. It appeared as often as not in the evenings, but it seemed to me at least that the fog came more readily on nights Gwen interacted with the souls of the departed. The dead had never bothered me—neither emotionally nor in any physical manner—but that didn't stop me from thinking they could, should they desire to.

An uneasy calm, which paired with the fog as nicely as a fine wine with a meal, hung over the quiet fishing village of Soledad as we reached it. Breeze whistling across rooftops replaced the usual chatter of friends and neighbors, and windows often outlined by the lights of lanterns or candles sat dark and shuttered. Even cats that lived in the packed dirt alleys between buildings stilled their mewling in deference to the situation.

It almost seemed as if the town had abandoned itself, but as we reached the docks, we found the missing citizenry. A good half of the village stood on the weathered, elevated planks of the wharf, their faces grim in the flickering light of a handful of upheld torches. The crowd parted as we approached, and I could see some measure of uneasiness drain from many of the faces, but only a measure. Loose boards clattered underfoot as we walked, and as we reached the forefront of the onlookers, I felt the weight of their gazes upon my neck.

Gwen leaned close to me and spoke in my ear. "Say something to them, John."

I turned to her. "What? Me?" I said in a low voice. "I've never been one for speeches. And I doubt even half of them would understand what I say."

"If you're here to help them, my love, then show it," she said. "Your responsibility, which you so pointedly reminded me of up in the foothills near our bungalow, demands it. Their fear is as much your enemy as whatever it is those pirates intend."

I sighed and turned to the faces, most of them familiar, even though Gwen and I had only resided on the isle for perhaps a half-dozen seasons.

"Um..."

Gwen poked me in the arm. "Louder."

I cleared my throat and tried to project my voice. "Hear me, friends. I know you're concerned about the presence of this, er...ship in our harbor. But know that Tom and I are going to investigate, and whatever the problem is, we'll resolve it. So please, head back to your homes."

The gathered masses looked at one another, either in incomprehension or dissatisfaction at the mediocrity of my address, I couldn't tell. Nonetheless, they started to disperse. Tom gave me a subtle thumbs up and a forced grin, while Gwen shrugged in the way she always did to express middling approval.

I ignored them both and turned to a man at my side, a tanned Spaniard who I knew fairly well. "Jorge, mind if we borrow your fishing skiff? We plan to approach the ship in the harbor to discuss their presence and to see if they have any demands."

He nodded and bowed his head, something I'd repeatedly told everyone around town not to do. My previous occupation as a constable gave me no real authority or standing on the island. Besides, it made me feel weird.

"Sí, señor John," he said. "Claro que puedes. Buena suerte."

"Um, thanks...I think." I glanced at Tom. He gave me a blank look.

Our trio piled into the small boat, which rocked precipitously as we entered, and Tom took the oars. As the big man put his muscles to work and drew us into the bay, I noticed how much the fog had thickened. The slight elevation of the docks combined with the burning torches had helped keep the mists at bay, but now at the water's surface, the fog nearly overwhelmed us. I could barely see the Mast's outline through the thick haze, but Tom knew where it anchored and rowed us forth.

Water slapped at the edge of our boat, and from the shore, I could hear the occasional cries of the nocturnal petrels, which the locals called *diablotín* due to the devilish nature of their mating cries. Otherwise, the night was still, which disturbed me more than it should've. The *Black Mast* was a mighty ship, with a crew of likely close to two hundred. Where were the shouts and cries and sung sea shanties? The curses, the thumping of boots on decks and the rattling of anchor chains? Why did the pirates remain so quiet? And why had they sailed here, yet refused to come ashore? I racked my mind, trying to come up with possibilities. Unfortunately, only one came to mind.

I jerked forward as our skiff collided with the frigate's hull, and I reached a hand out to make sure Gwen wouldn't be knocked overboard. Luckily, if you could call it that, her motion was stopped by the algae-slicked sides of the *Mast*. She collided with the ship with a muted thump.

"Oops. Sorry," said Tom, stowing the oars. "Lost sight of her in this blasted fog. Thick as the devil's pubis, it is. Err...I mean..." He glanced at Gwen.

She waved him off. "Oh, stow it, Tom. I've heard your foul tongue before, as much as you try to hide it."

"Are you all right?" I asked her.

"Fine," she said, and I believed her, at least in the physical sense. But a touch of the pallor I'd spotted earlier had returned to her face, and her right hand shook, though almost imperceptibly. Despite her cheeky display atop the foothills of the Isla de Perdición, I could tell she wasn't completely comfortable with the thought of setting foot aboard a pirate vessel.

I reminded myself that, if for no other reason than to put Gwen at ease, I needed to project an air of confidence, even if the current situation didn't particularly instill it in me.

"Ho," I called up the fog shrouded sides of the *Black Mast*. "Is there any man awake aboard this vessel? We've come from town to parlay."

No one responded, and as the cool mist swirled around my arms, I shuddered. For the first time, I thought perhaps I should've stopped by my home before descending into town, and not to grab a coat despite the sudden chill. As usual, I wore a pair of breeches, a loose-fitting shirt, boots and a belt, but it was my lack of a cutlass and pistol I now regretted. At least Tom had his axe—not that even his brawn would help in a battle against the *Mast's* crew.

A familiar sound reached my ears. Not a man's voice, but the rustling slip of rope on rope.

"Stand back," I said, mere moments before the hemp ladder unfurled, slapping the wet planks of the ship's hull.

I grasped the rough fibers of the lowest hanging rung and turned to my companions. "I'll go first. Tom, follow close behind me. Gwen, we'll bring you up last. Let me initiate contact with them, and for the love of God, don't say anything brash or untoward."

The two of them nodded, and I began to climb, pulling myself up hand over hand. The timbers above me creaked in response, and I felt the ladder pull taut as Tom mounted it below me. As I reached the ship's bulwark, I pulled myself over the railing and onto the deck

below. Fog shrouded much of the ship, obscuring everything past the edge of the main mast.

Tom joined me at my side, and together we hauled
Gwen, who'd hooked her feet over the bottom rung, up
behind us. As she approached the top, I reached over
the side of the ship to help her. She grasped my hand,
and I heard a familiar voice behind me.

"*Bonjour,* Driftwood."

5

I pulled Gwen over the railing and helped her steady her feet upon the gently rocking deck before turning toward the voice. Out of the fog, a number of figures had stepped forth—men, clad in a motley collection of baggy breeches and billowing shirts, either with or without sleeves, paired with doublets and jerkins of every conceivable make and design. The majority sported thick beards and kept their hair hidden under either a kerchief or a Monmouth cap, and not a man amongst the bunch sported shoes on his feet.

At the front of the crowd, two men stood out from the rest: one, a man with a sharp nose and a thin, pointed English moustache, wearing an elaborate dark green coat and a jaunty felt cavalier hat with a wide brim, and the other, a shirtless, well-muscled black, tall and lean, with an eye patch that couldn't completely hide the jagged scar that crossed his face from temple to lip. The former twirled the tip of his moustache between his thumb and index finger, while the latter stood motionless, his arms crossed and his one good eye set firmly upon me.

We stared at one another, none of us uttering a word, until Gwen's hesitant voice broke the silence.

"Who among you spoke?" she asked, joining me at my side.

"Zat would be *moi,*" said the man with the thin moustache, his voice flowing with the accent of his homeland. He removed his hat and swept it before him as he bowed. "Nicolas de Guerre, at your *service, mon cherie.*" He paired his bow with a debonair smile.

The timbers behind me creaked as Tom shifted his feet, but other than the sounds of his weight on the planks, the man remained as quiet as a mouse.

"As we boarded your ship, you said something," said Gwen, unfazed by the man's attempts at charm. "*Bonjour,* Driftwood. What did you mean by that?"

"*Bonjour,*" I said without turning my gaze from that of the two pirates', "is a French salutation. It means 'hello.'"

Gwen's fist slammed into the meat of my upper arm. "I know that, you fool. I meant the other part."

The Frenchman straightened, replaced the wide hat upon his head. "Ah, Driftwood. You cannot tell me zat zis *belle femme,* zis *petite amie* of yours...does not know?"

"Know what?" said Gwen, frustration replacing the hesitancy in her voice.

"It's...not what you think," I said as I turned to her.

"Unless," said the lean black in a thick pidgin English, "you dink dis man you call John done lied to you 'bout his past, in which case tings just 'bout exactly what you dink."

"I never lied," I said. "Although I may have...omitted information."

"John..." said Gwen, her eyes boring into me like an auger. "Explain yourself."

I sighed. I knew the truth would emerge eventually. I'd merely hoped to expose Gwen to the secrets of my past in a more governed manner.

I gestured to the two men across from us. "Nicolas has already introduced himself. He is, unless I'm mistaken, the quartermaster of this vessel. And the other man is Chinue Okadigbo, the bosun, but most simply call him the Jaguar. They're former...*acquaintances* of mine."

"Acquaintances," said Chinue with a flash of his brilliant white teeth. "Dat is a good word, one I will have to remembah. Much moah complex, I dink, dan *friend*."

"Don't lie, Chinue," I said. "You and I were never friends."

Gwen grabbed me by the arm and pulled me back a step, as if doing so would shield our speech from the ears of the *Mast's* crew.

"John, do you mean to say that you were once...*a pirate?*" she asked in a hushed voice. "You told me you made your fortune as a privateer!"

"I *was* a privateer," I said. "But I regret to say that I did not, actually, make my fortune as such."

Gwen released my arm and stepped back, her face falling. "Then, what they say...*it's true?* You engaged in *piracy?*"

"*Bien-aimée,*" said Nicolas. "Driftwood was not zimply any pirate. He was ze quartermaster of ze *Black Mast*."

Gwen took another step back into the fog, the blood draining from her face. Her eyes, which a moment ago had regarded me with the same hard, frosty look they sometimes acquired during our lovers' quarrels, now shimmered with a new emotion, one I'd never before seen in her. Fear.

I longed to rush to her, to take her in my arms and whisper apologies in her ears, to shower her with kisses and grovel for forgiveness, but I couldn't. Not with the full crew of the *Black Mast* waiting in the wings, watching me and waiting for my response. Not with Tom—my one ally should the situation deteriorate—at my back, his allegiances uncertain in the light of the pirates' allegations. And so I stood my ground, in the literal sense, but in the figurative, I fought back with every ounce of verve I could muster.

"Yes, Gwen, I *was* a pirate," I said. "And I did serve aboard the *Mast* as quartermaster. But that shouldn't serve as a condemnation of my moral compass. Like so many others, I was press-ganged to joined the crew of the *Mast* after they set upon me and the rest of the crew of our privateering vessel, the *Skylark*. And the fact that I rose to the position of quartermaster aboard the *Mast* had nothing to do with my thirst for blood or my capacity for wickedness, but rather my ability as a sailor and a lack of other able bodies to fill the position.

"As a pirate, I acted in the same capacity as I did as a privateer. I plundered the holds of other vessels, true, but never once did I strike down a man who did not engage me first, nor did I treat any captives in a cruel or unusual manner. Under my tutelage, we never left a plundered vessel without a means to ensure her safe travel to a nearby port, and I treated my own crew with fairness and respect. With God as my witness, I swear these words to be true, and if any of the crew of the *Mast* hear my statements and know them to be false, then I challenge you to stand forth and strike me down for my deception."

The silence stretched for a moment, and I heard coughs amongst the gathered pirates, but none said a word—at least not until Nicolas cleared his throat.

"Yes, well, would zat I could," he said. "But you speaks ze truth in zis *à propos* speech of yours. A pirate you were at ze face, but a lousy one at heart."

"Dat, I dink, be da way for Nicolas to call you a coward man," said Chinue with a sneer. "But he be much moah bettah with words dan me."

I ignored their jabs and glanced at Tom, who gave me firm nod as a measure of his support. Then I extended a hand toward Gwen. She peered at me warily, but the fear had faded from her eyes. In its place swirled a thousand unanswered questions. I lifted an eyebrow and tilted my head, trying to convey that I'd answer all her queries in due time, but I've no idea how she interpreted my facial display. Nonetheless, she took my hand, and I drew her to my side.

"And I thought you said you weren't any good at speeches," she whispered in my ear.

"I lied," I said with a hint of a smile, my heart buoyed by her return to form. "Now, then," I said, turning to Nicolas, Chinue, and their retinue. "As much as I've enjoyed exchanging pleasantries with you two rapscallions, I have to wonder why you're here? And, more importantly, where's Raphe?"

Nicolas crossed his arms and began to pace along the deck of the *Mast*, his bare feet creating little more than a whisper as they moved along the planks. "Ah, yes, how *drôle* zat you should ask zat, as zat is ze reason we are here. I don't suppose you have seen ze man, have you?"

"Seen him?" I asked. "How would I have seen him? Is Raphe not still the captain of the *Black Mast*?"

Chinue unfolded his arms and took a step forth, his dark skin glistening from the fog's tongue in the light of the moon. "As familiah as you believe yoahself to be with da man, you are no longah one of us, and you must refer to him as da Badger."

"Peace, Chinue," said Nicolas with a wave of his hand. "I zink we can afford Driftwood a wee bit of, how should we say, lee-way in zis regard. And to answer ze question, yes, Raphe Bartholomew is still our *capitaine*, alzough he is not aboard, and has not been for some time."

I rubbed a hand against my chin. "I don't understand. Did Raphe leave by force or by choice? And regardless, if he's left you, as I once did, why haven't you elected a new captain?"

Nicolas stopped his pacing and turned to face me, his face shadowed by his hat and framed by the lingering fog. "Zat is between us and him. Zuffice eet to say, we need him back."

"Why?" I asked.

Chinue took another step forth, his jagged scar gleaming in the moonlight. His voice, already stern, became passionate and fiery. "Because da man stole from us. Stole a treasah dat belong to de whole of da crew. One dat has now been lost, and now he must come to bear da judgment of his own men, as Captain befoah dem. Only den, once we heah dah man's plea and see da truth in his eyes, once we see if he can return de treasah to us, will we come to judge his fate."

The force of Chinue's response might've pushed me over the side of the *Black Mast* if not for the presence of Tall Tom at my back, but the big man might as well have been a mast himself for all he moved. I glanced at Gwen, and while she appeared shaken, there was a measure of relief in her face as well. So...the crew of the *Mast* weren't at the sandy foot of Perdición to engage in debauchery and violence, but rather in search of their lost captain. The question was what role they expected *me* to play in such a matter.

"Very well," I said. "So the Badger is missing, and you seek him out. But if you've sailed all this way to ask me if I've caught word of him, then I'm afraid your trip will have been in vain. I haven't heard mention of Raphe since I left the *Mast*, much less seen him."

"You mistake owah motives, Driftwood," said Chinue, his fingers clenching into a fist at his side. "We do not expect you to know where he is. We expect you to find him."

"*What?*" I said. "How would I do such a thing? If his capture means so much to you, I assume you've already tried to track him down, and to no avail. What, then, instills confidence in you that I could do such a thing?"

"Come now, *Constable* Mahlahkey," said Chinue with an evil grin. "Did you think we would foahget?"

"You misunderstand the duties of my former position," I said with a shake of my head. "Constables are responsible for the collection of evidence, not apprehending wayward suspects."

"Now, now, Driftwood," said Nicolas. "You must be less *modeste* about your abilities. Your training has given you a good eye, no? And look at us. You, as one man, are much less *visible* zan our crew. You can question and *interroge* where we cannot. And lest you forget, you know Raphe Bartholomew better zan any of us. For zis, and other *raisons*—" Nicolas shared a sidelong look with Chinue. "—you are, should we say, ideally zuited to ze task of finding him."

"You know the famed Badger?" asked Gwen.

I glanced at her. "I don't *just* know him. Before I set foot on this isle, before we met, before I'd ever even heard the name the *Black Mast*—he was my best friend."

Gwen stared at me incredulously.

"I'll explain in due time," I promised. "But I don't see how my friendship with Raphe has any relevance to his capture. If he's escaped your clutches, he could be anywhere in the Caribbean, perhaps anywhere in the world, depending on how long ago he left your side."

"Not zo long ago as you zink," said Nicolas. "He left our, should we say, *présence* a few short days ago. He was headed zouthwest from the Caicos, in ze direction of Tortuga."

"And did you check to see if that's where he went?" I asked.

Nicolas whipped his hand through the air, as if he were slashing it with an invisible cutlass. "Enough. Zis is your task, Driftwood. Consider eet a delayed *pénitence* for your departure from ze *Mast*. As your friend, Raphe

Bartholomew was kind enough to let you leave weezout paying ze price, but no longer. I may not yet be *capitaine*, but I act in ze wishes of ze crew. Find ze Badger, and bring heem to us."

I swept Gwen behind me with an arm as I broached my next question, fearing I already knew the answer. "And should I refuse?"

"Please, Driftwood..." Nicolas slowly drew his saber from the sheath at his side and brandished the well-oiled blade in the moonlight. "Pirates we may be, but we are not zo cruel at heart. Do not let zis play end in *tragédie* for you and your *petite amie.*"

Chinue fingered a long handled knife at his own belt. "And me dink you not so foolish as to run. Regulah man, maybe, but not a man who know da speed of da *Black Mast* when da wind fill her sails. Ain't no hole so deep in all da Caribbean dat owah jaws cannot reach to da bottom."

Perhaps it was my imagination, but it seemed to me the crowd of pirates surrounding Nicolas and Chinue surged forth as the black delivered his thinly veiled threat. Despite the fog, I could see in their faces—many of them familiar—a mixture of emotions: ferocity, determination, anger, and uncertainty, although some men might've even called it fear. Again I was glad for the presence of Tom at my back, although I felt that even with his support, our promise of safety about the *Mast* was rapidly eroding.

"Very well," I said as I swallowed. "Be sure that I'll give grave consideration to your...*request.*"

Nicolas and Chinue both smiled, but for a motion that was supposed to convey joy and goodwill, I felt utterly devoid of both.

6

"A pirate!" said Gwen. "Of all things! You could've lied about your past and hidden from me that you'd been a silversmith or a wainwright or even a butcher with a vendetta against small animals, but honestly, John? *A pirate?*"

Twigs crunched underfoot as we walked along the jungle path back to our bungalow. Tom followed us closely, though he wisely chose not to insert his tongue into the line of Gwen's fire.

"I told you I was a privateer," I said.

"Yes, *a privateer,*" said Gwen. "As in a sailor aboard a ship that has been commissioned by his majesty the King in service to the crown. Your ship had been issued a writ, John, allowing such acts of plunder as a consequence of war, but only against ships in the service of his majesty's enemies."

"You act as if a grand chasm exists between the two," I said. "In practice, privateering and piracy differ in little but their name."

My plea seemed to enter into one of Gwen's ears and out the other. "And not only were you a pirate, but apparently you were best of friends with the most notorious buccaneer in all of the West Indies!"

I rolled my eyes. "Notorious, yes, but not for his ruthlessness or depravity. He's known for his recklessness and flamboyance, more than anything else. And most of the stories involving him are pure fabrications, especially that one involving the twenty barrels of rum he lashed together and the flaming harpoon and the leviathan. The man was drunk and stuck a catfish with a knife, that was all."

Gwen folded her arms. "Oh. And how, pray tell, do you know this?"

"Because I've known the man since we were boys," I said. "And you should be glad of that fact. If not for him, we'd never have met."

Gwen lifted an eyebrow. "Go on."

I slapped my arm as one of the jungle's many blood-thirsty insects attempted to make a meal of me. "Raphe, who's two years my senior, grew up across the street from me in Wexford. We'd play frequently, and enter into all sorts of misdeeds that young boys are prone to do, and while I favored playing at knights, Raphe preferred to imagine himself as a daring seaman, climbing swaying riggings and braving the fiercest gusts of a storm. And so it was that as he aged, he joined the crew of a privateering expedition, whereas I stayed in Wexford and pursued a vocation in justice as a constable— which, before you ask, I did not deceive you about.

"Now, it was at this time that my family, which was of some means, sought to marry me off to the daughter of a local mill owner, a maid by the name of Ellinor. And as pleasant as the young woman was, I felt no passion for her, and possibly more importantly, I fancied myself much too young to engage in that most holiest of unions. I felt certain adventures awaited me if I simply sought them out.

"As I struggled with this impending arrangement, Raphe returned from his first privateering expedition, and he brought with him tales of excitement and wonder and warm, blue Caribbean waters—surely embellished, as he was always prone to do—but nonetheless containing enough amazement to spark inside me the flame that fueled my own sense of adventure. And so, in a fit of impulse, I signed on and joined Raphe aboard the *Skylark*.

"Now, as I believed, Raphe's tales had been embellished. Drastically so. Life aboard the *Skylark* was a brutal slog from the crack of dawn to the last light of dusk, day after day. But I didn't have long to regret my choice in the matter before we were attacked and boarded by the crew of the *Black Mast*. They gave us a choice to join or perish, and quite wisely, Raphe and I chose the latter."

Apparently, my tale had intrigued Gwen to the point of dousing the fires within her, as when she responded, her voice had sunk to a more pleasing register. "But what then? How was it Raphe became the captain of such a vessel, and you the quartermaster?"

Our feet brought us to the entrance of our secluded bungalow, and I paused outside the door. "That, I think, is a tale for another day. Suffice it to say both Raphe and I proved our mettle on more than one occasion, and the life expectancy on the vessel wasn't particularly great. For now, though, we have more pressing matters to discuss. Tom, would you care to join us?"

Tom stuck his hands in his coat pockets and stared at the ground. "Oh, um. Well, John, I wouldn't want to interfere with you and your lady's home life, and—"

"Let me rephrase that, Tom," I said. "Get in the house."

Tom obliged, though he insisted Gwen enter first. The big man shifted his feet as he stood behind one of the austere chairs that populated our sitting room, waiting as Gwen searched through the remains of our fire for a live ember.

"Have a seat, Tom," I said. The man's sense of chivalry was commendable, if a little exaggerated.

Tom sat reluctantly, and light bloomed as Gwen brought the ember to the wick of one of our candles.

"Do we have anything to drink?" I asked as Gwen searched for another candle.

"There's a pot of water over the fire, though I doubt the contents are still warm," she said. "And there's a keg of small beer in the pantry."

I grunted. "I'm not sure if the latter is quite strong enough for my current tastes. Tom, can I get you anything?"

The big man shrugged. "Whatever you're havin', I'll have one meself. You know me. I'm not fastidious when it comes to drink."

I slipped into the back of our bungalow to the pantry, where I collected a trio of mugs and half filled them with rum. I also snatched a bright green lime from a bowl of freshly picked fruits and, after slicing it in half with a carving knife, spread its contents evenly among the mugs. With the tankards in hand, I returned to the main room and topped the beverages off using the pot that hung in the fireplace.

Tom and Gwen accepted the drinks without question, though a quick sniff would've easily divulged their contents. With my own mug gripped tightly in my hand, I sat across from Tom. My chair groaned in response, though I had little sympathy at the moment for its tribulations.

I took a sip of my grog and stared at the floor, letting the liquid warm the already tepid interior of my throat.

The Black Mast.

I couldn't believe it had found me. Though I'd left the ranks of its crew little over two years prior, my time aboard the vessel seemed a lifetime ago. Part of that, I thought, was due to the changes I'd underwent since my departure. I'd matured in those two years. Gained a willingness to settle down and an appreciation for a dry bed, especially one warmed by a lovely companion. And, of course, I'd met Gwen. Her radiant features and infectious personality had hastened the demise of my adventurous spirit and turned me into the man she now knew and loved. But really, I'd pushed away thoughts of my days working under the shadow of the *Mast* primarily through sheer force of will.

I'm not sure if Gwen understood that. She questioned why I hadn't shared my past with her, assuming it was because of embarrassment or guilt, and I suppose those emotions played a part in my silence on the matter. But simply, I wished to forget. As much as Raphe relished in his role as an infamous pirate captain, I'd never harbored any secret desire for a life of marauding upon the high seas. Despite Gwen's roguish pet names for me, I fancied myself more valiant than that, and so I'd chosen, whether intentionally or not, to wipe the memory of the *Mast* from my mind. And I'd been quite successful...until today.

"John?"

I lifted my head at the sound of Gwen's voice. "Yes?"

"Are you well?" she asked.

She needn't pry further. I knew what she meant, and though I might be willing to open my heart to her in confidence, I didn't dare do the same in the presence of my tall, stalwart peace-keeping companion, Tom.

"Well enough," I said around a sigh.

The relentless chirping song of the jungle insects filled the void of our silence—that, and the slurping of Tom from his mug. The man would drink anything, which, despite his silence on the subject, hinted at his own past spent aboard long voyages at sea.

"Well then?" said Gwen.

I took a deep breath and gave my head a shake. "I don't suppose we have any choice. We must go after Raphe."

Gwen's drink languished untouched between her hands. "It's not the only choice. We could escape, I'm sure. And hide. Despite that black's claims, surely faster ships exist than the *Mast*. And I'm certain we could find a secluded corner of the West Indies where none of the crew would ever find us. As small as Soledad is and as few amenities as she offers, we could subsist on less. There's nothing tying us to this isle other than..." Her voice trailed off.

Other than the memory—and ghost—of her father, I thought, which was a draw more powerful to her than she was willing to admit. But that wasn't the most important counterpoint to her argument.

"No," I said. "Had we known the *Black Mast* came for us and we'd escaped prior to her arrival, then yes, I'd believe we could've disappeared. But now?" I shook my head. "This involves more than the two of us, Gwen. You don't know Nicolas and Chinue as I do. Raphe, for all his eccentricities, possesses a character flaw among men of his ilk. Mercy. It's a flaw Nicolas and Chinue don't share. If we don't do as they ask, they'll exact revenge upon us, and should we be absent, they'll not hesitate to burn Soledad to the ground in search of our whereabouts. I couldn't do that to the people of this isle, or to Tom."

The big man lifted his head from his mug. "Are you implying I'm not a person?"

"Quiet, Tom," I said. "You know what I mean. No, our only real choice is to find Raphe and convince him to return, or lacking that, find whatever treasure it is he stole from the crew and return it to them. Only then will Nicolas, Chinue, and the rest of those men leave us alone."

And only then will I finally be free from the yoke of the Mast and its memory, I thought.

"Well, then. It's settled." Tom slammed his mug on the small table between us and stood. "We sail for Tortuga!"

I glanced at the man. "Tom, what are you doing? It's the middle of the night. Sit down. And besides, I haven't even asked you to come."

Tom sunk into his chair. "Sorry, Constable. Just trying to take some initiative, I was. Though I take exception to that last part. If you think I wasn't going to join you on this foray, then you've lost your...uh...uh..."

"Keen deductive ability?" I offered.

"Right," said Tom. "That."

I glanced at Tom's mug and didn't spot a single splatter mark on the table. In fact, the man's tankard was bone dry. Had I accidently poured a little *too* much rum into his cup?

"So I take it you're not particularly...*perturbed* by the revelations about my past?" I asked the man.

Tom averted his eyes and scratched his neck. "Oh, um. Well. About that..."

The look on Tom's face said it all, but even if it hadn't, the man's gait aboard the deck of the *Mast*, the ease with which he'd pulled himself up the rope ladder, and his unflappable demeanor in the face of the most feared pirates in the West Indies said it for him. Apparently, we'd all been a bit light on the details of our own past journeys. Couldn't say I was surprised, though. The King's pardon had enticed many a man.

I turned to Gwen. "So, darling, what do you think? Should we allow Tom to join us on this quest of unknown proportions?"

"Wait, what?" said Tom, blinking. "*Us?*"

Gwen sipped her drink and peered at me. "He doesn't quite absorb information the way the rest of us do, does he?"

"I'm willing to chalk it up to the drink," I said. "Although to be fair, your brashness combined with your complete inability to accept established gender roles is a difficult concept for others to grasp."

Gwen smiled and lifted an eyebrow. "Only others?"

"Oh, I grasped it right away," I said. "But I'm still coming to grips with it, if that makes any sense."

Tom peered at the pair of us as if we'd lost our minds. I couldn't blame him. Our banter had that effect on others, as did Gwen's brazenness. But as often as I disagreed with her desire to involve herself in others' affairs, no matter how unsuited they were to her sex, I was glad she was willing to join me in my search for Raphe. For one thing, it meant I'd be able to keep her close and not worry about what ills might befall her at the hands of the *Mast's* crew should I fail, but more importantly, it meant she'd already begun to forgive me for my truth-based indiscretions.

"Why don't you head home, Tom?" I offered. "It's late, and we all need rest before the morrow. And don't worry. I'll be sure to call on you before we depart."

7

I stood on the port side of the *Mejillón*, salty sea spray drifting across me as we bobbed up and down on the ocean waves. Despite the ship's hold being empty, a powerful smell of old fish filled my nostrils, which wasn't surprising given the vessel's primary use.

The *Mejillón* was a fisherman's cutter, and small at that, with a trio of staysails affixed to her bowsprit, but she was the only vessel in Soledad seaworthy enough to transport us to Tortuga. I thought I might have to test my foreign language negotiation skills to convince the citizens of the Isla to let us use her, but given the uproar caused by the appearance of the *Black Mast*, the townsfolk had been unnaturally agreeable. With barely more than a kind request on my part, Jorge had rounded up his brother and a pair of cousins, and we'd set sail at noon the following day.

Of the *Mast*, there remained not a sign. Once the fog had burned away under the hot lash of the morning sun, the bay had revealed itself to be empty, and not even Gwen, with her sharp eyes, could spot any sign of her on the horizon. I could only assume such a silent departure would add to the legendary tales surrounding the ship and her crew, and surely the act would be attributed to none other than Raphe Bartholomew himself, despite his lack of involvement. Knowing the man, he'd be happy to take full credit for it, and he'd probably embellish the tale to include elements of strange magic and several busty wenches of questionable moral character.

I leaned further over the edge of the *Mejillón*—which, if my Spanish could be trusted, translated to the rather odd *Great Cheek*—and rested my arms against the smooth wood of the railing. The cool sea breeze filled my hair as readily as the sails, the canvas of which cracked fiercely as the winds abated and then burst back to life. Tom sat at the stern of the vessel, drawing a whetstone across the edge of his massive axe, producing a slick metallic song that paired nicely with the slap of the waves against the ship's hull. The bright sun warmed my face, and despite the tenor of our voyage, I found myself smiling.

I startled as I felt a touch on my arm, only to find Gwen, dressed in a billowing white chemise and ankle-length red petticoat, at my side.

She grinned. "Frighten you, did I?"

"Some," I conceded as I felt my heart rate recede. "Though not as much as you'll scare Tom once he sees you in that." I whistled.

Gwen flicked her hand at me. "Oh, as if that man's modest sensibilities have any impact at all upon what I wear."

"To be fair, they're not merely *his* sensibilities," I said. "Many people share them."

Gwen snorted. "I stopped caring about fashion conventions as soon as I moved to a land where said conventions would result in me drowning in my own sweat."

"Liar," I said. "I doubt you ever cared."

Gwen shrugged, but her smile validated my suspicions. She snuggled under the crook of my arm, taking one of my hands in hers, and turned her gaze toward the ocean to match mine. I relished in the softness of her body as it pressed against mine and the smell of her hair—freshly washed with soap scented of some fragrant, local orchid I couldn't quite place. I breathed of it deeply and sighed.

"John..." said Gwen.

"Yes?"

"I...wanted to apologize," she said, keeping her eyes on the horizon. "For my behavior last night. It was unwarranted."

I gave her a squeeze with my arm. "On the contrary. I'd say it was quite warranted, given the knowledge you discovered of my past—which, in turn, I must again apologize for. Not the past in and of itself, but for my neglect in telling it to you."

Gwen turned her face to mine. "And that, precisely, is why my reaction was unwarranted. Not that I wouldn't have wished for you to tell me earlier. But how can I be upset with you for holding back an element of yourself that you fear and most clearly regret when I did the very same thing? I should've told you of my...*abilities* sooner, but I was afraid of how you'd react. And I see now you felt the same way about your past as a pirate."

"Careful!" I said with a wave of my hand. "That's not a word you casually toss around a fishing vessel like this one."

Gwen frowned. "As if Jorge and his men understand any English."

"More of it than either of us of understand his tongue, I think." I tapped the fingers of my free hand on the railing. "So...am I to assume this means you forgive me for my past indiscretions?"

Gwen lifted herself on her toes and gave me a warm, slow kiss—a tender embrace of our lips that brought me back to the very first kiss between the two of us. Like this one, that kiss had been delivered on the rocking decks of a ship, with the wind in our hair as we travelled from Havana towards Perdición, Gwen in search of a quiet resting place for her father to spend the last of his days, and I in search of much the same, not realizing the true thing for which I'd been searching was Gwen herself.

As she pulled back, she drew her hand across my cheek. "I forgive you, dear. At least, for *this* particular incident. And besides—now that I've sat on my thoughts for the better part of a day, I find your past as a you-know-what rather...*exciting.*"

"Oh, really?" I said. "How so?"

Gwen lifted her eyebrows and looped a finger through the curls of her hair. "Sexually."

"Oh. *Well, then.*" I straightened and saluted—in the traditional sense, not the metaphorical. "In that case, the impetuous and roguish—not to mention ruggedly handsome—quartermaster Driftwood is at your service, my lady. Although I'm not sure a vessel of this size offers much in the way of privacy for extracurricular activities."

"True," said Gwen. "And if Tom might faint at seeing me in my current attire, then image what might happen if he were to be exposed to the sounds of our rutting."

I chuckled and smiled.

"So," said Gwen. "In light of the limitations of our current accommodations, why don't we clear our heads? Speak of something else. Why don't you tell me about Raphe?"

I snorted. "Really? You seem to be acquiring an alarming penchant for thinking of other men in lieu of making love to me."

I dodged the blow to my arm before Gwen could complete her swing.

"You really are a knave," she said.

"Assuredly," I said. "But apparently that makes you wet in the britches."

Gwen crossed her arms and frowned. "You're not making this any easier."

"Fine," I said, shifting to lean my backside against the *Mejillón's* railings. "What else about Raphe do you wish to know?"

"Tell me about the man behind the legend," said Gwen, tossing her head to let the wind carry the hair from her face. "You said most of the stories of his mis-adventures are false. So what of the man is true?"

I rested my elbows against the slick wooden bulwark and intertwined my fingers. "Well, that's the thing, you see. The stories of him both *are* and *are not* true. In many ways, he strove to mold himself in their image, and the more extravagant they became, the more they drove him to prove their veracity."

"Meaning?" said Gwen.

"Meaning he wasn't always the grandiloquent swashbuckling caricature of a man he's become. Once upon a time, he was heartfelt and sincere, and his desires in life consisted of the attainable rather than the impossible. When we were boys—and even older, when we left together aboard the *Skylark*—we wanted much the same things. A little adventure and some mystery, perhaps. But now?"

I shook my head and cast my glance past the mast and rigging of the *Mejillón*, past the starboard edge of the ship into the shimmering blue waters and crest-tipped waves beyond. "I don't know anymore. And I haven't seen the man in almost two years. How much has he changed since? Clearly he's now stooped to the level of theft from his own crew. If we do find him, will I be able to reason with him? Reach him on any sort of meaningful level? Will I be able to convince him to do right by his crew, and by me? And..." I squinted into the bright light. "And..."

"And what?" asked Gwen.

"And...I think there's something out there," I said, standing straight. "Way out there, past the starboard side. I saw a glimmer in the distance."

Gwen followed my gaze. "A ship?"

"Possibly," I said.

Gwen and I locked eyes, and I think we both shared the same concerns as to the probable affiliations of said vessel.

I felt the heat of the sun fade from the back of my neck. Gwen looked over the port side of our cutter and tilted her head.

"Well, whatever it is you saw, John," she said, "it may be the least of our worries."

I looked behind me, and in the far distance, a mass of thick gray clouds devoured a portion of the sky. A haze covered the sea below them, and a flicker of brightness from within their nebulous bellies carried with it promises of mischief, if not yet the accompanied peals of rolling thunder.

"Better you head below decks, Gwen," I said. "We appear to be headed for the worst of it."

8

Rain lashed my face in unrelenting waves. It hammered the sails of the *Mejillón*, rebounding off them with pattering clacks as it continued its descent toward the decks. There, it gathered in pools before the rocking of the ship sent it swaying back and forth and through the scuppers at the base of the bulwark, where it poured into the sea, mixing with the seething dark waters of the salty deep.

I passed a hand across my face to wipe the deluge from my eyes, but it provided only a momentary respite. My hair clung to my scalp like seaweed to a hull. As rain water poured down the nape of my neck, over my shirt and coat, and down my legs in never-ending rivulets, I wondered if there existed a square inch of my skin that didn't resemble the withered remains of a raisin.

I heard the clump of heavy feet over the monotonous dance of the rain drops, and Tall Tom appeared at my side. He clutched the bulwark and leaned over next to me.

"Do you see it, John?" he rumbled.

I glanced at the man, not for the first time envious of his wide, tri-cornered hat. While the headdress afforded him no greater measure of dryness than it did me, at least it kept the water out of his eyes. Mostly, anyway.

"Yes, Tom," I said. "I see it."

Or, rather, I saw enough of it for my imagination to fill in the rest. Past the edge of the ship in the twilight gloom, I spotted flickering lights. Hundreds of them, illuminating the edges of market stalls and lean-tos and the ends of at least a half-dozen piers that faded from my sight as they stretched toward town. The lights of Tortuga.

For two full days—two endless, dark, waterlogged days that had merged together in my mind as one exhausting endeavor—we'd fought the worst of mother nature's rage. To Jorge's credit, he'd managed the squall masterfully, ordering his men to swing the boom about in tandem with the wind's whims, furl the sails when needed and loosen them when the winds abated to levels of restrained strength. I assisted where I could, knowing full well what actions to take to keep the small vessel afloat and intact, but my extended stint on land had blunted my skills, at least to a degree, and given the language divide between Jorge, his men, and I, my well-intentioned actions could've unintentionally countermanded the Spaniard's orders. So, to keep myself engaged and out of the way, I helped navigate during the tempest, basing my directions primarily off my limited knowledge of the sun's whereabouts and the basest instincts of my gut. Given the ferocity of the storm and our inability to lay eyes on the stars at night, I was sure we'd tacked far off course, but lo and behold, the winds and my intuition had brought us straight to Tortuga.

Apparently, my skills had blunted less than I'd thought over the years. My capacity for withstanding rain, however, was about as I remembered it.

I clapped Tom on the back and smiled before turning to seek out Jorge. With such a small ship, I knew I'd soon find him, which I did, tightening the braces at the stern.

"Well, Jorge," I said. "I can't say I enjoyed the trip, but we made it through in one piece, and that says a fair bit about your nautical know-how. Now what do you say we dock this cheeky vessel of yours and find ourselves a place to warm up and dry off?"

Jorge wiped his forehead with his arm and peered at me, confusion written across his face. *"No sé lo que me has dicho, señor John, pero yo voy a atracar esta nave, y entonces espero encontrar un lugar para calentarme y secarme, si Dios quiere."*

"Right, um...good man," I said. "You do that."

He wandered off, probably in search of his brother or one of his distant cousins, and I headed below decks.

I found Gwen with her feet up, resting in a hammock and reading by the light of a gimbal-mounted lamp. Even the tiny amount of light it provided seemed bright to my eyes made dull by the muted evening skies, and the barest trickle of warmth that seeped from its flame made me eager for a roaring bonfire in a tavern's hearth.

I scratched my head as I sat in the hammock at my wife's right. "You brought books with you?"

"Of course I did," said Gwen without looking up. "I'm well aware of the length of the trip to Tortuga, and I doubt this'll be our last stop. The more important question is—how is it you didn't notice this fact until now?"

"What do you mean?" I said.

Gwen poked her nose over the edge of her book. "I've been reading for the better part of the past two days."

I wiped at my sodden neck. "I've been busy battling the storm, if you hadn't noticed. The men needed me above decks."

"They needed you, or you *needed* to be needed?" Gwen made her eyebrows dance.

"You're a confounding woman, you know that?" I nodded toward her choice of literature. "So, what are you reading?"

"*Macbeth*," she said.

"That tripe? Again?" I said.

"What's wrong with it?" said Gwen defensively.

"It's so pompous and overblown," I said, "not to mention as bleak as the eyes of a man with the plague. And that Shakespeare's been dead for, what...seventy years?"

"I don't see how that has anything to do with the quality of the work," said Gwen, turning her eyes back to the play. "And besides, I like it. I think you're just jealous the play features the Scots and not the Irish."

I rolled my eyes. "As if I had any lasting ties to that miserable, wet homeland of mine."

Gwen peered at my waterlogged coat, breeches, and sopping hair, but she neglected to make the obvious comparison. "Is there a reason you've come down and disturbed my leisure?"

"We've arrived at Tortuga," I said. "Jorge's in the process of docking us...I think."

Gwen closed her book and swung her feet off the side of the hammock. "You know, we really must have you expend some effort into learning that language. I've a feeling it would come in handy."

"I haven't the time for it," I said. "And besides, I'm not good with tongues."

"Oh, I don't know about that," said Gwen with a grin. "You use your own quite deftly."

I lifted an eyebrow. "Really, woman? You tempt me with thinly-veiled allusions now, of all times?"

Gwen shrugged. "Sorry. I've been cooped up down here for two days. And I read *Much Ado About Nothing* before moving onto *Macbeth*. You know how that always enflames me. Anyway, since we've now arrived at Tortuga, what do you propose as our first course of action?"

"Well," I said. "If Raphe's passed through town recently, we'll soon know it. Even if the townsfolk haven't laid eyes on him, they'll have heard the uproar that generally follows in his wake. I'd say our first stop should be The Salty Slattern."

Gwen lifted her brows slowly. *"Pardon?"*

"It's a local tavern, not nearly as bad as it sounds," I said. "The host is a woman by the name of Maggie Leach. If a rumor makes its way into town, it passes through her sooner or later."

"Very well," said Gwen with a sigh. "I suppose it'll be as good a place as any to ask about your erstwhile friend. I'll get my cloak and meet you on the main deck."

A fresh gust of wind creaked the ship's mast, and drumbeats pounded the timbers overhead as the rain intensified. "If it's all the same to you," I said, "I think I'll wait right here until you're ready."

9

Despite Gwen's strength of spirit, I had my doubts about having her accompany me into Tortuga's unseemly underbelly. As I recalled it from my days aboard the *Mast*, the city was little more than a playground for pirates. To those uninitiated in the ways of the seafaring brethren, said description would be sure to instill a cold fear into their hearts, evoking images of snarl-toothed villains wielding rusty knives and preying upon man and maid alike from the mouths of dark alleys.

Truth was, few people suffered any violence from roaming the streets of Tortuga at night, and those that did brought it upon themselves with their foolishness, bravado, and boorish attitudes. Instead, what one had to be wary of was pirates made boisterous by their drink, and enormous quantities of it were consumed in the town every day. Rum, of course, remained the drink of choice, whether neat or mixed with water or lime or the sweet juices of any number of tropical fruits, but beer and wine flowed freely as well, to the point that it was a wonder the streets didn't run with spilt violet spirits and foamy, golden suds—although based on the smell, they certainly were exposed to their fair share of a different yellow liquid.

Drunkenness quite often led to debauchery, but luckily there were brothels aplenty to satiate the needs of the pirates—and to ensure they were thoroughly liberated of their coin. The whores were quite skilled at the latter, and should they somehow fail in their endeavors, the local cutpurses were quick to pounce upon the unconscious forms of overserved partiers that chose to sleep in the streets.

Thankfully, however, the unyielding rain had the same effect on the city's inhabitants as it did on the urine stench, washing them out of the streets and sending them packing into whatever bits of shelter they could find. So it was that Gwen, Tom, and I barely encountered anything unbefitting of a lady's eyes as we made our way through the muddy, barren streets of Tortuga toward The Salty Slattern. In fact, the only interesting scene we chanced across was a bout of fisticuffs between a burly fellow wearing a waistcoat and breeches and a gangly, mustachioed man with a scarf wrapped around his head, neither of whom spoke a lick of English based on the insults they hurled as they punched one another into oblivion.

As we walked in the slackening rain, the Slattern finally showed herself at the top of a gentle slope, identifiable by her sign out front depicting a wench holding two mugs of ale.

Tom halted me with a hand to my shoulder as we reached the front door. "John, you know as well as I do this tavern is no place for the likes of Gwen."

I think Tom meant to hide his voice from my wife's ears, but the man's deep rumble carried much farther than he realized.

"And what sort of place is that, exactly?" said Gwen.

The tavern spoke for itself. A ruffian with a thick, black beard wearing an empty bandolier across his chest exploded out the front door, landing on his back in the street's thick mud with a splat. A mixture of cheers and jeers followed him from the interior of the pub, followed by lots of shouting and the muffled music of a fiddler.

The lights and sounds faded as the door swung shut. I pointed at the entryway. "That sort of place," I said. "Normally, I'd hold the door for you, my dear, but in this instance, I think it's better if I enter first. Not that you have anything to fear with me and Tom at your side, but still. I can act as a shield in case any drinks or darts happen to fly your way."

"How sweet of you," said Gwen. "Though do try to protect your face. As gruff as it is, I'm rather attached to it."

She smiled, and I winked in response, all while Tom shuffled his feet uncomfortably.

I pushed through the door, letting the tavern's ambience smash into me with the same force as any of the waves the *Mejillón* had battled on our way into port. The lights and heat I appreciated after my long bout with the rain and gloom, but the cacophony brought on by the patron's yells and clinked glasses I could've done without. I shouldered my way through the boisterous crowd, working toward the back of the establishment, and by some miraculous stroke of luck, I stumbled into a free table and a couple of chairs. I commandeered them posthaste, wondering if perhaps they'd been in use until recently by our new acquaintance, the drunk gunslinger with the muddy back.

Gwen took a seat as she shook out her cloak. I offered Tom use of the remaining chair, but he refused, citing some hierarchy based on my status as a constable which I'm fairly sure the man made up on the spot. As I wrung water from my coat, a skinny lass in a rusty brown gown and bodice popped by.

"Get you lot anything?" she asked.

"Ale," I said. "Wine if you have it. And something to eat. Hot, preferably." I fished out a pair of reales from my pocket, knowing full well a place such as Maggie Leach's wouldn't take credit from anyone, no matter how fine the hem of their cloak looked, and mine had seen better days.

I glanced around at the men who filled the rough plank and nail bar, sailors every one of them based on their distinctive attires, though which ones hailed from ships that flew merchant house flags as opposed to Jolly Rogers and Jacks, I had no way of knowing. I didn't spot any friendly faces—or any unfriendly ones, for that matter—and not a man there seemed interested in our presence. All of them were too far gone in their rum or focused on swatting at serving wenchs' bottoms to pay us any mind.

Barely had I gathered my bearings when the skinny maid returned, her arms loaded with plates and her fists full of foaming tankards. She deposited the lot on the table with a clatter, distributing platters loaded with portions of toasted crust and mysterious brown filling.

I poked my meal with a wary finger and took a sniff. "What is this?"

"Steak and kidney pie," said the wench.

I wrinkled my nose. "Made with salt beef?"

"I dunno," said the young woman. "What's it matter?"

"I prefer meat products that haven't traversed the entirety of the Atlantic on route to my mouth, that's all," I said.

The girl shook her head and turned to leave.

"Wait," I said.

The maid gave me a thin-lipped, eyebrows raised sort of look.

"We need to see Maggie," I said. "Tell her Driftwood's in town."

As she left, I endured a reproachful shake of the head from Gwen, but not Tom, as the man had lifted his bowl to his face and had half his head submerged in his pie.

"What's that all about?" I asked Gwen.

"You," she said. "What ever happened to the man who spent years subsisting primarily off hard tack and salt pork?"

"He counted his blessings the day he set foot off his ship for the last time," I said. "And filled as much of his belly as he could with fresh food instead of biscuits and beans. Honestly, before arriving here, I never could've imagined the wealth of fruits and plants and animals that thrive in these climes, and yet, with all that bounty, they serve this?" I pointed at my plate.

Gwen smiled. "And to think you were suspicious when I first had those island women show me how to cook local cuisine."

"Well, of course I was suspicious," I said. "I'm always wary of food I can't pronounce. *Picadillo? Cou-cou?* And what's that one with the stewed greens? *Callaloo?* I'm still not sure I'm pronouncing that right. But even though I was suspicious, I'm glad you did it, because I've found my tongue is quite accepting of the Caribbean palate."

I took a spoonful of the steak and kidney pie and put it in my mouth. It wasn't anywhere near as bad as I'd feared, but it lacked a little panache.

"Well," said Gwen. "When we return to our bungalow, I'll be sure to prepare for you a nice steaming dish of whatever jungle oddity we can find the ingredients for. But only if you—"

A boisterous voice cut through the crowd and drowned my wife's pleasant soprano. "Driftwood! Well, I'll be damned. Where the hell have you been?"

I recognized the voice instantly, and its owner looked much the same as I remembered her. A tall woman, full figured, with shoulder-length hair the color of sand, wearing a wide skirt and a flowing shirt that barely contained her abundant chest. Maggie Leach, the tavern's owner.

She clapped me on the back with a strong hand. I stood to offer her my seat, but before I could, the woman enveloped me in a hug, her bosom crashing into me like breakers against a shore.

I croaked out a response. "Um...good to see you, too, Maggie."

I heard a piqued clearing of a throat coming from Gwen's direction. As I extracted myself from Maggie's busty embrace, I took note of the decidedly frosty glare Gwen shot in my direction.

"Maggie, if I may introduce a couple individuals," I said, with a wave of my hand. "This is my good friend, Tall Tom." The man gave a perfunctory nod as he continued to eat. "And this is my *wife*, Gwen." She chose *not* to give the same perfunctory nod.

"Well, ain't you the prettiest little thing," said Maggie. "Goodness, me, how the time's passed. Congratulations, Driftwood!"

Maggie tried to pull me into another embrace, but I held her off with a free hand as Gwen looked on disapprovingly.

"Care for a seat?" I asked, in an attempt to distract the woman.

Maggie waved me off. "Keep it. I own this place. I take what I want."

As if to prove the weight of her words, she turned and grabbed the back of a chair from another table, one currently occupied by a boisterous man well into his rum. She jerked on the chair's top rail, sending the man toppling to the floor, and replaced it in front of our table, all while the man's friends erupted in a chorus of laughter.

"So, Driftwood," said Maggie as she settled into her chair. "What brings you to the Slattern? Word was you'd given up the life."

"I did," I said. "As should be plain from my present company. But apparently the life didn't leave me."

Maggie lifted an inquiring eyebrow.

"I can't go into much detail," I said, "We're searching for information, and I figured you'd be the best person to see about that."

"Yes," said Gwen icily. "John was quite insistent that rumors of all shapes and sizes make their way through here, and after making your acquaintance, I'm certain he's right. Why, I have to imagine there's not a man that passes through Tortuga without suckling at the Slattern's teat."

Gwen gave me a slant-eyed glance, and I returned the favor as her words sunk in.

Maggie smiled and slapped the table as she laughed. "Hah! I like her. She's funny."

"Don't mind Gwen," I said. "She has a unique way with words. Now, then. To business. Have you by any chance heard rumor of the Badger recently?"

"Couldn't stay away from your old mate, could you?" asked Maggie, leaning back in her chair.

"Something like that," I said.

"Well, you're in luck," said the head barmaid. "As it so happens, Raphe's in town. Arrived about a week ago, if memory serves me correct. Word is he's been spending most of his hours at the brothel across the street from the church."

Gwen snorted, despite her obvious attempts at severity.

"You find the juxtaposition of the two amusing?" I asked.

"I'm more surprised that Tortuga even *has* a church," she said.

"Best brothel in town, according to the men," said Maggie. "And the church allows for convenient forgiveness of sin, I think. But no matter. Driftwood, why don't you still your wife's flapping tongue so we can talk a mite?"

A crash of ceramic and splintered wood accompanied a chorus of shouts from across the bar, drowning out whatever acidic quip Gwen concocted for dame Leach.

Maggie rose. "Stay here," she muttered. "I'll be back. *Blackguards...*"

Gwen stared at me, her lips pressed together in a thin line as she shook her head stiffly.

"Don't give me that look," I said. "She's an old friend. Nothing more."

"An old friend with the manners of a *javelina*, apparently," she said.

I sighed, then devoured the greater portion of my pie, washed it down with a few gulps of ale, and motioned for us to go. Better to risk Maggie's ire at our premature departure than Gwen's wrath, till death do us part.

10

I'd anticipated Tortuga's church to be easy to find, as surely its belfry and steeple towered over the buildings surrounding it, but I hadn't anticipated how easy it would be to locate the whorehouse itself. The building stood a good two and a half stories, painted in a faded red that perhaps meant to evoke thoughts of a lady's privates. Its windows sprawled open, their shutters pushed aside as wide as possible, and harlots called out from them, trying to entice passersby with their wares, such as they were. Other women stood at the building's entrance doing the same, and I imagine they would've taken to the streets to ply their trade had the rain not been so incessant.

Inside, the building was dimly lit, hot, humid, and packed to its gills. Shouts and raucous laughter and the sounds of clinked mugs filled the air, much as they had back at Maggie's establishment, but other sounds reached my ears too, emanating primarily from the upper portions of the bordello: thumping and giggling and cries of pleasure. Perfumes lay thick in the brothel's air, alloying themselves with the earthy smell of unwashed bodies and the sweet scent of spilt rum to form a heady mixture that made me feel aroused and on the verge of illness at the same time.

Throughout our trip to the brothel, Tom had insisted such a place wouldn't in the least bit be appropriate for a woman of Gwen's rearing, and while I knew my wife could handle herself under virtually any situation, I was starting to agree with the big man's sentiments.

"You know," I said, leaning close to Gwen's ear so she could hear me over the din, "perhaps Tom was right. I'm not sure you should be exposed to an establishment of this nature."

As if to emphasize my point, a pirate with a black bandana and a large hoop earring slapped a strumpet on the rear right in front of us, eliciting a cry of—pain? or perhaps pleasure?—from her.

"Nonsense," said Gwen with a wave of her hand. "I'll be fine. But you? You're the one who requires supervision. You could get into all sorts of trouble if left unattended."

"Me?" I put a hand to my heart. "I have eyes only for you, Gwen."

She eyed me suspiciously. "And barkeeper Maggie's mountainous breasts, apparently."

"I tell you, she and I never engaged in any amorous activities," I said. "There's not and never has been anything between us."

"Except, of course, her mountainous breasts," said Gwen with an evil grin.

I sighed, exasperated. "You're going to milk this for all it's worth, aren't you?"

"*Milk?*" said Gwen. "Please tell me that choice of words was intentional, dear."

I rubbed a hand against my forehead. "Tom, you talk to her. I don't know how much more of this I can deal with... Tom?"

I looked around and realized the big fellow had vanished, which wasn't easy to do for a man his size.

"And where do you suppose *he* disappeared to?" asked Gwen with a raised brow.

I had a good idea. "Suffice it to say, I think we might be without his services for a while. Now let's see if we can find Raphe and get out of here."

With Gwen at my back, I shouldered my way through the crowd until I found a free strumpet: a thin girl, probably several years Gwen's junior, with a crop of black hair and a dress that revealed a goodly portion of her shoulders and bosom.

"Excuse me," I said, grasping her arm. "Perhaps you can help us. We're looking for someone."

"Of course y'are," she said, latching onto me as if she were a lamprey. "Lucky fer you, ya found 'er. Fancy a tumble?"

"He does not," said Gwen, who forcefully removed the girl's arm from my own.

The girl sniffed vigorously. "Hmm! Bringin' yer own bonny's 'gainst the rules, dontcha know. I've half a mind to call fer the bawd."

"You mistake our purpose here," I said. "We're looking for a man. A client, most likely. Name of Raphe Bartholomew Thatch. Sometimes goes by an alias. The Badger?"

The girl looked at me blankly, so I described him, replete with his distinctive black and blonde hair and the long braided beard that drooped from the tip of his chin.

"Oh. That tosser," said the girl.

"Is he here?" I asked.

She shrugged. "Beats the dickens outta me."

"Well, surely he's been seeing a woman here," I said. "Could you point me in her direction?"

"Who hasn't 'e been seein'?" said the girl. "But to answer yer query, he's spent mosta his time with...oh what's 'er name? I forget. Don't matter. You'll recognize 'er right off. She's the mestiza."

The girl pronounced the word oddly, like Miss Teaser, but I knew what she meant, and the phrase gave me something to look for in terms of appearance. I gave the girl my thanks, and with Gwen holding onto my shirt so as to not lose me, I performed a quick walking survey of the main floor in search of the woman.

In short order, we circled back to the front of the bordello, no richer in knowledge than when we'd started the brief quest. Although the darkness lingering in the building's corners could've hidden the mestiza girl, I suspected we couldn't find her because she was otherwise occupied.

As I glanced back and forth into the crowds, Gwen read my mind.

"So...what now?" she asked.

I took a deep breath and immediately regretted it as the sickly aroma attacked my olfactory senses. "Now, we wait—at least until some of these crowds disperse. Though who knows how long that'll take." I glanced out the front door. "I think I'll cool my heels outside for a while. This place is making me ill."

Gwen followed my gaze. "Really? Despite the rain?"

I gave her a look. "Would you rather stay in this hellhole?"

"Point taken," she said.

We stepped outside and managed to find a spot partially shadowed from the rain by the building's portico. Gwen lifted the hood of her cloak, while I, still damp down to my smallclothes, simply endured nature's whims. Across the street from us in a weed-strewn lot next to the church, a pair of old asses hitched to a rickety cart slowly chewed their way through a pile of roughage, their mouths working in tandem in a familiar down, over, back ruminating motion. With the pitter patter of the rain on the street in front of us and the brothel's bawdy laughter at our backs, we shared a few moments of the closest possible approximation to silence that we could currently achieve.

"So," said Gwen. "Is this what most of your escapades as a pirate encompassed? Staying up far too late, mucking about in homes of ill repute in search of scraps, all while being slowly turned into the main ingredient in a chilled soup?"

"More or less," I said. "Although most of the time, our piratical endeavors featured fewer busty barmaids and more malnutrition and dismemberment. And we rarely battled gigantic sea monsters or stumbled across ancient caches of Incan gold, either. Don't tell your father, though."

"As you well know, we don't talk that often," said Gwen. "But no, I won't. It would be downright cruel to corrupt his image of buccaneering after death."

A thought hit me. "Do you think I should tell him? That I was a pirate, I mean. I'm not sure if it would make him like me more or less, given I married you."

"You're not a pirate anymore, so I'm not sure the latter comes into play," said Gwen. "He'd probably find it titillating. Though I'm not sure it's helpful to my psyche for you to refer to him as if he were still among us."

"Sorry."

I tried to stow my thoughts for later, but I couldn't help but wonder what Paul's reaction might've been upon learning of my past. The man had obsessed over pirates, even if he hadn't really understood the realities of the occupation.

A drop of chill rain hit me in the back of the neck, making me jump. As I wiped it away, a tall man in a heavy cloak traversed the street across from us. I'd assumed he'd make his way toward the brothel at our backs, but instead he walked past and turned at the edge of the church, fading into the darkness.

I scratched my chin and grunted, though not entirely of my own design.

"What is it?" said Gwen.

I shook my head. "Hmm...nothing."

"It's bad form to lie to one's wife," said Gwen. "Especially in the shadow of a church."

"It's nighttime and it's cloudy," I said. "There aren't any shadows."

"It's also bad form to be an ass," she said. "Now, out with it."

I pointed in the direction of the chapel. "The man that passed us. As he turned, I caught a glimpse of his face. I could've sworn...it was Chinue."

"Are you sure it wasn't some other black?" said Gwen.

"No, of course I'm not sure," I said testily. "I saw him in passing, from a distance, and in the darkness. Still...I had a sensation as I laid eyes on him. A remembrance, of sorts. But how could it be him? If, aboard the *Mejillón*, I was right and the *Mast* was following us, then how did they beat us here? And why follow us at all if they pointed us to Tortuga in the first place?" I dug my fingers into the beard at my chin as I thought.

Gwen crossed her arms. "You know, there's a simple way for your curiosity to be sated."

"Being?" I asked.

Gwen pointed. "Let's follow the man."

11

I harbored my doubts about whether or not we'd be able to successfully tail the man, not only because of the rain and the darkness but also because of his cat-like instincts, but as luck would have it, his trail didn't extend very far. We spotted fresh, muddy footprints, which I naturally assumed were Chinue's, at the foot of a door set in the church's side, and when I tested the door itself, I found it wasn't latched. After cautioning Gwen to stay quiet, I grasped the door's handle and pushed on in.

A display packed with about two score votive candles greeted us, and by the pale, flickering red-orange light they provided, I could just make out the extent of the basilica. A dozen roughly hewn wooden pews lined the church's aisles, leading up to a simple yet elegant altar packed with crosses of bronze and a hand carved wooden crucifix. Blood seemed to ooze from the lash wounds on the Body of Christ, whether due to the tinted light of the candles or some trick of the painter's brush, I couldn't tell.

Above us, heavy timbers supported the church's strongly pitched roof, and a chandelier of black, wrought iron held at least a dozen unlit taper candles. At the front of the building shone a wide, circular window of stained glass, depicting the birth of Christ and containing no less than a hundred colored panes. Up in the rafters, small walkways traversed the church at the sides, disappearing past the altar into what I assumed might be the minister's living quarters. Back on the main floor, the muddy footprints extended in that same direction, past the altar and in the direction of a door, though they faded as they went, as the mud thinned and the light cast by the votive candles dimmed.

I took a step in the direction of the tracks, but Gwen halted me with a hand.

"John," she said. "I have a bad feeling about this."

"It's the ambience," I said. "Don't worry. It gets me, too. Something about darkness and empty places of worship makes you think as if the creator himself is watching. And perhaps he is. But it's not as if we're here to sack the place. Just don't pay too much attention to that crucifix. Its eyes are rather...*disconcerting.*"

Gwen shook her head. "It's not that. It's a more basic sensation of disquiet. I...think there might be a grave-yard nearby. Or perhaps a catacombs."

I narrowed my eyes as I looked at Gwen. "And what makes you say that?"

"I can sense it," said Gwen. "If there's enough souls of the departed nearby, it can give me a sensation. A chill at the base of my spine or a raising of my arm's hackles."

I glanced at her arms, but in the dim light, I couldn't tell if the hairs had raised. "Why have you never mentioned this before?"

"We've never left Perdición before," said Gwen. "And the graveyard there is quite small. Not enough to cause me any ill feelings."

"So what are you saying?" I said. "That we should be wary of ghosts?"

"I'm—"

A thump sounded behind me, strong and distinct, and despite my unflappable nature, I admit I jumped. I turned to face the noise, fearing the worst, but rather than the pale, shaking hand of a soul caught between worlds, I instead saw something most unexpected. Or rather, *someone*.

Raphe Bartholomew Thatch burst from one of the alcoves past the end of the altar, on the top floor by the rafters. He darted along the narrow walkway, the soles of his knee-high boots thumping heavily against the wooden planks, vibrating the whole of the chapel. His black and blonde hair streamed behind him, kept out of his face only by the toil of a bright red bandana that wrapped around his forehead and ended in a knot tied at the base of his skull. The man looked as I'd remembered him, outfit and all, except for the large brown canvas satchel that hung from his belt loop and swung violently as he ran.

"Raphe!" I called.

The man turned and reached for a flintlock in his belt, a wild look in his eyes.

Fear gripped my heart, and I reacted instinctively. I dove into Gwen, knocking her behind the nearest wooden pew, as Raphe drew his pistol. I anticipated a violent crack of gunpowder and wood splintered by speeding metal, but instead received only a call in return.

"John? Is that you?"

I peeked my head above the side of the pew to reply.

The pistol fired.

I ducked as the crack of a lead ball splitting wood reached my ears, but the sound didn't *fill* my ears. It came from above, to my right, toward the opening above the altar.

I looked again. Raphe's pistol pointed toward the opening as wooden fragments showered down onto the Body of Christ. Then, out of the gap appeared a man with a heavy cloak, the cowl now down and bunched around his neck. A black man, tall and lean.

Chinue dove forward, a wicked, curved cutlass in his hand. The air whistled as he took a mighty swing at Raphe, but the Badger danced back. Chinue's sword cut into a wooden pylon with a thwack. The black man put his boot into the pylon to pull the sword free as Raphe drew his own cutlass, but before the famed pirate could swing, the lanky black dove back himself and drew his own muzzleloader.

Raphe turned and jumped as Chinue's pistol erupted flame. A chunk flew from the pylon as Raphe careened into the wrought iron chandelier, sending it swinging as it showered us with taper candles.

"Raphe!" I yelled. "What the Hell is going on, man?"

"Language, mate," said the Badger, his rolling speech as distinctive as a horse's gait. "We're in a church, you know."

Gwen shoved me, and I realized I still lay half atop her. I shifted so she could see.

"*That's* your concern?" I called back.

Chinue ripped his sword from the pylon, a vicious sneer chiseled into his hard face.

"Look, old friend," said Raphe. "It's lovely to see you. Really, it is." He pulled another pistol from his belt and fired it at Chinue, sending more sparks and gun smoke and splintered wood flying into the air. "But this isn't the best of times to try and catch up."

Cutlass in hand, Chinue lunged at the chandelier, but Raphe set his feet into the metal and shifted his weight, sending the thing swinging away just out of the blade's reach. As it approached the other side, Raphe jumped. His arms flailed as he flew through the air, and I feared he might make an unplanned descent into our midst, but the man's luck held. He caught the opposing walkway's banister in the midsection, emitting a grunt as he did so.

As I heard his groan and Chinue's curse, another thump sounded from behind, and I turned. This time, I spotted a distinctive cavalier hat and heard another familiar, if not as welcome, voice.

"Now, now, Raphe," said Nicolas, standing at the end of the walkway on which Raphe had landed. "Zis running and ze chase. Eet is zo very unbecoming of you. Accept your fate and be done wiz eet."

Raphe stood and glared at the man, his eyes as wild as when I'd first spotted him. "The devil take you all."

Nicolas reached for his pistols. Raphe turned toward the front of the church and ran.

A shot fired. Wood splintered.

Raphe set his foot into the side of the banister as he reached the end of the walkway.

Another shot fired. Sparks flew.

Raphe jumped, and a shattering, sparkling crash filled the air as his body exploded through the church's stained glass window, sending hundreds of slivers of expensive colored piety dancing through the air.

12

I grabbed Gwen by the arm, pulling her past the rack of votive candles and out the church's side door, despite her protests.

"John, what are you do—"

"Not now, Gwen," I said. "For once, just follow. We must get to Raphe."

And figure out what the Hell is going on, I thought to myself, but I left it unsaid as I figured I'd engaged in enough blasphemy within a house of worship for one day.

As we burst into the street, the rain hit us in a violent deluge, having intensified mightily since our entrance into the basilica. The darkness combined with the downpour limited my vision, but my ears helped me decipher the chaos.

Gunshots rang above me, coming from the church's rafters, followed by the crack of their lead shot impacting the brothel's walls across the street. Shouts emanated from the bordello—more animated than the cries of pleasure we'd previously experienced. To our side, the snacking asses brayed loudly, frightened no doubt by the bangs and the smell of black powder. And over the jumbled roar, another sound: that of shuffling, boot-clad feet, scraping and slipping over rough wood.

I followed the noise and spotted Raphe—thank the Lord for his bright red bandanna—scaling the top of the building caddy-corner to the brothel. As his feet disappeared over the top of the wall, another gunshot sounded, this time coming from the top of the whore-house. I squinted in the rain, and by the light of the open windows, I spotted another dark figure. Though I couldn't discern a face, my gut assured me it was another of the *Black Mast's* crew.

"Raphe! Wait!" I shouted.

Gwen grabbed my arm. "John, honestly—"

Again I shushed her, knowing full well I'd pay for my actions later, but time was of the essence. A glimpse of red caught my eye as Raphe leaped to the roof of an adjacent building and disappeared behind a wall of the sky's worst.

My, but the man was spry! I suppose it came from years of climbing riggings and ladders to reach ships' tops and mastheads, actions I'd once mastered but long since lost. With Gwen at my side in a sodden dress that clung to her ankles, how could we possibly hope to catch the man?

Another buffet from a fired hand cannon and a frantic bray spurred me into action. I ran forward to the donkeys and their cart and began to loosen their reins from a nearby hitching post.

Gwen followed at my heels. "Asses, John? Have we now stooped to common thievery?"

"You forget, dear," I said, as the shouts across the street intensified and lights bloomed in the windows of numerous homes. "I'm a rotten, black-hearted pirate."

I lifted my wife and plopped her in the rickety bench seat behind the donkeys.

"But they're burros, dear," said Gwen, holding the cowl of her cloak tightly around her face to protect herself from the rain. "If you expect to catch Raphe—"

I hopped next to her, a thick switch in hand, as the asses stamped their feet. "—then the beasts will have to be properly motivated, that's all."

I cocked my arm and waited for the next gunshot. As I heard the blast of powder, I sent the switch flying into the donkeys' hindquarters. The beasts elevated their brays into awkward yells and tore out into the street, sending mud and pooled water flying and clattering the rickety wheels of the cart with such clamor as to wake the dead—should Gwen's presence alone been insufficient.

As I wrenched on the reins to turn the donkeys down the street's incline, a giant of a man burst out of the brothel, his breeches wrapped around his ankles.

"John! Wait!"

Tall Tom stumbled and fell into the mud as the asses caught their footing.

"No time," I called to the big man. "Follow as best you can!"

We tore around the corner and down the street, headed in the direction I'd last seen Raphe jump, our bodies jostling and bouncing as the cart threatened to dismantle itself under the donkeys' power. Wind whipped around us, sending rain lashing against the sides of buildings as well as our faces. I turned my eyes to the rooftops, trying to catch glimpse of Raphe, but I could only take quick peeks as I struggled to control the frightened asses.

"There he is!" said Gwen.

She pointed. I followed her finger to the telltale red bandana, bobbing as its owner leaped to another building.

"Raphe!" I called. "Slow down, damn you!"

I saw the man pause, perhaps in acknowledgement of my demand, but then he turned and ducked. A split-second later, a man lunged out of the shadows and sailed over him, falling off into the black, yawning void past the far edge of the roof. I heard him cry out, but the thump of his landing was muffled by the relentless hammering of the rain.

We sailed past Raphe, driven forth by the overzealous donkeys. Behind us, the man changed directions, his feet propelling him over the tops of the Tortugan roofs. I yanked on the reins, forcing the asses left around a corner, then again into an alley where we scared the wits out of a tabby and nearly trampled a drunk, then once more back onto the main thoroughfare.

Raphe had changed directions yet again. Gwen, with her sharper eyes, instructed me on which ways to turn as we followed him, playing a game of cat and mouse with the man—or ass and pirate, as the situation dictated. Our buttocks bounced off the cart's bench as we turned right and left, and I heard a loud crack as we turned a corner, not of a musket or pistol but emanating from one of the cart's wheels. I feared the thing might disintegrate on us, but somehow it held. Wherever we went, a trail of shouts, pistol fire, and lit lanterns followed in our wake.

After what seemed an eternity but was likely only a few minutes, our cart careened onto the Tortugan docks. As the wheels hit the wooden planks, whatever structural fault had produced the loud crack finally manifested itself. The entire cart collapsed on itself in a shower of wooden debris, dumping Gwen and me unceremoniously to the worn boards underneath. The donkeys brayed once more and ran off, dragging the decrepit remains of the cart—mostly just a bench and harness—off with them into the night.

I helped Gwen to her feet, blinking several times as I stared at her. "Are you all right?"

"Fine, thank you very much," said Gwen as she took my hand. "And you don't have to look so surprised. I can handle myself. I thought you'd know that by now."

"I do," I said. "My surprise is due to your dress. How in the world is it so free of mud? I'm coated to my waist."

"Don't be a ninny," said Gwen, and then, pointing, "There's Raphe!"

Sure enough, the man vaulted from a rooftop three piers down, the dock underfoot rattling as he landed.

Gwen and I took off after him, racing perpendicular to him along the marina as he ran down the length of the pier. We shouted for him to stop, and for once the man seemed to hear us. He waved as he ran but didn't slow, and I was left to wonder what in the world the man intended. As close as we were to him, surely Chinue, Nicolas, and the rest of his pursuers weren't far behind. Did he intend to dive into the sea and swim to all the way to Hispaniola? Or was the *Black Mast* anchored somewhere out in the bay, shrouded by rain as it had been by fog back at the Isla de Perdición? If so, why would head there? Even if he planned some convoluted double-double cross of the crew of the *Mast*, one man couldn't sail such a ship any more than a raft of sea lions could. Blast it, why couldn't the man slow for a moment and tell us what was going on!

We turned the corner onto his pier and followed him. Through the pouring rain, I could just see him at the end of the jetty, pausing beside a tiny skiff with a single sail, barely long enough for the man to lie down in. Surely he didn't mean to escape the *Mast* in *that*?

He dove into the vessel. I opened my mouth to call out to him, but a massive, howling wind tore the breath from my mouth, bowling Gwen and I over and forcing our bodies to the rough wooden planks beneath our feet. Raphe's skiff blasted into the bay like a cannon shot, sending spray careening off the boat's prow in a giant cloud. As the boat sped off, I could barely make out Raphe's voice on the wind—which made no sense, as the forceful gusts carried the man directly away from us.

"Farewell, John," came his wavering voice. "Bid the devils *adieu* for me, will you..."

I pushed myself to my feet and helped Gwen to hers as the wind whistled around us. It whipped Gwen's hair across her face and pulled the water from our clothing as the rain added more, but after a few mighty gusts, the wind slowed to a gentle breeze. As it did so, the rain—

omnipresent for the past two and a half days—dwindled and stopped. I wiped a hand across my face and glanced at the heavens, where the winds played with the clouds as easily as they had me and Gwen. They scurried along the sky, quick as mice, and within a moment, they'd opened a gap through which I spotted Castor and Pollux and caught a glimpse of the moon's pallid light.

"By my faith and begorrah," said Gwen, "what in the name of the almighty just happened?"

I stared at my wife. "Well, look at you. Spicing up your vocabulary, are you?"

"You're one to talk," she said. "Yelling all about Hell and damnation in a church, of all places."

I heard a bell ring in the distance, and looked up at the sound of a voice.

"Ho, zere, Driftwood."

Nicolas stood atop the building at the base of the pier, flanked by Chinue in his heavy cloak and a pair of stern-jawed pirates. "Don't tell me zat ze Badger escaped? Zat does not makes me 'appy, you understand."

I approached the man and his retinue, blood pumping in my veins from anger as much as the thrill of the chase.

"What in the world is this, Nicolas?" I said. "You ask me to seek out Raphe, and I do. Yet when I arrive, I find you already here. And I thought you sought a treasure he stole from you. So why do you try to kill him?"

The bell continued to peal, and a commotion brewed nearby. Shouts mingled with the muted roar of stomping feet.

Nicolas looked over his shoulder toward the sound. "Now iz not ze time, Driftwood. Just remember your part in zis. Or suffer ze consequences..."

Nicolas and the two pirates disappeared over the back of the building. Chinue sneered and ran a knife over his throat, no doubt as a reminder to the sorts of consequences Nicolas referred, before following the lead of his quartermaster.

Despite myself, I shivered. The man would do it. I had no doubt. And he'd likely take pleasure in the act. I felt my breath become heavy as I pictured Gwen, kneeling, on the deck of the *Mast*, Chinue at her side. A jagged blade in his hand. Me, immobilized and forced to watch. A flash of steel. A scream...

I felt Gwen's touch on my arm. "John...? The commotion. Soldiers, I think."

I shook my head and blinked. "You're right. Time we apply the switch to our own asses and get out of here before the cavalry arrives."

13

"Honestly," said Tom. "A thousand pardons, to the both of you. My absence was inexcusable."

"On the contrary," I said. "It was eminently excusable. We all have needs, Tom. Might as well admit that."

The big man shook his head. "No, no. Don't say that. It minimizes my own vice, it does. Besides, it's irrelevant to my fault in the matter."

We sat in the main hall of an inn—not Maggie's place, as Gwen wouldn't let us return—warming our feet and drying our clothes by a crackling hearth. Steam rose from the three of us, as well as from the bodies of the other patrons in the place, which were few in number given the late hour. The occasional chuckle or muttered French curse acted as our conversation's only company.

"You know," said Gwen. "Saying the phrase 'a thousand pardons' is enough. You needn't *actually* apologize a thousand times."

Tom removed his tricorn hat and passed a hand across his short, thin hair. "I know. But I just feel if I'd been there I could've—"

"Your presence wouldn't have aided us in the least, I'm afraid to say," I told the man. "In fact, if you'd added your heft to that cart, I've no doubt the thing would've exploded after a bare half-block."

"Speaking of which," said Gwen. "We must try to locate the owner of that wagon. Pay him recompense for our actions."

"Certainly," I said. "I'll add it to our to-do list alongside finding Raphe and avoiding a violent death at the hands of Chinue and his bloodthirsty brethren."

Gwen rolled her eyes, and I felt perhaps I'd been too sharp with my tongue. If marriage had taught me anything, it was that no shame existed in admitting fault in one's own actions.

"Sorry," I said, leaning over and taking Gwen's hand. "That was discourteous of me. You're right. We should. It's just that I'm a bit on edge regarding that business with—"

"The weather?" Gwen regarded me with a sidelong glance, but she gave my hand a squeeze, as if to recognize and approve of my apology.

"Yes," I said. "The weather."

"Funny bit of business, that," said Tom. "Rainin' harder than a man's..." He glanced at Gwen. "Um, well...rainin' quite hard, anyway. And then that violent gust of wind comes in and carries all the storms away with it? Downright odd, it was."

"You don't know the half of it," I said.

Which was true. He didn't. We hadn't had enough time—or the mental wherewithal—to fully explain it to him yet. After fleeing the docks, Gwen and I had hid while the French *militaires* had searched the streets, looking for the source of the commotion. While initially worried we'd be captured, we soon realized two things. First, the deluge during our donkey ride had been so intense that not a man or woman could've possibly recognized us from more than a few feet away, and more importantly, the *militaires* were far more interested in calming citizens so they could return to their drinking and whoring than they were in finding out the cause of the uproar.

Nonetheless, we skirted them and headed back toward the brothel. Halfway along the path we found Tom, muddy and soaked but with his privates thankfully covered. On Gwen's insistence, we'd holed up in the nearest inn, which, unlike Maggie's place, seemed to cater to a decidedly more international crowd—by which I mean not a single barmaid in the entire place spoke a lick of English. Luckily, between the three of us, we were able to recall the French word *vin*, although I'm sure if we'd lacked that, the maid still would've brought us something palatable upon taking a bite of our coin.

I hefted my cup of wine and took a long draught, hoping against hope the beverage might clear my head rather than fog it. As the fermented grapes soaked into my belly, I couldn't help but think back to Raphe's battle at the church and our chase. How had Nicolas and Chinue beaten us to Tortuga, and why had they enlisted my help when they clearly knew where to look for Raphe without me? And it had seemed the pirates had been far more interested in filling the man with lead shot than capturing him so they could extract from him the location of their stolen treasure.

Of course, if those questions engendered in me some level of confusion, then Raphe's actions left me in complete and total bewilderment. What had the man been doing in the church? He'd seemed quite rushed, and a look bordering on madness had filled his eyes, though to be fair the man probably hadn't anticipated Chinue's arrival. And then there was the issue of his departure. The timing of that gust of wind seemed far too fortuitous for it to be mere coincidence, but even if God had taken mercy upon the Badger's plight in granting that breeze, Raphe's demeanor hadn't been that of a man with his back pressed against the wall. He'd run straight for his ship—if it could be called that—as if he'd *known* the skiff would be able to grant him safe passage away from Tortuga and his pursuers.

The barmaid came by to see if we needed more drink, and I waved her off. Tom lifted a hand, but the maid had already turned her back, and she waltzed away before the big man could force his mouth around any more mangled French. It was then I noticed Tom's cup ran dry. Looking at my own, which was a few sips shy of full, I thought perhaps whoring was the least of Tom's vices.

"So," said Gwen, nursing her own beverage. "I suppose we should find a place to rest our heads for the evening. I can't say I know the French for 'bed,' but I'm sure I can convey the concept with a few hand gestures.

That's assuming these ruffians don't interpret my hand motions as something filthy and depraved..."

I shook my head. "Not yet."

Gwen narrowed her eyes and peered at me. "It must be past midnight by now. What else do you mean to do? Don't tell me you plan on harassing poor Jorge into setting sail tonight? I'd rather not spend the night in a hammock again, anyway."

I couldn't tell if that last bit had to do with comfort or privacy. While Gwen had been rather grabby during the trip to Tortuga, I couldn't imagine Maggie's unwanted advances and the musk of the whorehouse had done much to stoke the fires of Gwen's desire.

"No," I said. "We can't expect to traipse all over the Caribbean in the *Mejillón*. It's much too small, and besides, Jorge will need to return to his family. We'll find another ship. But that's besides the point. I wasn't planning on leaving in the middle of the night."

"So, what *were* you planning, then?" said Gwen.

I took a long sip of my wine and set it back on the table in front of us. "I mean to discover what Raphe was doing in Tortuga. And what better time to do so than under the cover of night?"

14

We pushed into the interior of the faded red brothel and were greeting with the same sickly scent as before. The intensity of the odor had lessened, likely due to a combination of the heavy winds that had blown through town and the lessened late night clientele. Still, it forced a wrinkle in my nose.

"I really don't see why we needed to continue this endeavor tonight," said Gwen.

I glanced at her. "It's called curiosity, my dear. Don't you harbor any?"

"I'd rather harbor some shut eye," she said, stifling a yawn. "Honestly, what's your aversion to sleep? It's delightfully refreshing, and I've heard it helps tighten the skin, among other things."

"Are you saying I'm getting saggy?" I said.

Tom cleared his throat behind us. "Look, I don't normally have any quarrel with your marital squabbles, but could we try to hasten things? You know, before the fates conspire to get me into any more improper situations."

Gwen laughed. "Oh, Tom. You act as if you have no say in the matter. What? Do you think your pants might drop to the ground of their own accord and you might trip and fall into a woman's privates?"

The big man blushed and muttered something about respect and a man's personal turmoil. I ignored him and began my search of the bordello, which was easier this time due to the diminished number of patrons. While I didn't find the girl I'd hoped to encounter, I did find someone almost as useful: an older woman, overweight and tired, whose services I doubted would be in much demand from Tortuga's visitors. Her presence in the brothel suggested a different sort of role for her.

Draped in a faded red dress that hung limply over her wide hips, she worked at clearing a set of tables of their cups. I tapped her on the shoulder. "Pardon. Are you the madam?"

The woman turned. A comb kept the majority of her gray-flecked hair out of her face, but a few strands has loosened themselves and attacked her nose. She tried to blow them out of the way, but they fell right back into place.

"Aye," she said. "What're ya lookin' for?"

"The mestiza girl," I said.

The woman eyed me before sizing up Tom and ultimately settling her gaze upon Gwen. "What? The three of ya? What exactly do you intend with 'er?"

"Not what you're thinking, most likely," I said. "We have questions."

"Time is money," said the bawd.

"We'll pay," I said.

She held out a hand, which I filled with a few coins from my pocket.

The matron shifted the reales in her hand, feeling their heft, before pocketing the lot. "Second floor," she said. "Third door on the left, most like. Keep it quick. And no samplin' 'er exotic charms without payin' a greater price."

Part of me wanted to give Tom an elbow to the ribs to make sure he'd heard, but I think Gwen had already shamed the big man enough. Besides, he'd never try such a thing in Gwen's presence. Unlike the brothel's lowly harlots, Gwen, by some reasoning of Tom's brain, was a *lady*.

We headed upstairs, found the door in question, and knocked. After a moment of silence, I heard squeaking floorboards, and the door cracked. A face appeared in the gap, one with long dark hair, coffee-colored skin, almond eyes, and a wide mouth. Rather than a smile, however, her face sported furrowed brows, sunken eyes, and drawn cheeks. A face of caution, not enthusiasm. A face turned cold by the realities of her chosen profession—if, indeed, the choice had been hers.

"Yes?" she asked. She eyed us with some concern, Tom more so than the rest of us.

"My name is John," I said, "and this—"

She stuck a hand out the crack, palm up. "No name, please."

I placed my hand on the door and felt the resistance from the woman's body on the other side. "You misunderstand our presence. I'm a...constable. I'm conducting an investigation, of sorts."

"Oh, so now you're a constable?" said Gwen. "You seem to break that out when it suits you."

"Shush," I said.

The half-breed's face contorted, whether because of our banter or my word choice I couldn't be sure.

"We're here to ask you a few questions," I explained.

"Question? What sort question?" The mestiza's English was curt and sometimes broken, but mostly effective.

"Questions regarding a former friend of mine," I said. "Raphe Bartholomew Thatch. Some call him the Badger. I was told you may have spent some time with him over the past few days, Miss..."

"No," she said. "No name. But...come in."

The door opened under the pressure of my hand as the mestiza woman relented. Inside her room, I spotted a simple bed frame topped with a lumpy straw mattress, a lone chair, an iron banded chest, and little else. As we entered, she retreated to the room's corner and sat in the chair, her arms folded across her chest. She stared at the floor, eyes empty and head bowed, and I began to wonder what in the world had drawn Raphe to the poor woman.

Not that Raphe was bigoted against those without fair skin. I'd seen him enjoy the company of women of all colors, and almost all shapes and sizes for that matter, but he'd always been drawn to women like himself—loud, boisterous, lovers of life and drink and laughter. Not quiet, withdrawn women whose faces betrayed the emptiness of their own hearts.

I glanced at Gwen who gave me a nod of her head as response, as if to tell me to get on with it.

I cleared my throat. "So then... I take it Raphe was here with you?"

The woman nodded.

"How long?" I asked.

She shrugged. "Three, four night."

"Do you know what he was doing in Tortuga?"

The mestiza gave me a blank stare.

"Let me rephrase that," I said. "Was Raphe with you tonight?"

She nodded again. "Early. Yes."

"And when he left, did he tell you where he was going?" I asked.

"No," she said. "But I see him. He go church." She pointed out her window to the building in question.

"Had he gone there before?" I asked.

"Yes," said the woman.

I rubbed my beard. Interesting. Multiple visits to the church indicated there was something there Raphe valued. Had he hid the treasure he'd stolen from the rest of his crew there?

"Do you know why he visited the church?" I asked.

"No," said the mestiza.

"Come, now," I said. "Think. Surely he mentioned something to you about it in the three or fours days he spent here."

The woman's arms drew tighter around her body. "No. By the winds of Yocajú, I tell you he not."

"Yoca *who*?" I asked.

Gwen pressed a hand against my shoulder. "John...we're not getting anywhere. It was a good thought to seek her out, but she clearly has nothing to tell us."

Tom shuffled his feet and nodded, likely eager to leave the place—or to have us leave his presence.

"Not yet." I turned back to our quarry. "Before I go, answer me one question. Why was Raphe here?"

The half-Indian woman glanced at me. "You stupid? This whorehouse."

"Please," I said. "You're not Raphe's type. So tell me. Why you?"

The woman shrugged. "I not know. He ask me question. And visit church. That all."

"What kind of questions?" I asked.

"About me," she said. "My life. My people. I not know why."

I furrowed my brows. That didn't make sense. "Was there anything...*odd* about his behavior?"

"He strange man," she said. "Yes."

I waved my hands. "That's not exactly what I meant. Raphe was always loquacious—meaning he talks a lot. And his personality is very distinct. Rakish, jaunty, dismissive. I'm trying to find out if there was anything *else* about him that seemed out of place."

The whore stood and gazed out the window. I thought she might not answer, but after a pause, she did. "He talk to him, lots."

"Him?" I said. "You mean himself?"

"Yes, and no," she said. "Him, and bag he carry."

I recalled the large brown canvas satchel I'd spotted hanging from Raphe's belt loop as he'd burst into the church's main hall. "Are you saying he spoke to his knapsack?"

The woman nodded.

"Well...what was in it?" I asked.

The mestiza turned and looked at me. "I not know. I only see one time. It look like..." She pressed her lips together and furrowed her brows. "I know not word. *Cob.*"

"You mean maize?" I asked.

The woman shook her head.

"Describe it, then," I said.

The woman gestured with her hands, forming a shape roughly the size of a melon. "Shell. Color of sand." Then she whipped her fingers around in a spiral.

I glanced at my wife for some help.

"I think she's describing a conch," said Gwen.

I sighed and scratched my head, feeling more puzzled by the moment.

15

Outside the front of the church, a pastor clad in heavy brown vestments gestured wildly at the broken stained glass shards on the street. He pointed at the gaping hole in the front of his building, all the while cursing in Spanish in a most unholy fashion. Beside him, a pair of the French *militaires* spoke to one another in their own romance language, clearly not anywhere close to as upset by the turn of events as the priest. By the looks of things, neither half of the conversation understood the other. Certainly, I couldn't decipher any of it, but I got the general gist.

Gwen, Tom, and I watched the scene unfold from the darkness of an alley adjacent to the brothel. After some more animated gestures on the part of the Spaniard, one of the Frenchmen spoke and pointed down the street. The Spanish priest threw up his hands, and together, they walked off. I supposed they might wish to record the priest's testimony as part of the public record.

Once they'd disappeared, I motioned Tom and Gwen forward, tiptoeing across the street on light feet.

"This is madness," said Gwen under her breath.

"I concur," said Tom. "It's not wise to return to the scene of a crime. You of all people should know that, John."

"Nonsense," I said. "Those *militaires* will keep that pastor busy for hours."

"Then why are you walking as if trying to sneak past a sleeping guard hound?" said Gwen.

I looked at my own feet and saw the truth of her words. "Fine. So perhaps they'll be back. You can't fault me for my caution. Now stow the blather and come on."

I slipped to the church's side entrance again and paused outside the door.

"Tom," I said. "You hide in the empty lot here while Gwen and I search the church. If you see the pastor or those French soldiers return, hoot like a barn owl twice in quick succession to warn us."

"What? Why me?" said Tom.

"Because you're big and you have a sharp axe," I said. "It'll help you ward off any gremlins that waylay you in the night. Besides, you still need to pay your penance for your pantless escapades."

Tom mumbled and shambled off, and I opened the door for Gwen.

Inside, the church was as we'd left it. The votive candles burned orangey-red, illuminating the scattered wooden detritus from the pistol fight. Taper candles strewed the floor underneath the chandelier, and by the entrance, bits of glass glimmered in the flickering light.

After a cursory examination of the interior, I set my eyes to the muddy tracks on the floor. I'd never fancied myself much of a woodsman—despite Gwen's proposal to escape the *Mast's* crew and live in solitude off the land, I doubted we'd survive more than a few weeks in such environs—but mud on a floor I could track. I followed the steps back past the crucifix, through an entryway, and stopped at the mouth of a dark corridor.

I couldn't see a thing, but luckily, a lantern hung lifeless from a hook on the wall. I took it and retreated to the votive candles, where I used a sliver of fatwood to transfer the fire to the lantern's bowels. The candle inside roared to life, and I closed the lantern's shutter to protect the flame.

With a bit of light by which to see, I returned to the corridor and continued to follow the tracks, but my trek ended shortly. The muddy prints brought me down the hallway and ended within a small room—a library, packed with perhaps two hundred or more books. A compact writing desk with two austere chairs pushed under either side of it hugged one side of the tight chamber while bookshelves pressed against the other walls. A miniscule window hovered over the desk, but given its size, I doubted a man could read by its light alone even in the noonday sun.

"So," said Gwen, startling me. "Would you care to explain what, exactly, you hoped to find here?"

"Well, in truth, I'd hoped to find Raphe's stolen treasure," I said. "Not that I expected him to leave it lying about in the open, mind you. But this does change my thinking somewhat."

I set the lantern atop the writing desk, shedding some light on a pile of books that sat there. The largest of the bunch caught my eyes. I flipped open its cover and found it to contain a series of exquisite, hand-drawn maps of the Caribbean. Given the detail of the drawings, surely the book was highly prized, but I doubted such a tome could be part of the Badger's treasure.

"So, what?" asked Gwen. "Are we to assume your friend Raphe snuck out of his room at night so that, instead of satiating the fires in his loins, he could *read?*"

"As I already mentioned, that mestiza woman isn't his type," I said. "So I suppose it's possible. The question is why? To my knowledge, the man never shared your passion for the humanities."

I picked up a smaller tome from the desk and flipped it open. The title read: *The Jamaican Fool, an Almanac of Jamaica, Cuba, Hispaniola, Porto Rico, the Antilles, Caicos, and all the Waters In-between, For the Year of Christ 1678.* I flipped through it, noting its contents, which contained the usual fare—weather forecasts, knowledge of the winds and tides, planting dates, and the like. As I surveyed the pages, I noticed a few jagged tears at the binding.

Gwen picked up another book from the pile and opened it, revealing the title. *A History of the Taíno and their Sundry Cultures and Customs, as translated from Friar Ramón Pané's Seminal Work on the Subject, by James Cordwith III.* Gwen thumbed through it, as I did with mine.

"Perhaps Raphe came here in search of knowledge," she offered.

"You may be right," I said. "There appear to be some pages missing from this almanac, though there's no way of knowing what information said pages might've contained."

I picked up another couple books, but both of them appeared to be in Spanish. One was a nautical text, filled with—I think—information on ocean currents and wind patterns, and the other was something titled *Mitos y Leyendas de las Indias Occidentales*.

A fierce yawn from Gwen brought my eyes up from the printed words.

"Tired?" I asked.

Gwen tried to stifle the involuntary action. "What can I say, John. It's dreadfully late. I know you wish to see this thing with Raphe through to its conclusion, but I don't see how breaking into this chapel, for the second time in one night I might add, will help much with that. Nor do I see why it couldn't wait until the morrow."

I sighed and took Gwen's hand. "You're right, of course. On all accounts. I guess I got caught up in the chase. Comes from my background as a constable, I suppose. It's just that, once the oddities regarding Raphe's behavior started to mount, I was sure there'd be some logical explanation for it. Some piece of evidence that would shed light on it all—and on the motives of those involved. But I should've known better..."

As the words faded from my lips, I paused, my ears straining. I thought I heard something. Words. Phrases. And not in English.

I poked my head from the entrance to the library and peered down the hallway. At the end, I saw the reflections of a flickering light, and not those of the votive candles. They accompanied some muted Spanish cursing.

"God's teeth," I said. "Blast Tom and his tired eyes! Why didn't that man hoot twice like I told him?"

"The pastor?" asked Gwen.

"Yes."

I set foot into the hallway, but I hesitated. The light appeared to be intensifying, and there was something else. I heard more than one voice.

"What is it?" asked Gwen.

"The soldiers," I said. "I think they're here, too. And they're headed this way."

"Oh, wonderful," said Gwen. "Just *wonderful.*"

My mind swirled as I considered our possibilities. We could run, but we'd have to go right by the pastor and the soldiers to leave the church—at least, I wasn't aware of any other way out. But surely they'd try to stop us. I could fight them, of course, but I didn't have any weapons on me, and the Frenchmen were armed. I'd seen their pistols and sabers as they'd conversed outside the church. That put me at a huge disadvantage, never mind the fact that I'd be preoccupied with protecting Gwen during the affair. And besides—I couldn't very well attack a man of God, could I? Maybe if I merely knocked him down...

I heard thumping, and I turned to see Gwen fumbling at the bookshelves.

"What are you doing?" I asked.

"I'm shelving these tomes to make it seem as if no one's been here," she said. "Perhaps if the pastor thinks we've just arrived, we can convince him we're pilgrims looking for a place to rest our heads."

"Really?" I said. "You think he'd believe that after what's already happened to his church tonight?"

Books thumped as Gwen pushed them into slots. "Well, do you have a better plan?"

I glanced back out into the hallway. The light hadn't brightened, meaning the men hadn't closed on us at all. "Perhaps I can distract them. Some of these books are quite heavy. I could use them as missiles. Or maybe they won't find us. Perhaps if we wait..."

Thump, thump. More books being put away. A creak. "Oh, yes. Lovely. What a wonderful plaaAAAAN!"

I spun, only to spot a flutter of Gwen's dress as she fell into a yawning void, one that had contained a bookshelf a mere moment ago—a bookshelf, I now noted, that was still there, but had swung back on a hinge.

Hearing the voices from the church proper intensify, I grabbed the lantern and dove after Gwen, pushing shut the bookshelf door behind me.

16

Thankfully, the void into which I'd entered contained more than a never-ending well of darkness. There were walls of rough stone, a spiral staircase of worm-eaten wood, and at the bottom of it all, Gwen, lying prone on a floor of packed dirt made damp by the rains.

I took her in my arms as I reached her. "Gwen! Speak to me. Are you hurt?"

She held her head and squinted, but responded immediately and with conviction. "Yes. I'm fine. I just hit my head on that blasted staircase."

I breathed a sigh of relief. "Oh, thank God."

"Might as well," said Gwen as she rubbed the base of her skull. "I don't see who else might've freed us from that quagmire."

"Speaking of which," I said. "What in the world did you do?"

"I don't know." She glanced at me with those beautiful pale eyes of hers. "I was simply placing those books upon the shelves, and the next thing I knew the wall disappeared out from beneath my hand, sending me toppling into the darkness and down here. Wherever we are..."

Gwen turned her eyes to her surroundings, as did I. And I nearly jumped.

Stacks of bones—human ones—lined the walls: skulls and clavicles, femurs and tibias, ribs and vertebrae and hips. Worms and beetles had long since stripped the flesh from them, leaving behind only pale grey reminders of our mortal bodies. Roughly three feet off the floor, a row of skulls stretched into the darkness, the hollow eye sockets seemingly staring through my skin and muscle into the depths of my soul.

Gwen snorted. "Told you."

"Come again?" I said, ripping my gaze from the bodies of the dead.

"I knew there was a catacombs nearby," she said. "I could feel it."

"Oh. Yes, yes. Right." I helped her to her feet. "Very prescient of you."

"Not at all," said Gwen as she tried to wipe dirt from her dress. "Prescience is foresight, of which I have none. Trust me, if I'd had any idea I would've opened a portal behind a bookshelf and fallen down the stairs I would've worn a sturdier dress and protected my head. In truth, my abilities are much less. More of a subtle sensation. A feeling in my core."

"Like indigestion?" I offered.

Gwen punched me in the arm. I could've avoided the blow, but I didn't flinch. I deserved it.

"You're such an ass," she said.

I bared my front teeth and waggled my hands behind my ears, trying to make them look long and floppy like the ears of the beasts in question. Gwen rolled her eyes and shook her head, but she couldn't prevent a smile from creeping onto her lips.

"Come on," I said, lifting my lantern. "Let's find a way out of here before our friends upstairs investigate."

The catacombs branched to our right and left, but I chose the path straight in front of us that led back toward the front of the church—at least, that's what I believed. Having descended a spiral staircase of unknown length, and with no view of the sky or outdoors to speak of, I couldn't be sure. After a few paces, I began to doubt myself, but I figured the catacombs couldn't be very large, so I let my feet take me where they may.

After passing piles upon piles of bones, Gwen's thoughts apparently started to approximate my own.

"Where in the world do you suppose all these dead came from?" she asked. "Tortuga can't have more than...what? Five or six thousand inhabitants?"

"Of European descent, yes," I said. "But I have to think once upon a time, many more natives than that lived here. And I can only assume where they've all gone..."

I shuddered at my own choice of words. Once upon a time, I'd assumed the dearly departed all either headed to the depths of Hell or passed through the gates to the kingdom of Heaven under the watchful eye of St. Peter, but now I knew better. Another fate, one much more nebulous, also existed for the dead.

"Gwen," I said, suddenly feeling nervous. "It occurs to me that standing together with you in a catacombs packed with the bodies of dead Indians, who likely don't speak a word of English and bear an understandable grudge against anyone with pale skin, isn't the smartest of ideas."

"Oh, stop it," said Gwen. "The dead can't hurt us."

"Are you so sure of that?" I asked. "It's true they cannot touch us. I've seen you try and fail with your father. But I've also seen the man manipulate objects, and more than one of the Spaniard women in Soledad has called upon you to help with mischievous ghosts who rearrange the cupboards. Whose to say they cannot injure us should they will it?"

"Relax, John," said Gwen. "In all my years I've never seen such a thing. Besides, do you see any ghosts here?"

I held the lantern out before me and gazed down the corridor, but all I spotted were bones and darkness. "Well, I suppose—"

Something trailed along the nape of my neck. I screamed and jumped.

Gwen laughed as she pulled her hand back from my collar. "Oh, dearest. You're too easy."

"Not funny." I frowned as I rubbed my neck. "*At all.*"

"Oh, don't be that way," said Gwen. "Come. Give me a kiss to make up." She wrapped her arms around my midsection and leaned forward.

"You must be kidding me," I said. "Of all places to be amorous, you choose a dank, dark crypt?"

"It's secluded, at least," said Gwen.

"What ever happened to being tired?"

"What can I say," said Gwen. "Being chased by soldiers and falling down a set of stairs lit my blood afire.

The former in particular was rather exciting, in retrospect. And you know I have a thing for graveyards."

"You're an awfully troubled young woman, you know that?"

"Yes," said Gwen. "And you're stuck with me, whether you like it or not. You gave me your oath."

She forced her kiss upon me, which I accepted without much resistance, but after I'd satiated the hunger of her lips, I pulled away.

"You know," I said. "You raised a good point, however. Why *aren't* there any ghosts down here?"

Gwen sighed, frustrated. "Probably because these individuals are all long dead."

"So?" I asked.

"The veil around me is thinned. In my presence, ghosts have more influence than they do outside of it. Their capacity for speech is increased, for example. But even around me, the long departed have difficulty coming back."

I raised an eyebrow.

"I've told you this before," said Gwen, looking exasperated. "And don't ask me why. As if I had any idea. You might as well ask me why the sun rises in the east and sets in the west or why the winds blow from the northeast."

"Now, now," I said. "No need to get agitated. I was just curious."

"Yes, you're very good at that." Gwen flicked her hands down the corridor. "Seeing as you've killed the mood, let's keep moving, shall we?"

I obliged, leading us to a junction in the path. As I stood there, pondering which way to go, Gwen snapped her fingers.

"Yes?" I said.

"I suffered a thought."

"And would you care to share it?"

"Raphe's treasure," she said. "He must've hidden it here. That must've been his true purpose in the library."

I chose to turn right, responding to Gwen as I walked. "If only that were true, but sadly it isn't."

"And how are you so sure?" said Gwen.

I turned and smiled at her. "As keen as you are with elements of the *supernatural*, so am I with the eminently *natural*. There are no prints in the earth down here except for our own. With the rain over the past few days, if Raphe had been down here, we'd see evidence of it."

Gwen sniffed dismissively, as if my insights into the real world were somehow less impressive than hers into the realms of the dead. Regardless of the intent of her sniff, however, it served to fully quash whatever remnant of the mood Gwen's advances had created.

We walked in silence, turning here and there before ultimately coming to a set of worn, stone steps. We followed them up, and after passing through a rather cramped mausoleum, we found ourselves in a fenced-in graveyard. In the near distance, I spotted the church's belfry by the light of the moon. When we finally returned back at the lot where we'd left Tom, we found the big man pacing furiously.

"Remind me never to ask you to make birdcalls, again," I said.

Tom was too relieved at our presence to be upset by my jab. He swallowed the two of us in a massive hug.

"Oh, thank goodness," he said. "Where've you been?"

"We took a slight detour," said Gwen. "Might've been longer if my husband weren't such a prude."

Tom blinked. "I'm not going to ask."

"Tom, please take Gwen back to the inn," I said. "I'll meet you there shortly."

"*What?*" Gwen stepped back and crossed her arms. "You mean to tell me you still have plans for the night? At this hour? And after all we've already been through?"

Gwen had a right to be upset. I hadn't dropped any hints that I intended to make one final trip before the sun's rise, but unlike our visits to the brothel and church which had been driven primarily by my burning curiosity, my remaining task was purely pragmatic in nature.

"I swear, I won't be long," I told her. "And I promise I won't do anything mischievous or illegal. Now, to bed with you. Before you collapse."

Gwen gave me a sour look, but for once, she acquiesced. Tom took her by the arm, and I set about my remaining business.

17

I felt a light touch on my arm. "John..."

I mumbled and floated away on my own personal cloud.

"John..."

The steady pressure on my arm transformed into a mild shake.

I blinked and immediately regretted it. Sunlight streamed into Gwen's and my room at the French-speaking inn, a small space made seem lavish only by our visit last night to the mestiza's quarters.

I squinted against the light. "Urgh."

Gwen sat next to me on the lumpy bed. "Come on, John. It's time to wake."

I nodded toward the window. "Urgh?"

"It's about ten, I think," said Gwen. "Far past your usual waking hour."

"Urgh..."

"Yes, well, you did go to bed just shy of dawn, most likely," she replied. "But nonetheless, it's high time for you to be up."

I raked my tongue over my teeth. It moistened my mouth, and helped me find my voice. "A moment. I'm still trying to banish the fog from my head."

"I'm not sure that's possible," said Gwen. "To my knowledge, that's a permanent feature of your mind."

I tried to come up with a witty rebuttal, but the best I could manage was another "Urgh."

Gwen stood and folded her arms. "This is most unlike you. You're usually the first one up."

I rolled onto my side and forced my feet over the edge of the bed. I yawned and dug a fist into my eyes. "Yes, well, two days of fighting the elements aboard the *Mejillón* followed by a near sleepless night can do that to a man."

"What took you so long, anyway?" asked Gwen. "I thought you said you'd be right behind us."

"My excursion took longer than expected," I said.

Gwen raised a brow.

"All in good time, dear. Let's grab some breakfast."

"I already did," she replied. "Though Tom might still be stuffing his face. That man can *eat*."

I shrugged. Given his size, it wasn't particularly surprising.

As Gwen watched me, likely to ensure my cooperation, I threw on my boots, laced my breeches, and donned my shirt, the last of which was starting to acquire a unique salty and savory fragrance, despite the best efforts of the rain.

Once dressed, I headed downstairs into the common room with Gwen, where I found Tall Tom nursing a mug over an empty plate.

"Please tell me that's your first," I said.

"Third," said Tom.

I frowned and pushed my brows together.

"What?" said Tom. "It's small beer. And besides, I needed somethin' to wash down my meal."

"Three somethings, apparently," I said. "So, what's for breakfast?"

"Fresh bread. Eggs. And halved fruits," said Tom. "Not sure what kinds. One with tiny orange seeds and another with bigger, black ones."

"Very descriptive," I said, grabbing a chair.

I flagged down one of the tavern maids and mimicked the action of eating to her as I passed her a couple coins.

"So," said Tom as he took another draught from his ale. "Got back late last night, I presume?"

"Far *too* late," said Gwen, joining me in a seat at my side. "And up to no good, if you ask me. Probably out whoring. Or burying his face in that Leach woman's breasts."

I rolled my eyes. "Really? You know me better than that, Gwen."

"Oh?" Gwen gave me one of her mischievous grins. "Then what *were* you doing?"

"I said, *in good time.*"

Gwen snorted, and her smile disappeared. "Whatever it was, you're being very secretive about it."

"I thought you liked surprises," I said.

"It depends on the surprise," Gwen said. "A pleasant meal paired with a fine vintage and a kiss at the end, yes. A polecat between the bed sheets, not so much."

I glanced at Tom and back at Gwen as I tried to determine if the latter had ever actually happened to her before I was interrupted by the arrival of my meal. The maid set before me a plate of eggs cooked until just firm, their bleeding yolks a bold yellow, served over toast slathered with butter and with a side of guava and papaya—the source of Tom's mysterious large, black seeds.

I took a bite of the egg-soaked bread, and as the mixture hit the pit of my stomach, I realized how much I regretted passing up the majority of last night's meal. I inhaled the entire plateful in the briefest of moments—barely enough time for Gwen to ask me about my clandestine nighttime activities thrice more.

As I wiped the last of the tender, orange papaya from my chin, I finally relented to Gwen's nagging. Without explaining myself, I rose from my seat and waved for her and Tom to follow. I led them out the inn, down the muddy streets of Tortuga, past the shops of carpenters and ropers, past food carts and loudly snoring drunks, all the way to the docks, where, as far as I could tell, there wasn't any lasting evidence of rampaging ass-induced damage.

As we walked down a pier, perhaps two down from where we'd chased Raphe, Gwen's self-imposed silence finally broke. "Would you care to share what, exactly, the purpose of this expedition is?"

"Remember how I said I didn't think the *Mejillón* could serve us for the remainder of our journey?"

Gwen nodded.

I stopped and held out a hand. "Well. Meet your new home for the foreseeable future. The *Tickled Pink*."

She sat at anchor in front of us—a sleek Bermuda sloop, fore-and-aft rigged, about seventy feet from stern to prow, with a half-dozen guns on either side of her. She sported a single mainsail in back, but a trio of triangular jibs stretched between her bowsprit and her lone mast. Her red cedar hull beamed bright, clean of seaweed and barnacles, and based on her narrow beam, I knew she'd be a fast lass.

Gwen eyed me dubiously. "*The Tickled Pink?*"

"Get it?" I said. "It's funny because she's a sloop, not a pink. See? Look at her stern, and see the curvature of her bottom? She's rounded, not flat."

"I get it," said Gwen, holding up a hand.

"So, what's the problem?" I asked.

"Well it's an incredibly silly name for a ship, don't you agree?" said Gwen. "I mean, what sort of captain would name a vessel in such a manner?"

"Ah, yes," I said. "About that—"

I didn't get a chance to explain, as a voice hailed us from the ship's decks. "Ho, there, Mr. Malarkey. Am I to assume you've assembled your meager crew, such as it is?"

A woman stood on the edge of the bulwark, grasping one of the ship's bowlines. She wore tight breeches and a fitted waistcoat without an undershirt, showing off her lean, muscular arms and glistening bronze skin. Her auburn hair hung in a tight braid over one shoulder, and her eyes, dark and husky, hid behind long lashes. She smiled at us.

"Hopefully the crew is included in the cost of the charter," I joked. "Captain Handy, let me introduce my wife, Gwen, and our acquaintance and sometimes body-guard, Tom. Gwen and Tom, meet Captain Jane Handy."

Tom removed his hat and bobbed his head, but Gwen stood there, tongue in her cheek.

"We've already brought your things over from the *Mejillón*," said Captain Handy. "Let me pop down and I'll lower the gangplank." She hopped off the bulwark and disappeared.

Gwen stared at me. "You're kidding, I hope."

"Oh, don't give me that," I said. "It's not what you think. Sailors harbor a fear of transporting women on board a ship. You should've seen Jorge's face when I first told him you were coming. The only way I could circumvent those superstitions was to find a vessel where there was already a woman aboard. As it so happens, there's not many of those. Which brings us to the *Pink*. But she's a fine ship, and fast, if I'm not mistaken."

"So, let me get this straight," said Gwen. "Is it *sailors* that harbor this fear, or *pirates*?"

I squinted at her. "I'm confused. Are you angry I chartered a ship captained by a woman, or that said ship is a pirate vessel?"

"Can't it be both?" said Gwen.

I held my hands out in appeal. "Look. It's Tortuga. What did you expect? The Royal Navy?"

"What I expected," said Gwen, "was a ship that wouldn't incriminate me by its mere presence, and one with a competent captain at the helm."

"Well, that's a rather sexist assessment, especially coming from you," I said. "By all accounts, Captain Handy is an exceptional sailor."

"She looked quite competent to me," said Tom, rubbing his chin. "Especially from the backside..." He whistled.

Gwen and I both stared at him.

"Is that a euphemism?" I asked. "Or are you not entirely sure what that word means?"

He cleared his throat. "I...um...never mind."

The gangplank thudded as it hit the pier.

"All aboard," called Captain Handy, her voice light on the westerly winds.

Gwen snorted and turned her eyes to the ship, but as she gazed at the vessel, I could tell her displeasure was fading. Gwen wasn't much of a sailor, but even she could see the *Pink* was built for speed and ideally designed for our voyage.

My wife kept her gaze on the sloop. "You still haven't explained how it is you intend to track your old friend, Raphe. It's not as if we found anything to advise us of his intentions or motives last night."

"Fair enough," I said. "But I've since realized I was too reliant on my training as a constable and not enough on my abilities as a sailor. The winds—as *peculiar* as they've been—have blown in a westward direction ever since Raphe sailed off in that skiff of his. And the man's boat isn't meant for the open seas. Therefore, if we head west at a brisk pace, staying to the shallows and keeping our eyes trained on the shore, we should find Raphe sooner or later."

And if we couldn't find him, it very well might be because the man had sunk to the bottom of the ocean, but I didn't want to dwell on what that might mean for us and the crew of the *Mast*.

Gwen glanced at me, the frost having mostly melted. "They brought over my possessions? Including my books?"

"So said Captain Handy," I replied. "We'll be sure to check before we weigh anchor."

Gwen sighed, shook her head, and boarded the ship. I followed in her wake.

Captain Handy stood at the side of the gangplank. She snorted as I set foot on the *Pink*, and I wondered if she'd overheard Gwen's and my conversation. I hoped not. The last thing I needed was to start the next leg of our voyage on the wrong side of the ship's command.

18

I leaned over the *Tickled Pink's* side, watching the moonlight play over the shallow waves of the sea. A tickle settled onto the tip of my nose, and I tried to displace it with a gust of air blown from between my lips. I succeeded, but sadly, my actions didn't entice the winds into doing the same to our sails.

After leaving Tortuga, we'd loosened the ship's canvas, catching the westerly winds and making good time as we skirted the coast of Hispaniola. But that's when our plans went awry.

As we'd turned the northwest corner of the island, by the old French fort of St. Nicolas—who bore no relation to the *Black Mast's* quartermaster, to my knowledge—we'd turned our sights to the straight that separated the Isle of Guanabo from Hispaniola proper, but despite the determination of the *Pink's* crew to lead us in that direction, the wind had other designs. No matter how hard we tacked, the wind pushed us farther and farther west, away from all land and into the waters of the windward passage.

I'd feared the rogue winds would carry us all the way to the coast of Cuba, but following an afternoon of struggling against their might, the forceful gusts had died as swiftly as if by a knife through the heart, just as the sun dipped below the horizon. The rapid change brought mutterings from the ship's crew, and I even heard one claim of an *unnatural* hand at play in the weather. Normally, I would've let such superstitious nonsense roll off me like rain from a greased tarp, but following the bizarre circumstances of Raphe's departure from Tortuga, I wasn't entirely as sure as I'd used to be.

The doldrums had lasted through the night, into the following morning, and throughout the entirety of the day, leaving us stranded in open waters. By the navigator's charts, we sat some twenty miles southwest of Cuba's tip, and the ship's lookout hadn't spotted hide nor hair of Raphe and his miniature skiff.

If not for the specter of the *Black Mast* and her pirates' threats, I probably would've lazed the day away alongside the crew of the *Pink*, who seemed like an agreeable bunch as I grew to know them, but I couldn't force my mind to rest. I kept revisiting my brief encounter with Raphe in Tortuga, and wondering at his presence there—as well as that of Nicolas and Chinue.

I heard a gentle creak of wood behind me, too faint to be caused by the heavy foot of a man or anyone without a hardened sailor's expertise.

"Quiet night, isn't it, Captain Handy?" I said without turning.

"A little *too* quiet for my liking." Jane Handy rested her elbows on the ship's bulwark and proceeded to crack her knuckles one by one, even those of her thumbs. "Whenever it gets this still, it makes me think a powerful storm is brewing elsewhere. And chances are it'll find us if we don't move out of the way, first."

"There's always a powerful squall brewing some-where," I said. "But I doubt said storm's force has any correlation to the calm on a sea some hundreds of miles away."

"So you don't believe in forces beyond our compre-hension?" asked Captain Handy.

"I believe in a great many things," I replied.

Handy lifted an eyebrow, but I didn't elaborate. Waves lapped gently at the side of the *Pink*, serenading us with their steady rhythm.

Handy turned and rested her backside against the railing. "Tell me, Mr. Malarkey, if you don't mind. What sort of man travels to Tortuga with his wife in tow, ac-companied by a tall, handsome, axe-wielding friend, and seeks passage aboard a vessel such as mine in the wee hours of the morning?"

I felt my eyebrows knit together. "You think Tom is handsome?"

"Answer the question."

I cocked my head at the woman. "Is my coin not as welcome here as I thought?"

"Not at all," said Captain Handy. "I just like to know the nature of the men—and women—I host aboard my ship."

"I told you," I said. "We're in search of an old friend of mine, at sail in a small single-masted skiff. The reasons for our search of him are private."

"You've sailed before." Handy posed it not as a question, but as a statement of fact.

I nodded. "Aboard the *Skylark*. A privateering vessel."

"I'm sure you did," said Handy. "But that's not precisely what I meant."

I glanced at her, my eyes impassive.

"You seem quite comfortable aboard my ship," said Handy, with a flick of her reddish-brown braid. "Where *else* did you serve?"

"You really wish to know?" I asked.

"Is there a reason I wouldn't?"

I sucked on my teeth. "Heard of the *Black Mast*?"

Jane's eyes widened.

I nodded.

"How did you escape, then?" she asked, her voice quieter than it had been. "From everything I've heard...well, that sort of thing just doesn't happen."

"Not to most," I agreed. "But the captain, the renowned Badger, let me go. Of my own free will."

"Did you know the man, then?" asked Handy.

I paused before responding. "He was my best friend. And I his quartermaster. He's our quarry in this charter."

Handy whistled. She pressed her palms together and tapped her fingers against her upper lip before responding. "You're either an exceptional liar, or a man I'd love to spend an evening swapping tales with. Either way, I'm starting to think perhaps I *shouldn't* have taken the promise of your coin."

"Too late now," I said. "Unless you mean to throw me overboard. But I don't think you're the sort to do that. Especially not to a member of the brotherhood."

"*Former* member," said Handy with an evil grin. "By your own admission."

"Ever heard of the *Málaga Merchant*?" I asked.

"The merchant vessel rumored to hold over four hundred thousand reales in gold in her belly?" Captain Handy raised a brow. "What of her?"

I leaned in. "We took her. And if you ever expect to receive the full amount we agreed upon, I'll need to have my neck above water to tell you where I stowed my share."

Handy smiled, and in the moonlight, her teeth seemed a little *too* pointed. "I was merely joking."

"I suspected as much. But it doesn't hurt to reinforce your sympathies with silver." I turned my eyes back out to the still seas. "So, Captain Handy. I've told you about myself, albeit briefly. Why not tell me your own story? How is it a woman managed to gain command of her own vessel?"

"Democratically, of course."

"Surely there's more to the tale than that?" I asked.

Handy nodded. "There is. But its telling will have to wait until another time. I discourage my men from activity long after dark, and I adhere to my own guidelines. Don't stay up too late. It'll set a bad example."

She pushed herself off the railing and walked away, her feet barely more than a whisper over the sea-worn planks of the deck. I cast my eyes back out to sea.

"Oh, and Driftwood?"

I turned. "Yes?"

Handy smiled. "Nothing. Just making sure you were telling me the truth."

19

For a moment, I had nothing more than the lapping of the waves and the sighing of timbers to keep me company, but those were soon displaced by more footsteps: faint, as with the last set, but not as quiet. Not as experienced.

"What brings you above decks, Gwen?" I asked as I turned to face my wife.

"To see what keeps you awake," she said, joining me at the side of the ship. "You should be resting. I doubt you've yet recovered from your experiences aboard the *Mejillón* and in Tortuga."

"I slept well last night," I said. "You know I don't need as much rest as you do. Only when I stay up until three or four in the morning do I deteriorate."

Gwen sniffed. She turned toward the open waters and rested her elbows on the railing, intertwining the fingers of her hands together. "So... I see you've been making friends with our freewheeling captain. You know, for as taut as her muscles are, in other ways, she seems quite...*loose.*"

I sighed. "Not this again. I swear, Gwen, nothing untoward occurred between us. If you honestly think I'd philander, then you're seeing even more ghosts than usual."

"Relax," she said. "I'm teasing you. I overheard your conversation from the nearest booby hatch. And besides, I've no fears of you wandering off like a dog, sniffing at other bitch's hindquarters."

"Are you sure of that?" I said with a raised eyebrow. "You've been constantly chiding me throughout this trip, at the inn and the brothel and now here, peppering me with barrages of tightly knitted brows and sour frowns, which are displeasing even coming from your coral-colored lips."

Gwen wrapped one of her arms around mine. "*Lovingly* chiding you, John. Or at least so I thought. I never intended my barbs to actually harm you."

"They have."

"Well, then, I'll stop," said Gwen. "Just know that my intent was merely to make you squirm, as you do me with those infuriating bottom-pinching fingers of yours." She trailed a finger along the length of my arm. "Although if you like, I could try to make you squirm in *other* ways tonight."

She gave me that head tilted, puckered lip sort of look she always did when she was behaving mischievously. She knew it would make me smile, and despite my best efforts, I couldn't prove her wrong.

I chuckled and shook my head. "You're incorrigible."

"I like to think we takes turns being so," said Gwen.

"You're probably right," I said. "But despite either of our desires, I think you'll find even less privacy here than we had aboard the *Mejillón*. The *Tickled Pink* may be far bigger than Jorge's cutter, but she also hosts ten times the crew."

"We could try the hold," said Gwen. "I think there's a tarp down there we might be able to hide under. Or you could dangle me off the edge of the poop deck and hope for the best."

"And risk waking Captain Handy in the cuddy?" I asked. "I don't think that would go over well."

We shared a laugh over that, but as our mirth faded, I heard other voices. Animated ones.

The skin on my forearms prickled. Apparently, I'd been so focused on my conversation with Gwen I hadn't realized we shared the decks of the *Pink* with others, despite my own statement regarding the heavy population aboard the ship. My cheeks warmed as I thought of what the compatriots of our small, floating nation might've overheard.

I needn't have worried. A pair of pirates—one bald, heavyset, and with a faded tattoo on his neck and the other tall, skinny, and disheveled—argued over something, completely oblivious to their surroundings.

"I'm telling 'ya," said the heavyset one, "the shrouds're fine. Now quit messing with 'em and give me a hand."

"But Cap'n always told me they gotta stay tight," said the tall pirate. "Without 'em, the whole mast might snap like a twig, and then we'd really be over the barrel."

"Don't be a fool, boy," said the bald one as he grappled with the spar at the bottom of the mainsail. "The wind ain't blowing so hard we'd lose the mast. Now help me with the boom before a man gets knocked overboard."

Perhaps it was partly out of curiosity that I approached the two men, but it was certainly the sailor in me that forced my hand—and my mouth.

"Pardon me, men," I said. "Far be it from me to countermand your captain's orders, but what in the world are you doing?"

The heavyset pirate did a double take as he saw me. "Good God, man, don't just stand there! Either step back or lend a hand with this boom!"

"In what capacity?" I asked.

The man opened his mouth but paused before speaking. He tilted his head toward the sky, squinting as he gazed upon the stars. Then he brought his head back down and shifted his eyes from side to side. After a moment, he grunted.

"Is everything all right?" I said, wondering if perhaps the man was suffering some sort of spell.

"Aye," he said. "Must've been a false alarm, I guess. Mandrake, leave them shrouds be and let's head to bed. Capn's orders. You know how she is about evenin' discipline." He glanced at me. "Best you be headed below decks, too, mate."

"Just about to," I said.

The bald man and his tall friend made their way to the hatches and hopped on down. As they disappeared, I glanced at Gwen.

"Did you find that as odd as I did?" I asked.

"Actually, John," she said. "Now that I think about it—"

A shriek from the gun deck cut Gwen short. Numerous shouts followed it, and the sounds of at least a dozen pounding feet. I heard the door to the captain's cabin wrench in its frame as a cluster of the *Pink's* crew burst out of the hatches and onto the main decks. I grasped Gwen instinctually, hoping to protect her from whatever ill might follow, but the pirates beat a path straight to Captain Handy, who met the men at the mast.

"Silence! Silence!" yelled Handy as the men tried to speak over one another. "One at a time!"

A small man, barely five feet tall, with a salt and pepper beard stepped forth. "Captain! It was Fat Porter and Mandrake! I saw them, just now, in the hold!"

"What?" said Handy. "Speak sense, man."

"It's true," said another pirate, a wide man with a hook nose. "I spotted 'em as well, Captain. Thought it was a dream, but when I blinked my eyes, they stood there, plain as day."

Others nodded.

"Walked off toward the tiller."

"Saw it with me own eyes!"

"Plumb disappeared, they did."

"'Tis the blasted doldrums. Told ya they was unnatural."

Handy glanced at me and Gwen, a grim look stretching her face.

"What is it?" I asked, though I feared I knew the answer.

"Fat Porter and Mandrake," she said. "Two of our own, but they died in a fierce storm over a year ago. Knocked overboard by an unsecured boom."

I glanced at Gwen, both of us holding our tongues.

The pirates continued to mumble, but Handy cut off their complaints with a loud hawk. "All right. I don't care what anyone saw, it's time for bed. And that includes the two of you." Handy pointed at me and Gwen. "And Malarkey? I'll speak with you in the morn, once the sun warms our flesh and banishes the shadows."

I swallowed. Hard.

20

I awoke to the creak of timbers. I cracked my eyes and blinked, but in the tight confines of the hold, everything appeared black, even with my eyes open. Scents of mildew, slow rot, and a faint hint of pitch filled my nostrils, alongside the ever-present salty smell of the sea. I glanced to my side and could just make out Gwen's sleeping form in the hammock next to me, and when I listened for it, I could hear the gentle melodic rhythm of her breathing and the rustle of fabric as her chest rose and fell.

A bead of sweat trickled down my brow, which I wiped away with my thumb. The air hung thick and heavy, and I could only hope the day would prove cooler than initial indications suggested.

I swung my feet over the side of the hammock and stood, taking care not to wake Gwen with my noise. Sneaking past the darkness-shrouded forms of other sleeping men, I slipped to the nearest hatch and pulled myself up to the main deck.

The first glimmers of dawn had begun to paint the sky, but to my eyes, even their minor glow seemed bright. I blinked again as I drew myself to full height.

To starboard side, I spotted a few early risers like myself, checking the lines and knots and going through the myriad rituals that swallowed the better part of every sailor's day. At the port side, I caught sight of more of the same, as well the distinctive giant silhouette of Tall Tom as he gazed over the side of the vessel in the direction of the rising sun.

"Morning, Constable," he said as I joined him.

Apparently, I wasn't the only one capable of identifying a man by the sound of his feet.

"Morning, Tom," I said. "You're up early."

"Aye," he said. "It's a common side effect of going to bed early. You should try it."

"What? Turning in at a reasonable hour?" I asked. "Perhaps I should. It would've saved a fair bit of commotion last night for sure."

"Commotion?"

"You didn't hear?" I asked.

Tom looked at me blankly.

"Never mind," I said. "I'm sure you'll learn of it soon enough."

In retrospect, I probably should've warned Captain Handy about Gwen's unique abilities upon chartering her vessel, but I hadn't thought it was pertinent to our agreement. Besides, I hadn't expected any ghosts to manifest themselves during our trip. Not that I was naïve enough to think no blood had ever been spilt upon the *Tickled Pink's* decks, but I didn't expect any souls to haunt her at sea.

Tom ignored me and shook his massive head. "Not even the barest scrap of wind. *Again*. These doldrums are infuriatin'. Not to mention odd as the town drunk's ramblin's. 'Tis the windward passage, after all."

"It's actually a misnomer," I said.

"What's that?"

"The windward passage," I explained. "The trade winds frequently die here, despite the strait's name. I've known many a sailor refer to this region as the 'windless passage' for just such a reason."

Tom grunted. "Why must you always ruin my ruminations with your logic and sense?"

"It's a curse I've battled my entire life," I said. "If you think it annoys *you*, you should speak to my wife."

"No need for that," said Tom. "I'm gettin' more than my fill of the both of you on this journey."

"You know," I said, "you didn't have to come."

Tom gave me an eyebrows raised look. "And what sort of friend would I be, then?"

"Not nearly as good a one as you are." I clapped the man on the shoulder. "I haven't said it yet, but thank you. Your presence here is a comfort, and I've been glad to have another set of eyes to help watch over Gwen."

"Not that she needs it, accordin' to her," said Tom. "But I know what you mean."

I stood there, with my hand resting on the man's back, until a rumble from my belly interrupted the moment.

Tom glanced at my complaining stomach. "I'd wager Maggie's beef and kidney pie is sounding pretty good 'bout now."

"Sea voyages do have a way of lowering one's culinary standards," I said. "Honestly, I'd be willing to settle for just about anything at the moment. Even hard tack. Last night's dinner is a distant memory. I wonder if the cook's in the galley yet?"

A lookout cried out from above. "A sail! A sail! Two points to port!"

All the men on deck rushed over to our side of the ship to test their eyes against the lookout's, but with the dawning sun sending bright rays over the horizon, I, for one, couldn't spot a thing.

A familiar feminine voice called out behind me. "How does she stand?"

"She's a small ship, Captain," replied the lookout. "With blank sails. She's caught in the doldrums, same as us."

Captain Handy elbowed her way to the railing beside me and gave me a sour glance, as if to convey she hadn't forgiven me for whatever role I'd played in last night's ghostly appearances. Today she'd traded her waistcoat for a simple white shirt, the tails of which she'd tucked into her breeches.

She reached a hand into the folds of her shirt near her bosom and—though I've no idea where she might've hidden it—extracted a small bronze spyglass, which she extended and held to her right eye.

"I see her," said Handy. "Though it's more like two and a half points, if you ask me." She lowered the telescope and offered it to me. "You might want to have a look."

I took the spyglass and held it to my eye, casting its lens about twenty-five degrees from the prow. With the glare of the sun impeding me, it took me a moment to locate her, but eventually I did.

Raphe's skiff sat dead in the water, as still as a corpse, and her sail hung flat. Raphe, his bright red bandana acting as a beacon in the early morning sun, propped his back against the vessel's thin mast. He gestured wildly, and though the spyglass didn't afford me improved hearing to pair with its superhuman sight, I guessed from the motion of the man's head and hands that he was speaking. The question was to who—or rather, what, as I was certain the man had left Tortuga alone. While I couldn't be certain, he seemed to be yelling at an object roughly the size of a man's head, which reminded me of the mestiza's words.

"I think he's lost it," I said. "It looks like he's talking to himself."

"After only two days?" said Tom. "What sort of pirate loses his mind at sea so quickly?"

As I watched through the scope, Raphe stood and peered in our direction. He held a hand to his brow, then fumbled in his boat and produced his own spyglass. He looked through it straight toward us—and clearly spotted us, based on his reaction. He nearly fumbled the telescope overboard, juggling it in comical fashion, all the while screaming at the same object of his previous ire.

Then, inexplicably, the boat shot off.

"God's teeth," I said, pulling the scope from my eye. "It can't be."

"What is it?" said Handy, taking back her collapsible bronze eyepiece.

"It's Raphe, all right," I said. "But his ship... It just took off."

A murmur grew from the crew.

"That's impossible," said Captain Handy as she searched for the skiff through the glass. "There's not even the faintest hint of—"

A powerful gust tore through the air, rocking the *Pink* and filling her sails with a loud crack.

I heard oaths from the gathered sailors, including a choice one from Captain Handy herself, but she quashed any hints of disquiet with a few sharp commands.

"Stow your superstitious bellyaching and get to your posts, men," she shouted. "We've a ship to catch!"

21

As I stared into the dark, boiling clouds ahead of us and tried to peer through the shroud of rain lashing across the horizon from the farthest reaches of the sky to the frothing surface of the sea, I couldn't help but think: *Not again.*

The day had begun with such promise. Following the sudden onset of the winds, Captain Handy had summoned all hands on deck. The men—at least those who'd still slept—swarmed from the hatches, headed to their stations to loosen the sails, swing the boom into place, and tighten the jib lines, while Captain Handy herself rushed to man the wheel. Within moments, the crew had the *Tickled Pink* skimming over the waves as blithely as a porpoise.

As I watched the men work, my years of sailing under the ensigns of both the *Skylark* and the *Black Mast* kicked in. I felt a jolt of energy shoot up my spine as we embarked on our chase, and I longed to throw myself into the fray alongside the men, but I forced myself to hang back. Each man had his own responsibilities, and despite my knowledge and enthusiasm, my assistance would likely only serve to cause more work for the others. Instead, I mounted the shrouds, pulling myself up their weather-worn rungs, past the gaff all the way to the masthead. The lookout there eyed me oddly, as if wondering what space, exactly, I expected to share with him atop the small platform, but as I intertwined my arms amidst the shroud's ropes, I assured him I wouldn't stay long.

The fierce wind gusts might've loosened the bowls of lesser men, but not those of a former quartermaster and pirate. A man who'd faced down the barrels of two score guns, including at least a dozen 32-pounders, pointed at him out the side of a Spanish man-o-war, all while battling cold rains that stung the eyes and numbed the hands and while riding thirty foot swells as if they were mighty salt-water steeds.

No, the wind didn't bother me. It filled my lungs with freshness and my heart with desire—and besides, other than the strong gusts, the weather couldn't have been more perfect. The sun's bright morning rays streaked through the sky, warming my face, and the wind cooled my skin to a point where I could be comfortable with or without shirt. I felt my heart soar, too, confident in the knowledge that with the *Pink's* sails full, we'd soon converge on Raphe and take him aboard, at which point I could finally have him answer my questions.

The minutes passed as I clung to the shroud next to the Jacob's ladder, my eyes trained on Raphe's small skiff in the distance. The wind blew fiercely, trying its best to tear my arms from the ropes. I saw a sailor at the stern toss out the chip log, pulling with it the knotted line. I counted the seconds in my mind, and at the count of thirty, I'd seen a full twenty-two knots—twenty-two!—pulled into the water. Such speeds were unheard of, and yet, as I continued to wait in the shroud, it didn't appear as if we were gaining on the Badger.

I stayed in the rigging for perhaps a half hour, and in all that time, despite the unnaturally strong wind, we couldn't close to less than two hundred yards of the skiff. It made no sense. Raphe's boat, with a single sail no greater in size than an inn's front door, couldn't hope to outpace us, in a ship built for speed and with every last scrap of duck thrown on the wind, and yet she did. It was as if our two crafts played a silent dance. Our sloop would gain on her, and then the skiff would gain speed. Back and forth, back and forth, like partners toying with each other to increase the anticipation, except that we never managed to join together as one to fulfill our urges.

I thought to cry out to Raphe, to try and reason with the man to slow his vessel and join us aboard ours, as clearly I didn't mean him any harm, but such an effort would be wasted. The wind stole the words from our mouths as soon as they exited, and the lookout at my side was forced to communicate with Captain Handy by hand gestures and pointing alone.

Eventually, I lowered myself back to the deck, positioning myself at the ship's stern so I could maintain view of the Badger and his skiff. Hours passed, with the powerful winds showing no sign of abating and Raphe's skiff likewise showing no sign of slowing. The gusts pushed us south by southwest, past the rocky islet of Navaza and into the vast expanse of waters beyond. They seemed intent on carrying us all the way to Cartagena on the southern continent, but as the afternoon stretched toward evening, the winds suddenly shifted, carrying us to the west as if we were on some sort of bedeviled children's carousel.

It was shortly thereafter that I realized our good fortune. The shift in the winds had pointed our craft, and Raphe's as well, straight toward Jamaica. Though for reasons beyond me we couldn't catch my old captain, certainly the large island would halt his speedy craft's endeavors. He'd be forced to dock in Port Royal, and from there we'd be able to track him down in short order.

For the first time in the day, things were going swimmingly—until I noticed the storm.

It covered Port Royal, and perhaps all of Jamaica, obscuring the port with black clouds and driving rains. After two days spent aboard the *Mejillón* in such conditions, I had no desire to test my mettle against another of nature's battles. But what choice did we have? At least we wouldn't have to fight the elements long before weighting anchor, as the storm's borders didn't extend far past the edge of the island.

"Driftwood!"

I nearly jumped at the sound of Handy's voice.

She joined me at the base of the bowsprit, her auburn braid a tangled mess after having been ravaged by the wind for the majority of the day. "What in the world have you gotten us into?"

"I thought you were at the helm," I said.

"I left Günther in charge. He's capable enough."

"I'd hope so," I said. "He's your second-in-command."

"Stow your wit. I've no stomach for it." Handy narrowed her eyes and peered toward the oncoming storm. "And you still didn't answer my question. What have you gotten us into? Ghosts of the departed. Prodigious winds. Now a storm that hangs over Jamaica like a plague when it should be out roaming the seas and gaining strength? And let's not forget your friend Raphe Bartholomew's bewitched dinghy."

With the demands of the chase, Handy had never approached me to discuss what, precisely, we knew about the presence of the two dead pirates, and while I could try to explain Gwen's abilities to her, I decided to forgo said explanation in the face of all the other oddities I couldn't explain.

"These things you've mentioned aren't of my doing," I said. "And I know little more about them than you."

Handy gave me a narrow-eyed glance that said she believed me about as far as she could throw me, but out of respect—or perhaps fear—she held her tongue.

She took another look at the roiling clouds and tilted her head at them. "Well, be that as it may, you'd best prepare yourself for that mess, and I'd best prepare my men—although it's really the ship that needs the attention. And you might want to consider what course you wish to take if that storm's as bad as it seems. With evening coming and those clouds and rain, there's a good chance we'll lose sight of your old pal Raphe—assuming he doesn't acquaint himself with Davy Jones before he makes it to shore."

I couldn't make myself believe the latter. As wicked as the squall seemed, Raphe's skiff had fared above its capacity thus far, and the man would only need a little luck to navigate the thing to port before the rains pushed the lip of his craft below the edge of the sea. The question was: would our luck hold in tracking him?

22

"Luck," said Gwen with a snort. "As if we've even so much as sniffed any of that since we set sail from Soledad a few days ago."

I shook the rain from my hair and used my hands to press some of it from my clothes. "Oh, that's not true. What about that incident at the church where you found passage into the catacombs? You can't curse the fates when they freed us from near-certain captivity."

Gwen glared at me, her damp hair clinging to her face like so much seaweed. "The same fates that left me with a lump on my head and a backside caked with mud? I think I'll call them whatever names I deem appropriate."

We sat on a stack of empty vegetable crates in a Port Royal warehouse not far from where Handy and her crew had docked the *Tickled Pink*. Straw covered the floor, likely in an attempt to keep the contents of the warehouse from becoming coated with mud, but the efforts hadn't precisely worked. Muddy straw now stuck to boxes and walls as well as the floor, and a pervasive mildewy odor, reminiscent of the interior of a barn minus the horse droppings, filled the space. Above us, rain hammered the warehouse rooftop in a steady, relentless beat.

As I gazed at Gwen, I couldn't help a smile from creeping onto my lips. My wife had once again chosen to throw modesty to the wind and garb herself in unfashionable undress. She wore a thin apricot-colored chemise dress which, while quite appropriate for the Caribbean heat, didn't fare particularly well in the rain. After getting thoroughly drenched during our dash from the *Pink* to the warehouse, the dress clung to my wife's body, revealing the curve of her hips and the swell of her breasts. If not for her pale skin contrasting against the yellowish-orange of her dress, one might assume she wasn't wearing anything at all.

"Does something amuse you, my love?" asked Gwen.

I wiped the goofy grin from my face. "Hmm? Oh, nothing. I was simply *savoring* the rain's effect on your outward appearance."

"You must be joking," she said. "I look like a drowned rat."

"Not drowned," I said, taking her in my arms. "Merely sodden. And the fairest sodden rat of them all. One with a sleek and shining coat, long whiskers, and a tail as bare as a hog's hide."

Gwen lifted an eyebrow. "Oh, really? Is that how one measures the attractiveness of a rodent?"

"Of course," I said. "I have it on good authority from a tabby I once housesat."

Gwen drew her hand across the curve of my shoulder and down my arm. "Oh, John... Never has a woman been wooed with such a coarse, repellent metaphor. Your mastery of prose is akin to that of an illiterate chimney sweep."

I pulled Gwen closer. "I would've gone with a drunken pirate of ill-repute, but that works as well."

"You're drunk?" asked Gwen. "And here I thought you spent your time above decks today manning the helm."

Gwen smiled and I snorted. I pulled her body against mine, feeling the dampness of her dress through my own damp shirt and breeches. Though she leaned back from me, the smolder in her eyes and the wetness of her lips indicated she'd gotten over her distaste of the rain and acquired a hunger for something other than the night's meal. I leaned in, my own lips parting.

Someone of a feminine persuasion cleared their throat.

I turned to find Captain Handy standing not more than five feet from Gwen and me, Tom at her right. Handy shook her head from side to side slowly, while Tom held his hands behind his back, twisting his lips and looking uncomfortable as he so often did in such situations.

"You've barely been off my ship for half an hour and already you're pawing at each other like a tomcat and his queen," said Handy. "I'd hate to see what happens following a voyage that's longer than a day and change."

Gwen pulled her face back from mine, her cheeks darkening, but she didn't exit my embrace. She kept one arm wrapped around my midsection and smoothed her dress with her free hand.

"Do I detect a hint of jealousy in regards to our marital bliss?" asked Gwen.

"*Marital bliss?*" Handy snorted. "God, no. Don't get me wrong. I'm all for happiness. And I don't mind a tumble in the hay every now and then, but I've never had much difficulty finding a mate to share *that* with. Can't imagine I would in the future either, should the desire strike. Isn't that right, Tom?"

"Right." The big man nodded, then blinked as he stared at the bronze-skinned woman. "I mean...err... *what?*"

Handy laughed. "Oh, you're a racket. I like him." She jerked a thumb at the big man.

"Told you," Gwen whispered in my ear.

I assumed she referred to her own prediction of Captain Handy's promiscuity, but I didn't think it was the time or place—if ever there was one—to discuss such a thing.

"So, did your men find anything?" I asked.

"Of the mighty Badger and his majestic seafaring vessel?" asked Handy. "Not so much as a lock of his distinctive bicolored hair. Although I think some of my crew stumbled across a dinghy for sale that could seat three. Should we find your man, we should relay the news in case he wants to upgrade."

I grunted in response. After passing into the storm, visibility aboard the *Tickled Pink* had dropped from a few miles to all of fifty yards. We'd lost sight of Raphe immediately, and although the wind had carried us up around the southeastern tip of Jamaica and right into

Port Royal, we had no way of knowing exactly where my old captain and his skiff had disappeared to. Once we'd fastened the *Pink* to some bollards on the pier, Captain Handy had sent a handful of her men to scour the docks in search of Raphe's boat, but apparently they'd been unsuccessful in their search.

Of course, I'd been well aware of our possible failure in that regard, so while Handy's men had searched the docks, I'd asked Tom to head to a pair of the nearest seaside taverns and ask the innkeepers and gossips about Raphe. The man's eccentricities—which if our adventures in Tortuga were any indication, had only intensified over the years—made him memorable.

"So, what of you, Tom?" I asked. "Any luck?"

The big man kept glancing at Captain Jane, as if unsure he'd heard her correctly earlier. "Um...right. Well, yes and no. Nobody's seen him tonight, nor heard word of him. And I got some funny looks when I asked about him, to boot. Turns out there's a fair price on his head."

"Wait," said Gwen. "Raphe's wanted in Jamaica? Why?"

"There was an...*incident*," I said. "With a play. I'll explain later. Go on, Tom."

"Yes, well, as scuttlebutt has it, Raphe was here a few months ago," he said. "And you'll never guess what rumor told he was up to."

"And what would that be?" I asked.

"Treasure huntin'," said Tom with a nod. "And not just any treasure, but lost Indian riches. A picaroon over at The Midshipman's Roll says he recalls Raphe talkin' 'bout it while he was here. Said the man was askin' 'bout the local Taíno Indians and some golden idol."

I dropped my arm from Gwen's side and blinked as a memory worked its way free from the crevices of my mind. "The Taíno? And an idol? You're sure?"

"It's what the picaroon said," said Tom. "I can't vouch for the statement meself. But the old dog did seem sure of himself, despite his wooden leg..."

Gwen stepped back and glanced at me. "I know that look, John. What is it?"

I stroked my chin, letting my fingers dig into my beard. "Well, it could be nothing, but..."

"But what?" said Gwen.

I took a deep breath. "There's a legend, one an old jack aboard the *Black Mast* by the name of Lugger Slim would spout off about any time someone would pay him an ear. A legend of a hidden Taíno treasure cache, right here on Jamaica. I never paid him any mind. I thought the old fool had bats in his belfry. He spoke with a slur, as if he'd suffered a stroke years back, and he carried a blasted parrot on his shoulder, for God's sake!

"I was certain the other members of the *Mast* paid him as little heed as I did, but perhaps Raphe believed him. It would explain the picaroon's claims, and his presence here now. Not to mention that book we found at the church library in Tortuga. One of them was about the history of the Taíno." I snapped my fingers. "And the mestiza at the brothel! She said Raphe had questioned her about her life. I'd wager she's half Taíno, and Raphe was looking to see if she knew anything about the treasure."

"A whore?" said Gwen. "Why would he possibly approach a prostitute regarding the location of a legendary treasure?"

I started to pace. "Most likely because she spoke English. The majority of the Taíno don't, and they're notoriously unfriendly towards those they perceive as *conquistadores*. With good reason. Most of them died following the arrival of the Spanish. But it may also have been circumstantial. Raphe is no stranger to brothels. I'm sure he headed there for his own physical relief, but once he found the girl there, he decided to question her."

"But John," said Gwen, "none of this makes sense. That black man, Chinue, said Raphe *already* stole a treasure. If Raphe has it in his possession, why would he return to Jamaica, the treasure's supposed home?"

I stroked my chin again. "Good point. But perhaps the *Mast's* crew weren't completely forthright with us. It always struck me as odd that Raphe would steal a treasure from his own men. For all his idiosyncrasies, he's never struck me as a traitor or a thief."

"He's a pirate," said Gwen, crossing her arms. "Thievery is his livelihood."

"You know what I mean," I said. "Look, it's possible Nicolas and Chinue lied. What if Raphe didn't steal a treasure from them? What if, instead, he'd abandoned them to seek out the treasure on his own? You saw how those two referenced my own departure from the *Mast*. They don't take kindly to brethren who give up the life—which might explain why they seemed intent on killing Raphe on Tortuga, rather than questioning him regarding the treasure. Although..."

I paused, both in thought and in my pacing.

"Although, what?" asked Tom.

As plausible as my own explanation seemed, I couldn't quite make myself believe it, for a number of reasons. The miraculous timing of the winds, both as Raphe sped away from Tortuga and again as we'd spotted him aboard the *Pink*. His odd behavior. How he'd seemed to be talking to someone in his skiff this same morning. And the satchel I'd seen him carrying, the one the mestiza woman had remarked upon.

I shook my head. "Although...I think he does have a treasure. Perhaps the treasure referenced in Lugger's legend, the one located here on Jamaica. And perhaps something's forced him back."

"What sort of thing?" asked Tom.

I held my silence. I didn't want to voice my thoughts, both for fear of sounding crazy as well as fear of the truth should I be correct. What if the treasure...had been somehow *cursed*?

I waved Tom off. "That's not important. What's important is we find Raphe."

Captain Handy snickered. "And how do you propose to do that? Did your old parrot-wearing colleague retire to Port Royal to enjoy the whoring and debauchery his years aboard the *Mast* earned him? Do you plan to ask him?"

"I'm telling you, Slim was a kook," I said. "He had no more idea of where to find that treasure than I do."

"So how did Raphe locate it?" asked Gwen.

I think she meant the question rhetorically, but I answered her nonetheless. "He must've raided Governor Morgan's residence for the map."

That tidbit caused a stir amongst all souls present.

"What?"

"Huh?"

"Governor Morgan?"

"Look," I said. "There's more to the tale than I've time to tell here, but suffice it to say the one material shred in old parrot-wearing Slim's story was that Captain Henry Morgan, now acting governor of Jamaica, retained in his possession the one and only map of said treasure, which he acquired during his sack of Campeche in 1663. Now I've no idea if the map exists or if the treasure is even real, but I do know, from speaking to other seamen who were with Morgan at the time that the Governor came into possession of a large number of maps during that raid. And word is his arrest in 1672 was, at least in part, over his refusal to share the maps with the servants of the Crown."

"So...what?" said Gwen. "Are you saying you think Raphe stole this map from Governor Morgan?"

I wagged a finger. "I doubt it. That's not Raphe's style. And taking it would've further risked invoking Morgan's wrath, which...well, that's a story for another day. No, I suspect Raphe must've copied it instead." I sucked on my lips as I glanced first at Tom and then at Gwen. "And if he did, so must we."

23

The pounding rain had waned to a steady drizzle, but as recompense for the increased visibility, whatever deity watched over the isle of Jamaica had decided to toss some thick fog into the soup of our existence. It slunk through the jungle, hugging the ground before curling up the trunks of rain-slicked trees like a sun-hungry creeper vine. There the fog hung, clinging to palm fronds and the wide, scoop-like leaves of the cordia trees like a diaphanous spider web.

As I sat in the near-complete darkness of the tropical jungle, I used a free hand to wipe some of the moisture from my brow. In all my years traversing the vast expanse of the West Indies, from Barbados to the western tip of Cuba, from the northernmost isle of the Bahamas down to the atolls of the Serranilhas, I couldn't recall a single memory of weather such as what we now experienced. I'd curse the mixture of rain and fog for what it was—an abomination—but by showing my own trepidation of it, I might instill fear into the hearts of those around me, and for the time being, they seemed more annoyed than frightened. Gwen, in particular, seemed ready to bite off the head of anyone who so much as referenced the rain.

"Remind me, again, what our purpose here is?" she said.

Gwen, Tom, Captain Handy, her squash-nosed quartermaster Günther, and I sat on a small rise above Governor Morgan's mansion alongside a couple other pirates from the *Pink*, overlooking the property through a gap in the jungle foliage.

The place was enormous. Walls of pale gray stone and mortar that would've reached to Tall Tom's chin circumnavigated the property, which I estimated at perhaps two dozen acres. The governor's stately residence sat near the front of the acreage: a square, two-story plantation-style home, surrounded on the main and upper levels by a wide balcony, edged with a whitewashed railing featuring five balusters to a section. I couldn't see clearly amidst the drizzle and fog, but I was certain given its layout the mansion contained a square courtyard at its center, and likely featured a full basement beneath it.

"Surveillance," I said, pointing at the roof of the ostentatious dwelling. "I need to know the routes of the guards."

"But there *are* no guards," said Gwen.

"Not that we've seen," I said. "But I'm certain there must be some. They're probably inside to avoid this blasted weather..."

"And who could blame them," said Gwen. "But we've been sitting in this damp misery for an hour, at least. If they haven't shown their heads yet, I doubt they will."

"You should give your husband some credit, milady," said Tom. "Having patience is smart, it is. Better safe than sorry, me mum always said."

I glanced at Tom and his tricorn hat and blinked. That was about the most self-assured statement he'd ever made to my wife, although he still insisted on calling her 'milady.' I wondered if Captain Handy's presence had emboldened the man—or addled his thoughts.

"To be fair, Tom," I said, "Gwen has a point. I think we've all sat here long enough."

"So, let me make sure I understand the plan fully," said Gwen. "You intend to trespass on Governor Morgan's property, where you'll shimmy up the side of the mansion and make your way to his private study on the second level where you might, hopefully, *possibly*, find this mystery map of yours—a study you're only aware of, I might add, because five years past you captured a ship loaded with rum and sugar financed by Morgan, and one of the ship's crew—an eminently trustworthy fellow no doubt—told you all about Morgan's mansion from his lengthy visits to the place."

"We treated those men well," I said. "The man had no reason to lie to me."

"You treated them *well?*" said Gwen. "You forced the crew to enact an impromptu play in which their captain took on the role of Morgan—in this performance, an incompetent, blundering buffoon—and Raphe played himself as the rakish, conquering hero."

"That was Raphe's doing, not mine," I said. "And besides, it helped take the edge off the raid. Honestly, many of those men found it as funny as we did."

"And I'm sure Morgan also found it hilarious when word reached him of the incident," said Gwen sarcastically. "Which is why he set a price on Raphe's head, and why I'm sure he'll sport a wide smile on his face when he executes you for trespassing, instead of merely imprisoning you for eternity like he would any other common thief."

"As I said, the play was Raphe's doing," I said. "I doubt Morgan has any idea who I am. And I thought you weren't worried about the guards capturing me."

"I wasn't until you mentioned they're probably all waiting inside like a pack of hungry wolves!"

Handy glanced at her men before shifting her gaze to Tom. "Are they always like this?"

The big man shrugged. "More often than not. But they seem to make it work."

"Look," I told Gwen. "You know I'll be careful. I'll be as quiet as a shadow. No one will have any idea I'm there. If I smell even a hint of trouble, I'll be out the mansion's windows and back over the wall before a guard can get off so much as a warning shot. And God forbid something happen, we have a backup plan. Right, Tom?"

He nodded. "If you're not out within the hour, Handy's men'll cause a commotion at the gates, while me and the others will come in after you."

"Just so we're clear, Driftwood," said Captain Handy. "This'll be costing you extra, whether you end up needing our services or not."

"Add it to my tab," I said. "I promise I'm good for it."

Gwen sat there with her arms crossed, her eyebrows furrowed, and her lips pressed together. She'd let anger control her speech and fuel our dialogue—I suppose because the emotion was easier to display in front of others than concern—but I knew the reasons for her harsh language, and I understood them.

I leaned close to her. "I promise you I'll be safe."

"You cannot promise what you cannot control," said Gwen in a low voice.

I gave her a peck on the lips. "I love you."

"I love you, too," she said.

Without giving myself time for self doubt, I turned and scuttled down the hill. In my pirate days, I would've had to relieve myself of weapons due to their bulk and noise, but since I'd become accustomed to having Tom's axe at my back, I rarely carried with me more than a slim poniard in my boot.

I had it with me now, but I hoped I wouldn't need it.

I paused as I reached the wall, stretching my ears to see if I could hear any voices, but I couldn't detect any over the metallic buzzing of the cicadas and the occasional whooping gleep of the coquí frogs, so I placed my palms on the rough stone and pushed myself over into the manor grounds. From there, I wasted little time, rushing through the lingering fog to the near side of the plantation home. With an experienced ease born from years of climbing rope ladders and traversing ships' riggings in driving rains, I pulled myself up the railing to the second floor balcony.

None of the lanterns nearby had been lit, nor did any light shine through from the windows, as I'd already taken note of during my watch. I also knew I'd find a door hidden at the far end of the home, past the corner, but why bother when so many windows beckoned? I tested the nearest shutters and found them amenable to my touch, so I spread them wide and clambered inside.

The darkness inside was suffocating. I'd expected some light from *somewhere*—a bit reflected from a lantern hidden around a corner or at the base of a set of stairs—but if there was some, I couldn't spot it. For the first time, I was glad of the rain and fog, as they'd shrouded me from the moon and prepared my eyes as best they could for the task ahead.

I turned to my right, recalling my conversation years ago with the sailor regarding Morgan's extensive collection of maps, including all those he stole during the raid on Campeche. Gwen had been right to question my memory, but I recalled his description as if I'd been there to hear it the day before. Morgan's study was on the second floor of his home, at the far end of the right corridor, situated to the left, facing the courtyard.

I blinked as I thought of it. How *did* I recall our talk so well? Perhaps I had to admit to myself that old Lugger Slim's tales of golden Indian idols attracted me more than I'd ever thought.

I moved over to the runner that spanned the length of the corridor, hoping its plush carpeting would help silence the sound of my boots. From there, I quickly made my way down the hall to the last door on the left. I held my breath as I pressed my weight against the door's handle, praying for silence from the hinges but preparing myself for the worst.

For once, lady luck watched over me. The door gave in silence, revealing an unlit room, populated only by a writing desk, a number of bookshelves, and an enormous box chest that reached to my navel and likely weighed as much as a stallion, even empty.

I closed the door behind me, and as my first order of business, I snuck over to the room's window. I cracked the shutters, taking note of my position in case I needed to make a hasty escape, then slid them back into place. Then, I scoured the room for a candlestick, which I found upon the desk with a good length of candle still in it. I moved it under the seat of the desk to minimize the spread of its light, then with a fire steel I kept in my pocket, I lit the candle with a few targeted strikes.

As the candle bloomed to life, I moved to the box chest and lifted its weighty lid. From within the darkness inside, at least a hundred oilskin tubes peered back at me, each of them labeled with nothing more than a three digit number.

I swallowed. Perhaps I should've instructed Gwen and the others to give me more than an hour.

Trying not to let myself become overwhelmed, I snatched a few of the tubes and set myself down by the dim light of the candle.

I'd barely finished glancing at the third map when I heard the voice.

24

"Who are you?"

A chill ran down my back, and my muscles tensed. I looked up from the maps to find a young maid, clad in a simple blue and white long-sleeved gown and matching bonnet, standing inside the door.

A thousand thoughts raced through my head. How had the young woman spotted me? I thought I'd positioned the candle such that none of its light would seep under the crack of the door. Had I generated noise, either through the step of my boots on the floor or my handling of the box chest? Or had I tracked mud onto the carpeted runner which she'd followed?

And how in the world had I allowed her to creep up on me without notice? I mentally lashed myself. I thought my ears more acute than that, and yet somehow the young woman had managed to follow me, open the door to the study, enter into my presence, and close the door behind her, all without my knowledge.

I blinked. She'd closed the door behind her. Why would she do that, unless...she hadn't tracked me. Unless she'd planned on meeting someone here. Someone else.

The maid peered at me curiously. "Pardon, sir, but I can't place your face. Are you new here? A porter or a guardsman, perhaps?"

I took a step toward the windows, ready to fling myself through them should the girl scream, but thankfully she didn't. Perhaps she feared the repercussions of her own actions should she be found here. She might be involved in something illicit. An affair, perchance.

"I... Uh..."

Words eluded me. What could I say to free myself from the predicament? A plea? A threat? Should I flee through the windows, or try to overpower her? I didn't want to harm the poor girl. She was just a maid, after all.

The young woman frowned and blinked twice, tilting her head to one side and then the other. She opened her mouth to speak but paused before anything came out.

I couldn't understand why she wasn't doing *something*—either screaming or running or trying to bargain with me for my own silence. Perhaps she wasn't here to meet someone. Perhaps she'd been sleepwalking, or her mental faculties prevented her from participating in any activities more complicated than sweeping or dusting.

And then it hit me. The closed door. She'd never opened it. I reminded myself to kiss Gwen when I returned to her arms.

Summoning my most confident air, I spoke. "Why, dear...don't you recognize me? I'm Adolphus Morgan."

The maid stared at me blankly.

I raised an eyebrow. "Henry's cousin, on his mother's side? I've been here for the past week, absorbing the local customs and enjoying the wonderful weather." I lowered my brow back to its rightful spot. "I kid of course. The weather's dreadful."

I finally seemed to reach the young woman. She took a step back and lowered her head. "*Oh.* I'm dreadfully sorry for interrupting, then. I was walking—I'm not entirely sure why, to tell the truth—when suddenly I found myself here. I sensed the light, and...well, I should be going."

She turned toward the door, but I halted her with a quick word. "Now, now, then. Don't run off. I've a question for you."

"Certainly," she said. "I'll help if I can."

"You've...worked here long?" I asked hopefully.

"Yes, sir," she said with a bob of her head. "For years, since I was little. Governor Morgan always took care of me. At least until... until..."

The girl furrowed her brow and her face fell, as if deep in thought.

I stepped forward, waving a hand to distract her. "No. Don't think of that. Focus, please. I need your help."

My wave seemed to work. "With what, sir?"

"I'm looking for a map," I said. "My cousin wanted me to take a look at it, but he, er...didn't tell me exactly where he left it. I thought, given you've worked here your whole life, you might know where I could find it?"

"Well, you've come to the right place. It should be here, sir," said the maid. "What map were you seeking, precisely?"

I took another step forward. "Well, it's a *special* map, you see. One Henry told me about in confidence. One that leads to a special, treasured location here on Jamaica. Does something like that sound familiar?"

The girl shook her head. "I'm sorry, sir. Nothing like that—"

"Don't give up so easily," I said. "Think. *Really* think. Surely you've seen him glance at it before, or spoken on the treasure it leads to. A fabulous golden idol, worshiped by the natives?"

The maid looked up. "Oh. Oh, yes, I think I might have an idea."

I smiled. "Excellent. Now, pray tell, within which of these tubes might I find it?"

"Oh, I doubt you'd find it here," said the maid.

This time, it was my own face that fell. "I wouldn't?"

The young woman shook her head. "Sir Morgan doesn't keep valuables like that in his office. He has a special chamber, deep in the basement beneath the house where he keeps such things. I'm not supposed to know about it, but I stumbled across it years ago while playing hide and seek with the other servants' children." Her eyes narrowed. "Funny Governor Morgan didn't direct you there himself, though."

I pressed my advantage while I still had it. "Err, well, you know my cousin. Always so absent minded. Now, why don't you take me there. And, in a tribute to your childhood, why don't you keep your mind focused on that. In fact, we can play a game of hide and seek ourselves. But this time, it'll be the two of us hiding from the rest of the household."

The young woman cast me an unsure glance, but after a little more cajoling, I was able to convince her. It wasn't that difficult. She was still extremely disoriented. As we left the study, she didn't even acknowledge that she walked right through the door without opening it.

25

As I pulled myself up a rickety wooden ladder and through an underbrush-obscured hatch outside the walls surrounding Governor Morgan's estate, I couldn't help but think to myself that mucking about in musty catacombs two out of every three nights wasn't exactly how I'd always pictured myself in retirement.

I shut the hatch and stood, ineffectually dusting my damp pants in the shadow of a towering banyan tree, or strangler fig as some called it due to the way the plant wrapped its smooth, ropy boughs around the trunk of an unsuspecting tree, strangling it until it died. Spanish moss hung down from the dangling limbs of the stranger, conspiring with the churning fog at my feet to add to my overall sense of foreboding, but I ignored the combined effect. I'd already run into a ghost and escaped not only unscathed but enriched by the experience. What further matter of disquiet could the night possibly hold for me?

I worked my way around the perimeter wall of the estate toward where I'd left Gwen, Tom, and the rest of my entourage. I instinctually glanced at the sky, hoping to gather some hint as to the time, but of course the drizzle and fog, who'd chosen to continue their torment throughout the night, didn't allow me that small boon.

Though my eyes were ineffective in the gloom, I soon heard hushed voices over the song of the jungle, and I knew I was close.

I pushed a fern aside as I approached. "Well, I guess—"

A sword slid from its sheath and at least two pistols cocked in my direction. I paused, but before I could convey my identity and the notion that we really should've established a verbal cue beforehand so they'd all know I approached rather than a snooping guardsman, a mass of damp hair, flailing limbs, and soft flesh barreled me over.

"Oh, John! Thank God, John! Thank God!" Gwen rained kisses down on me from above as the weight of her body pressed me into the damp leaves and squelching mud underneath. "I feared the worst. Oh, I was certain you'd been captured!"

"Well, I—"

Gwen's open palm collided with the side of my face, setting my head to spinning.

"That's for being such a fool!" she said. "Don't *ever* do something as foolish as that again, do you hear me?"

I tried to answer that I could hear her—barely—over the ringing in my own ears, but she crushed the breath from my lungs with a powerful hug before I could respond. Instead, I just hugged her in return and patted her back as she ran through the gamut of her emotions.

When finally I could draw breath again, I sat up and pushed Gwen to her knees. Between the dampness and the gloom, I couldn't tell if Gwen was crying, but a sniffle from her direction indicated as much. I drew a thumb across her cheekbones, feeling the warm tears I suspected would be there.

"I promised I'd be back," I said.

"Yes," she said with a hint of a warble in her voice. "But we've already established you're a dreadful liar."

I glanced at the rest of the crew, who'd replaced their cutlasses and pistols into their belts and bandoliers. Again, the night's darkness impeded my ability to discern subtleties, but I swear their faces were drawn in concern, even Captain Handy's.

"How long was I gone?" I asked. "More than an hour?"

Tom scratched his neck and avoided my gaze. "Might've been more. To tell the truth, none of us were sure, what with the darkness and clouds. But we were planning the specifics of the raid as you showed."

"So I suppose it was good timing on my part, then," I said.

"Earlier would've been better," said Gwen, still testy. "What took you so long, anyway?"

"I had to take a bit of a detour," I said. "The map wasn't in the study."

"No?" said Gwen. "So you weren't able to locate it?"

"That's not what I said," I replied. "As it turns out, the Morgan estate has quite an extensive basement. More like a complicated network of muddy tunnels, black as night corridors, and secluded rooms that could be used for anything from storage to torture. Or dark magic, should the desire strike. Quite cheery, really. Anyway, the map was down there, in an old chest in one of the storage chambers."

"Hold on a moment," said Captain Handy, holding up a finger. "While that sheds light on your delay, that doesn't explain *how in God's name* you found the damned thing."

I made my eyebrows dance. "Would you believe I'm that shrewd?"

"Not even Tom would believe that," said Gwen, which elicited a mumbled 'Hey, now...' from the big man.

I leaned over and gave Gwen a long, slow kiss, fulfilling a promise I'd made to myself earlier. "Let's just say I'm glad to have you as my wife."

Gwen glanced at me with curious eyes, but she didn't press me on the issue, for which I was thankful. I'd be happy to tell her about it later, but seeing as Captain Handy and her men still didn't know about her abilities...

"Well," said Tom, "I think I speak for everyone when I say we're glad to have you back. And surprised you found what you were lookin' for, especially after that delay and considering how cockamamied...err, I mean... Well, anyway." Tom spread out his hands and gestured with his fingers.

I looked at him blankly.

"The map," he said. "Let's see it."

I shook my head. "Tom, I didn't take it. That might tip Morgan off—should he somehow make it down to that spider web-infested hellhole of a storage chamber. And besides, it's raining and dark as a swarm of bats. Even if I did have the thing on me, I wouldn't take it out now."

Tom rubbed his neck and stared at the ground. "Oh, um...right, Constable." I could tell he was abashed by the fact that he'd reverted to calling me by my undeserved title. "But if that's the case, then how—"

I cut the man off by tapping the side of my head. "It's all in here, my friend. Have faith."

Captain Handy trailed her hands along the length of her braid and squeezed, forcing some of the rainwater that had collected there onto the forest floor. "Well, I for one'll be glad to leave this blasted place and its rain behind us. So...where are we headed?"

"East." I rose to my feet and helped Gwen to hers. "We won't need to travel far. At least...I don't think we will."

"You don't *think*?" Captain Handy squinted. "What's that supposed to mean?"

I sighed. "I mean, the map pointed to a destination in the jungle at the base of the Blue Mountains, up the Morant river and past a small village which, based on its given name, I can only assume is Taíno in nature. But maps such as these are rarely precise. If they were, all the world's golden idols would've long been uncovered. Luckily for us, however, we needn't find the treasure. We need only find Raphe, and I think he'll be much easier to track than an ancient, head-shaped lump of precious metal."

Günther grunted. "The Morant's mouth is Maroon territory. They're a savage bunch, and not particularly friendly to our kind. Could be dangerous."

"Then we'd better hurry and return to the *Pink*," I said, "while the night is still young, and she can offer us her protection. Now, move it, all of you."

26

"We really must talk about this aversion to sleep you're developing," said Gwen with a yawn. "It can't be healthy. For me, especially."

We sat in the prow of one of the *Pink's* cockboats, while Tom worked the oars and a pair of Handy's men sat at the stern to counter our weight. Tom's powerful strokes propelled us along the surface of the Morant, and if not for the occasional wet slap of the oars and the glistening drops that clung to their blades, I could've believed Tom had navigated us through the clouds and into the furthest reaches of the sky.

The night's drizzle had ceased, and the clouds had finally thinned, letting loose an intermittent shimmer of the nearly full moon's light, but as bright as the orb might be, its gaze couldn't burn away the lingering fog. The mist had settled and pooled in low lying areas, filling the river to the brim with a wispy, floating sea of white—which worked perfectly to our advantage.

"Although I'm certainly more of a night owl than you," I said to Gwen, "even I wouldn't willingly be out at this hour—*again*—unless the situation demanded it. This fog is perfect cover for our approach, and if Raphe came this way earlier tonight, it only makes sense we follow. If we waited until the morrow—or the following evening, for safety's sake—his trail could've gone cold."

"Yes, God forbid Raphe get any sleep, either," Gwen said. "Although, come to think of it, your colleagues from the *Black Mast* didn't appear at Perdición until twilight. Was becoming nocturnal one of the prerequisites for working aboard that vessel, I wonder?"

"Not as such, no," I said. "Though perhaps my time aboard it did instill in me more of an *appreciation* for the advantages night can offer."

"Stated like a true villain," said Gwen.

Our boat rocked as we ricocheted off a submerged rock.

"Sorry," said Tom.

Gwen glanced into the thick fog. "You do know apologies are used when someone is at fault, right, Tom?"

"Err, right," said Tom. "Sorry, milady. Or...well, you know what I mean."

I grabbed a sounding pole from the bottom of the boat and tested it on the river's waters. It came back wet to four feet. Not much, for a boat loaded as ours was, but enough.

"Getting shallower?" asked Tom.

I nodded. "And narrower, too."

The banks of the river had started to encroach on our boat, and with them came the spindly, intertwined arms of the mangrove trees that populated them. Those at least kept mostly to themselves, unlike the boughs of the tall rust-colored copperwoods which reached high overhead into the void generated by the river's path.

I recalled the map in my mind's eye, but as we floated along in the darkness, surrounded by the fog and dense foliage, I found I honestly had no clue where we'd gone. I knew we'd followed the river right when it forked as we'd needed to, but as to when we'd find the Taíno—that was more of a guessing game. I hoped it would be soon. I didn't think the river would carry us much longer.

As we approached a bend in the river obscured by a thick cluster of trees, I detected a growing rushing sound. I trailed my hand through the waters at the side of the boat, but they seemed to pass us by at the same speed as before, and Tom didn't appear to be struggling against the strength of the stream, so I doubted we approached any rapids.

Tom's heavy strokes pushed us around the corner, and the source of the noise came into view. The river widened before us creating a large pool, at the base of which towered a sheer cliff face roughly the height of ten men standing upon one another's shoulders. The flowing mass of the Morant poured over the top, cascading into the foaming waters below and creating a shimmering sheet of spray. The falling water banished the fog, pushing it to the furthest reaches of the pool where it spilled into the roots of the mangrove trees.

I couldn't tear my eyes from it. Presented as it was under the light of the full moon, the lake was idyllic. Under other circumstances, I would've fancied testing its waters in a spirited, bare-skinned dip with Gwen at my side, but I couldn't very well do so with Tom and the others onboard—not to mention Captain Handy and the dozen of her men that followed us in the *Pink's* other two cockboats.

I blinked as I settled my eyes on the pool's far side. If not for the mast, I wouldn't have spotted it in the fog: Raphe's dinghy, tethered to the root system of one of the mangroves.

I muttered a hasty prayer of thanks as I pointed it out to Tom. He propelled us toward it with his oar strokes. In less than a minute, we'd thumped into the roots ourselves, and I'd jumped into Raphe's skiff while Handy's men secured our cockboat.

Gwen chose to stay seated in the prow of our boat. "You must be kidding..."

"Excuse me?" I asked.

"Well, don't get me wrong, love," she said. "I trust you—except perhaps when you insist you'll be fine during an unarmed, solo invasion of a governor's mansion. But with that said...I suspected our chances of finding Raphe by following this map of yours were akin to a one legged man's chances of winning a dancing competition."

I chuckled. I'd heard that particular turn of phrase before, though expressed in a more vulgar fashion. "Well, I'll be sure to remind you of my keen wit during our future disagreements. But don't cheer too loudly. We haven't found him yet."

I searched the craft, although I wasn't entirely sure what I expected to find. Not Raphe, certainly, nor his treasure, if indeed he'd uncovered it. Perhaps I hoped to find evidence of who—or what—he'd been talking to when I'd first set Handy's spyglass on him, or some sign of what the man hoped to achieve, but in that I failed. The boat contained only the barest of essentials: oars, rope, dried foodstuffs, spare canvas, and a compass.

"Disappointed, Driftwood?"

Captain Handy stood in the prow of her boat as she and the other of our trio slithered through the pool's waters and docked at our sides.

"Not at all," I said, looking up. "We found Raphe's craft, if not him. I'd call that a resounding victory."

Captain Handy scoffed as she jumped to shore. "What hogwash—although sincerely delivered. You'd make an excellent politician."

I ignored the captain's gibe and pointed into the woods at the waterfall's side. "There's a path cut into the cliff face that leads up past this cascade. I'd be willing to wager that rather than head into the jungle's heart, my old friend took the obvious way forth. Care to argue against me, Handy?"

The woman shrugged and rolled her eyes, but I didn't take it to heart. The agreement we'd reached regarding her ship and her crew's services didn't specify how I'd recompense her for fog-riddled, middle-of-the-night boat rides into the heart of the Jamaican wilderness. Likely her biting commentary stemmed from her desire to return to her ship to catch some shut eye, same as everyone else.

After helping Gwen from the boat, I led the way up the narrow path. The climb took us some fifteen minutes, due mostly to the breadth of the trail and the looseness of its footing, but eventually we made our way to the top. From there, the trail continued, winding in and out of the forest but mostly sticking to the river's edge. As we reached another bend, my ears again notified me of something unexpected, but not with the same pounding of water on stone as before. This sound was more chaotic. More festive. More *human*.

I waved for everyone to stay quiet and crept forward to the edge of the trees.

I poked my head out as I surveyed the scene. Down the path, lit by a massive bonfire and at least two score torches, I caught sight of the Taíno village we'd been searching for. In a wide clearing, I spotted a half dozen wide cylindrical dwellings with conical roofs, each large enough to house at least twenty or thirty Indians. The sides of the buildings were constructed of sticks and a faded bark-like material, while the tops were of thatch—not of straw as was typical in England but rather thick bundled palm fronds.

The homes ringed a wide communal space, which at this hour of the night I would've expected to be deserted, but instead it was filled with revelers. Brown-skinned Taínos, all of them dressed in loincloths and little else, including the women, danced in a circle, raising their hands and lifting their knees in rhythm to their chants. Some wore elaborate carved masks while others sported shiny baubles braided into their long hair, clenching spears or bows in one hand while they gestured with the other. In the center of the circle on a high pedestal sat some sort of talisman or idol—I couldn't really tell with the Indians in the way—but I had a sinking suspicion I knew what it was.

Next to the bonfire over a pit of coals, a woman turned two long spits, each packed with the carcasses of small animal that looked like crosses between squirrels and beavers. The scent of the charring meat drifted on the wind, earthy and fatty with a distinctive hint of burnt hair, but there was something else to the odor as well. A heady aroma, herbal in nature, perhaps arising from the fire's fuel.

"Would you look at that," said Gwen as she sidled up next to me. "A real Indian tribe. I'd thought such groups had been displaced from these isles long ago. And they seem to be performing a ceremony. I wonder what? Father would've found it fascinating, I'm sure."

Tom joined us and quickly averted his eyes. "Oh, by the stars! They're *naked!*"

"They're not naked," I said. "They're wearing loin-cloths."

"So sporting a strip of fabric over one's genitals counts as being clothed, now, does it?" asked Tom.

"You know, Tom," said Gwen, "some day you're going to have to explain this moral balancing act of yours that prohibits you from laying eyes on a woman's body unless you're paying her."

Tom opened his mouth to complain, but I shushed the two of them before they could engage in further horseplay.

"Quiet." I extended my finger toward the near side of the village to a structure that had caught my eye. "See that?"

I pointed at a small enclosure fabricated out of two inch thick reeds, topped with thatch, and wrapped with lengths of hemp rope to add support. Based on the size,

I guessed it was a pen for animals, but this evening, it was being put to use for a beast of a different sort, one with long black and blonde hair half hidden under a bandana.

Through the thin gaps in the reeds, Raphe's outline was just visible. He seemed to have loosened a lone shaft from his wicker prison, which he extended through the reed wall—much to the ignorance of the Taíno. I didn't spot a single guard outside Raphe's prison. Apparently, the Indians had more confidence in the sturdiness of their enclosure than I did.

I felt Captain Handy's presence at my back before I heard her voice. "Don't tell me. Is that—"

"It is," I said.

"I see," said Handy. "So apparently *some* of the stories about him are true, at least those regarding the precarious predicaments he finds himself in. And in a not totally unrelated topic, Driftwood—I think it might be worthwhile to revisit the agreed upon payments for me and my crew."

"Don't be so rapacious," I said. "You're giving pirates a bad name. I'll be sure to pay you handsomely—*if* you help me come up with a reasonable solution for extracting Raphe from that enclosure."

My mind raced as I set it to the same task. Raphe's cage was at least on the correct side of the camp for us to reach it, but there was a wide gap between the village and the forest's edge. Even under the night's shroud, there was no way we'd reach him undetected—especially not with all the torches and the bonfire's blaze. And even if we did, the structure actually looked fairly solid, despite its rustic construction.

"How 'bout this?" proposed Tom. "I'll sneak around to the far edge of the camp with a few of Handy's men. We can either go through the forest or swim across the river. The natives seem engrossed in their festivities, so they probably won't notice us. Once we're in place, we'll fire off a few shots from our pistols to draw them out. While they're distracted, you all rush in and free Raphe while we disappear back toward the river."

"Could work," said Handy. "Driftwood, what do you think?"

I considered Tom's hastily fabricated plan as I watched Raphe, who was extending the pole he'd freed further and further from his tent—a pole, I realized, that had been modified in some manner. It curved back at the end.

What in the world are you up to, Raphe?, I asked myself.

I didn't have to wait long for an answer. He managed to grasp a torch pole with his makeshift crook and pulled, toppling the thing into the roof of his enclosure. As crazy as it might seem, I swear that as the fire started to catch, I caught sight of the man fanning the flames with his hands, encouraging them to spread.

27

The flames swelled, and surprisingly quickly given the weather we'd endured. I don't think any of the Taíno had noticed yet, but they would. Soon.

"New plan," I said. "Gwen, stay here. Tom, come with me. Handy—your men have pistols, right? Good. Follow at a distance and shoot anyone that tries to kill us."

"John!" said Gwen.

I grasped Tom's arm and darted off toward the village, pulling the big man along with me before Gwen could voice her objections. I already knew that if she had reservations about my plan to infiltrate Governor Morgan's mansion, she'd *truly* dislike my current plan— if it could even be called such a thing. But as I'd learned through personal experience, even the best laid plans could be undone by the heedless actions of a lone wolf, or badger as the case might be.

"John," said Tom as we ran. "This might be a good time to share with me your intent."

We'd covered half the ground to Raphe's burning enclosure and still no one seemed to have noticed us.

"You know those broad things that jut out from the side of your neck?"

"My shoulders?" asked Tom.

"Exactly," I said. "Keep running and put one of them into Raphe's shack."

My old captain noticed us about the same time the Taíno did. A cry went up, followed by several more shouted in a language I couldn't understand, all of them carrying hints of shock, alarm, or confusion. One final cry followed them all: Raphe's, as he took stock of the developing situation.

"John?" he cried. "John!"

Raphe dove to the ground as Tom and I barreled into his hut. I felt the sharp impact of the wooden poles resist my body, but only for the barest of moments. Then the entire structure exploded, sending burning thatch and flaming reeds flying through the air amid a shower of sparks.

The Indians' cries intensified, turning from confusion to fear. Through the fiery haze, I saw revelers fleeing from the common area, some pointing and gesturing with their weapons while others covered their heads.

Raphe recovered from the shock of our attack quicker than I did. He grasped my arm tightly and pulled me to my feet as he regarded me with the same wild eyes I'd seen on him back at the church in Tortuga, though slightly more muted, perhaps because no one was firing a pistol at him—yet.

"John," he said. "Is it really you?" He squeezed my arm again, as if I were a piece of fruit at a market.

"Who else would it be?" I said.

Raphe laughed nervously. "Heh. Who indeed?"

Tom rose, brushing burning embers from his jacket, and grasped my other arm. "Let's go."

I turned, but Raphe's hand stopped me.

"Wait," he said.

"*Wait?*" I looked at the man incredulously. "What do you mean, *wait?*"

"I need my things," he replied, and he had the nerve to smile as he said it.

Before I could stop him he'd darted into the village. I glanced at Tom, who sported the same baffled look on his face I was sure I did upon my own.

"Part of the plan?" he asked me.

"Oh, come off it, man," I said. "There is no plan. Just stay alive."

Tom pulled his axe from his belt, and I, lacking anything but my small boot knife, picked up a hefty pole from the wreckage, its end smoldering from the fire. I turned to follow Raphe, only to find the man had already made his way to the pedestal in the middle of the clearing and was stuffing the object into the brown canvas satchel he'd taken to carrying from his belt loop.

As he did so, the manner of the Taíno turned from fearful to angry. Many of those who'd fled now took stock of the situation and realize their erstwhile prisoner had turned into a thief.

Raphe raced back toward us as the Indian tide turned. A spear whizzed past him, sticking itself into the dirt. It vibrated from the strength of the throw, eliciting an unmanly 'Eek!' from my old friend.

I squawked something similar as a brown-skinned man came at me out of the gloom with a knife. Before I could react, Tom leveled him with a blow to the chest from the flat of his axe. Rather than thank him, I slammed my burning pole into the face of another on-coming attacker, which I reasoned he'd appreciate more at the moment.

As Raphe neared us, I tossed my flaming club to the side, spun, and ran. Tom followed suit. Two spears flew past us, and the air whistled as arrows plunged into the gloom at our sides.

The air split with a crack as smoke and fire erupted in front of us—pistol fire from the guns of my pirate brethren. Missiles of wood and flint and lead flew in both directions, making me suffer a momentary flash-back of my raids on ships as a member of the *Black Mast*, a flashback that was only enhanced by the presence of the man at my side.

"Go! Go!" I yelled at everyone. "To the boats! Now!"

They didn't need much convincing. A few more pistol rounds split the air, but as I reached the bend, I saw far more posteriors than faces, including, thankfully, that of my wife as she followed my particularly insight-ful commands.

Raphe ran beside me on the forest path, his flowing locks streaming out behind him, while Tom took up the rear. Questions for the man filled my head to burst-ing—What was he doing here? How had he been cap-tured? Did he have the idol?—but I stored them for a moment when my lungs wouldn't burn from exertion and where death didn't follow me on the wings of the wind.

Gwen, Handy, and the crew of the *Pink* massed at the top of the cliffside path, staring at our boats below as they considered their options.

I didn't give them a chance to decide. Never breaking stride, I grabbed Gwen by the arm and dove off the side of the waterfall.

Gwen screamed, as did I, as we plunged into the dark pool below. The churning crash of water filled my ears, and darkness enveloped me, but it did so smoothly and without pain. The darkness of night, not of unconsciousness.

I pushed my way to the surface, Gwen's hand still grasped in my own. She gasped as the others splashed into the water all around us.

"John!" she sputtered. "You fool!"

"We survived, didn't we?" I said.

"But how did you know the waters would be deep enough?" she asked.

I tried to wink, but I only succeeded in getting water in my eyes. "I didn't. To the boats!"

Gwen and I managed to swim to our rowboat before the deadly rain began again in earnest. As I reached my hands out of the water to grab the boat's gunwale, an arrow whistled through the air and embedded itself in the hull, vibrating with a twang. As I stared at it, my eyes widening, my survival instincts kicked in.

I pulled my boot knife and sliced the mooring line as I shouted to the other pirates and crew. "Use the boats as shields. Push them into the shallows before you man the oars! Go!"

Gwen and I gathered Tom and pushed out toward the river proper. Our other two pirate escorts joined Raphe at his skiff, while Handy and her crew grabbed the remaining pair of boats. All together, we traversed the pond, looking no doubt like a quartet of turtles slowly turning into porcupines under the steady twang of the Indians' bows.

The rest of the evening passed by in a blur of sweat and fear and exhaustion. I'd expected the Taíno to leave us be after our dive from the edge of the waterfall, but apparently Raphe's actions had angered them more than I'd thought possible. They descended the cliff path and hounded us with shouts and curses and arrows for miles, and perhaps it was a delusion brought on from lack of sleep, but I could've sworn I saw their canoes at our backs through the lingering fog on more than one occasion.

Tom and I took turns on the oars, each of us putting the full strength of our backs into our escape, all while Gwen hunched low in the prow. Handy's two cockboats, with more men available to throw at the oars, pulled away after some time, leaving only Raphe and me as targets for the Taíno's wrath.

Eventually, with the moon sinking in the sky, my muscles burning from exertion, and the cries and bow shots of our attackers becoming a distant memory, I stowed the oars and slumped against the side of the cockboat. For once Tom didn't take my place, instead letting the gentle flow of the Morant carry us the rest of the way to safety. As I lay there, I mumbled some half-hearted taunts in Raphe's direction, but I've no idea if the man responded or even heard me—surely my voice couldn't have carried far given my state.

Gentle snoring reached my ears—Gwen's lullaby, as she lay curled in a ball at the tip of our boat. I stared at the sky with heavy eyes and blinked slowly, a delirium settling over me. More than tired, my mind felt fuzzy. Overwhelmed, perhaps, by the day's events. Or perchance the herbal nature of the Indian's fires had addled my wits in some capacity.

Either way, I nodded off. My mind drifted to an elysian plain, where the wind blew through knee-high grass and the sky sparkled like a bowl of Ravenscroft crystal. I lay under a wide oak tree, its leaves rustling as the sun slowly drifted through the sky. Eventually, it dipped such that its rays were no longer guarded by the tree. I felt its warmth on my face, growing in strength—at least until a lone cloud passed through the sky and paused in front of the sun.

"Don't move."

I blinked, my fantasy shattering like the crystal bowl I'd envisioned following a fierce hammer blow. A dark figure stood over me, and I recalled Günther's words about the Maroons living near the river delta, but as my eyes focused, I realized the figure above me was more swarthy than truly dark-skinned. And he wore the distinctive knee-length white-banded red justacorps of an English officer. And he had a musket barrel pressed against my nose.

28

I grasped the rough, rusted iron bars of our cell window and stared outside into the heart of Port Royal. A pair of gulls perched not far from the ledge of my window in Fort Charles, calling to one another in their distinctive, honking manner. Beyond them, people bustled back and forth along the length of the docks, purchasing the morning's catch from industrious fishermen. The skies had cleared overnight, and between the bright sun, balmy temperatures, and brisk salty sea breeze, a more perfect day I couldn't have imagined, even in my knee-high grass-filled dreams.

I would've, however, preferred not to spend such a day in a dank, foul-smelling prison.

I lowered myself from the window onto a pile of musty straw and yawned. Gwen sat to my left, arms crossed, and Tom sat on the far side of the cell, his head hanging between his knees.

"It's all my fault," he muttered. "If only I'd stayed awake. I should've seen 'em, I should."

"Please stop, Tom," I said. "We all fell asleep. It's no more your fault than the rest of ours."

The big man shook his head. "Not true. You've had more late nights than me. That sort of thing is sure to catch up to a man. And you can't expect milady Gwen to have lasted through the evenin'. Not a frail thing such as her..."

Gwen glared at Tom. "A what now?"

Tom swallowed. "Um...nothing. But I still claim the fault as my own."

I twinged as I adjusted my position against the wall. Gwen glanced at me, and for the first time since we'd been unceremoniously tossed into the prison cell, I detected something other than anger in her voice.

"Your stomach?" she asked.

"It's fine," I said. "They didn't get me that badly. I'm a bit tender is all."

After our unwelcome wake-up call at the hands of the British soldiers, we'd been dragged from our cock-boat onto the decks of the *HMS Vigor,* a well kept brigantine with about two thirds as many guns as the *Tickled Pink*—the latter of which I'd caught no sign of. Nor had I seen any evidence of Handy, the two rowboats crewed by her men, or Raphe and his increasingly infamous skiff. Apparently, they'd all managed to escape while Gwen, Tom, and I enjoyed some much needed shut eye. At least, I could only hope as much.

After a few moments of waiting aboard the ship, during which the soldiers in charge of holding Gwen in custody got to experience the full extent of her verbal wrath, we had the pleasure of being introduced to the captain of the *Vigor,* one Edward Gallant, who immediately soiled his good family name by planting a boot in my gut. While Gwen screeched in horror and I tasted the remnants of my last meal as it freed itself from my stomach, the captain read to us from a writ the basis for our arrest: for aiding and abetting the known pirate, freebooter, swindler, thief, trespasser, and general ne'er-do-well, Raphe Bartholomew Thatch. At least the good captain had the decency to show me Governor Morgan's signature at the bottom of the writ before throwing us in the brig and dragging us to Fort Charles.

I pressed a hand to my stomach, remembering the unpleasant feel of the kick, and it growled in response.

Gwen sniffed. "And here I thought you were bruised. Turns out you're simply hungry."

"Perhaps it's a bit of both," I said.

Gwen's stomach added its voice to the chorus, and I realized the bite of her tongue was due to her own hunger.

"Do you think they'll feed us soon?" asked Gwen, hugging her arms around herself a little tighter.

"I hope so," I said, and I meant it. Few things could make Gwen as unpleasant as a hole in her belly. "But in all honesty, I suspect we won't have to wait here long."

"And what makes you so optimistic?" asked Gwen.

"Captain Gallant—who I think should seriously consider a name change—said Governor Morgan wanted to see us. It's no secret why. The man wants Raphe. So he'll come by in short order for the same reason I pushed to follow Raphe late into the night. Because he knows how slippery the Badger is, and he'll know that time is of the essence."

I thought back to the early morning hours before the sun had risen, as Raphe's skiff had floated at our side on the Morant. Where did the man slither off to, anyway?

"And do you think Governor Morgan will be willing to set us free?" asked Gwen. "Once we plead our case to him?"

"If we lead him to Raphe?" I said. "There's a chance..."

"That doesn't sound promising," said Gwen with a snort.

I shrugged. "The first step to freedom is getting out of this cell. From that point on, a number of opportunities will present themselves to us."

"What I don't understand is how they found us," said Tom, his head still hanging low. "Seems quite the coincidence, them being there when they was."

I grunted instead of voicing my opinions. Likely Morgan's guards had followed my muddy footprints in his home to the map, a map which the governor probably knew Raphe desired, if he paid any attention at all to the city's rumor mill. On the bright side, I was fairly sure the governor had no idea it had been me, and not Raphe, who'd broken into his home last night.

Despite my optimism, another hour passed without the slightest jingle of the jailor's keys or his powerful sweaty stench passing us by. I stood to stretch my legs and turned my eyes back out the small window toward town. I felt the strength of the breeze as soon as I neared the bars, and in the distance, I spotted a dense thicket of dark gray clouds.

They hung over the border between Jamaica and the sea, crackling with energy as they approached from the west. I shook my head. The blasted weather couldn't make up its mind. First storms, then abnormal winds, then none at all. Then more winds and storms and now, apparently, another tempest. Could it be a pattern? Would winds be next? Or was it simply a byproduct of the wild gesturings of a drunken sea god?

I almost chuckled, despite myself. To think I'd harbored some inkling that perhaps Raphe—beyond all reason—had played a hand in the vagaries of the weather, and all because the winds had favored his craft as he'd made his escape from Tortuga. But they'd also abandoned him in the windward passage, and I'd be willing to bet the rains had almost capsized him as he made his way to the mouth of the Morant.

I squinted at the clouds. They didn't cover the sky, like my two previous bouts with storms at sea had, but they were abnormally dark, and they seemed to be approaching Port Royal rapidly.

I wasn't the only one who noticed. Men in the docks took down sails and battened the hatches on their sloops and schooners, pointing and gesturing at the oncoming storm.

A flash of lightning arced in the distance, and by my own count of the ensuing thunderclap, I judged it to be about a mile and a half away. I watched it approach, thankful, if not for being imprisoned, at least for a roof over my head and solid ground at my feet.

Another flash came, closer this time. A mile. Then another, even closer. Three-quarters of a mile, at most. The storm bore down on us with alarming speed. Another flash dazzled me and made me jump, followed by a near instantaneous boom of thunder.

I stepped back from the window, my heart racing. I glanced at Gwen and Tom, who both regarded me with curiosity mixed with a little fear, whether induced by the storm or the look on my own face, I wasn't sure.

"Is everything all right?" asked Gwen.

Another flash and clap. Then another. We all jumped.

I don't know what spurred me into action—perhaps a feeling of disquiet that stirred in my gut—but I tore Gwen from the wall and pulled her down face first next to me as I lay on the ground.

"Get down!" I said. "Tom, you too. Now!"

The next blast filled my eyes with searing light and nearly tore my ears from my skull with its force.

29

My head rang as chunks of mortar rained down around me. Spots swam in front of my eyes, and dust choked my lungs. I coughed as I struggled to my knees. Partially blinded, I felt at my side. My hands settled on Gwen's form, and through her dress I could feel her warmth, her curves, and the swell of her ribcage as she drew breath. I sighed in relief.

"John, is that you?" came Gwen's voice through a wall of chimes.

I nodded, then realizing she might not be able to see me, I added a simple, "Yes."

She coughed and lifted herself to her knees as well. "You know I appreciate your advances, sweetheart, but is this really the time?"

My hands had drifted of their own accord. I pulled them back. "I was...simply checking on your wellbeing."

I felt her wink, even if I couldn't completely see it. "Sure you were."

"Tom, are you well?" I asked.

My vision was returning, and the noise in my ears was slowly dying, as well.

The big man's booming voice cut through the noise. "God's breath! What in the Devil's name just happened?" Then a pause. "Sorry, milady. My tongue got the best of me."

"Don't be an idiot, Tom," said Gwen. "As if I care at this point."

"Or ever did," I said.

"Are you three done?"

The voice, jaunty and jovial, came from the direction of the wall—or where the wall had been. As I turned to face it, I found myself staring through the settling dust into a gaping hole, and within it was a face framed by long black and blond hair and topped with a bright red bandana.

"Raphe?" I said.

"I've been shocked by your presence the past couple times," he said. "Only fair I return the favor, don't you think, mate?"

I tried to collect my thoughts. "But—"

Another flash and boom cut me off, and before I could regroup, Captain Handy's voice cracked, whiplike, through the hole.

"More moving and less talking, if it please your highness," she said. "We're breaking you out of a prison, if you hadn't realized it."

"Right." I grabbed Tom's arm and forced him toward the gap in the stones. "You first, big man. You've brought up the rear too often this trip."

He opened his mouth to argue, but I booted him in the rear and forced him out. Gwen and I followed in short order, slipping out the hole and skidding down a short embankment to the street below where a cluster of the *Tickled Pink's* crew had gathered.

The winds howled around us and thunder claps sounded intermittently, all while black-gray clouds swirled overhead. Surprisingly, not a drop of rain fell from the churning masses. The gusts felt hot and dry and raised the hackles on my arms.

My eyebrows drew together, and not entirely of my own free will. "Raphe... The lightning."

"Not now, mate," he said, grabbing my arm. "Later. Once we're free of Port Royal."

I swallowed my tongue and followed Captain Handy, who'd already set off down the road, pausing only to make sure Gwen shadowed me. With the help of the storm, the streets had cleared themselves of passersby, though a few people gawked from open windows, staring either at us or the gaping hole in the side of Fort Charles.

"Where'd you anchor the *Pink*?" I asked as we ran.

"Out past White's Line," said Raphe. "South of the old church grounds."

We passed a pair of buildings, and through the alley between them, I caught sight of the sloop, sitting free at sea a good two hundred yards from shore.

"But there's no dock out there," I said.

"Good thing we can all swim," said Raphe.

"But what about the cockboats?" I asked. "Or your, err...*ship*, such as it was."

"Boat," corrected Raphe. "Let's not mince words, mate. And we left them aboard the *Pink*—except for my skiff, which I abandoned. Swimming's faster."

"Maybe for you it is," muttered Tom. "You don't have to hold your hat in one hand. Makes swimmin' blasted difficult, it does. Almost lost it last night in that dark as night lagoon."

I was surprised Tom wasn't more concerned about the axe he'd lost—the English had impounded it upon our capture—but I also thought he had little to complain about in terms of swim attire, especially compared to Gwen. Then again, Gwen's chemise dresses put up much less resistance in the water than anything with internal ribbing and layers of petticoats would've. Perhaps a lack of modesty was only one of her reasons for wearing them. If so, there was much more of a method to her fashion madness than any of us gave her credit for.

I checked on my wife to make sure she was keeping up—and found her smiling through her labored breaths.

"Gwen?" I asked.

"I'm a criminal," she said, her eyes wide. "A wanted criminal. An escapee—from a fort, no less. I never would've believed it when we set out."

My heart fell. "Gwen. I'm sorry. You have to believe me, I never intended—"

"Nonsense," she said. "Don't apologize. It's exhilarating. I'm finally starting to understand your prior life choices."

She flashed me a smile, and I sensed an ill-contained hunger from her eyes—though not necessarily one derived from the pangs of her stomach.

"Settle down, there, you libertine," I said.

"Says the man who fondled me in a prison cell," she retorted.

We turned a corner and found ourselves face to face with the sea. Without even slowing her gait, Captain Handy dove headfirst into the waters and started swimming toward her ship. Her men followed suit.

Raphe paused, his foot even with the edge of the drop-off. "Race you? For old time's sake?"

"Let's just try to keep from drowning, shall we?" I said. "And make sure no one else suffers the same fate."

A bell rang from the direction of the fort, the one they used to rouse the men at arms. I had a feeling someone had noticed the change in condition of their prison.

"And one more addendum," I said. "Don't get caught."

"Way ahead of you." Gwen ran past me and dove into the sparkling blue waters, barely making a splash as she entered.

Raphe glanced at me with narrowed eyes, as if curious about Gwen's demeanor, and I realized the two had yet to be introduced. While there'd be time for wasted breath later, there wasn't now. I filled my lungs with as much air as I could and dove in after her.

30

I pried myself from my hammock in the bowls of the *Pink*, Gwen's soft breathing at my side acting as a constant reminder of her presence. I suffered a moment of *déjà vu* as I stood, recalling the moment a mere two mornings past as I'd risen early to check on the status of the doldrums. The *Pink's* hold smelled of pitch and mildew just as it had that day, and Gwen had yet to change out of her apricot-colored dress.

I blinked. How long had I slept? Had I imagined it all? The winds and storms, Port Royal, the ghost in Morgan's mansion, the golden idol and wild natives, and the unnatural lightning? It all seemed like the stuff of a fever dream.

Perhaps I could've convinced myself of such a thing—the light creeping through the gaps in the timbers seemed faint, as it should in the early morning hour—except for the lingering soreness in my belly, which was distinct from the hunger I also felt.

I fumbled my way to a hatch and pulled myself up to the main deck. The sun hovered low over the horizon, filling the sky with brilliant shades of purple and violet, but of rainclouds and thunderstorms, I saw none. The breeze blew gently, tousling my hair and caressing the sails with its warm tongue. It felt good on my skin. Predictable. Natural. For once...

I glanced around and spotted a number of crewmen I recognized—Günther with his bulbous nose, a wide-bellied pirate with a perpetual scowl, and a bearded individual with a scar under his eye—but it was the man who leaned against the edge of the port side of the *Tickled Pink* who I approached.

"Is it morning, or evening?" I asked him.

Raphe turned to look at me. "John. You're up."

"Morning, or evening?" I repeated.

He lifted a brow. "Really, mate?"

"Really."

"Evening." He crossed his arms. "Did you take a blow to the head during our escape?"

"I'm fine," I said. "But it's been a long few days. I felt a bit fuzzy upon waking and...well, I had to make sure."

Raphe narrowed his eyes. "Fuzzy?"

I ignored him. "Have you happened upon any food recently?"

"Check the galley," said Raphe, blinking away whatever bothered him. "The cook recently put a pot over the fire."

I made some indistinct hand gestures and told Raphe I'd be back shortly. When I returned, I sat down and settled myself against the bulwark, a steaming bowl of stew warming my hands. The meal smelled of pork fat and cloves and hot peppers, but such was my hunger that I spooned it down as if it were the world's finest repast.

"None for me?" asked Raphe.

"You didn't ask," I said between mouthfuls.

Raphe grunted, and I used the silence that followed as an opportunity to finish my meal. Once done, I set the bowl to my side and belched.

"I see your manners haven't improved," said Raphe.

"They're fluid, depending on the company."

He sniffed. "Nice to see how highly you think of me."

I imitated my old friend and responded with a grunt. Then I leaned back, clasped my hands over my belly, and took a deep breath, filling my lungs with the fragrance of the seas. Raphe took my lead, bending over the railing and casting his eyes into the darkening waters.

A breeze fluttered the sails, and waves lapped at the *Pink's* hull with steady, subtle slaps. The deck rocked beneath me gently, like a mother trying to soothe a crying infant.

I glanced at Raphe, taking in the full measure of the man—his streaming hair and bright bandana, his knee high boots and tight breeches, his billowing shirt that had seen better days, his belt loaded with pistols, and the sharp cutlass he often called by the pet name Magdalena. Other than the wild look I'd seen in his eyes a couple times—a look which he thankfully didn't sport at the moment—he appeared as I remembered him.

Between the sounds of the sea and the motion of our ship, I was drawn back into the well of my own memories. The *Tickled Pink's* mast turned dark in my mind's eye, and suddenly I was surrounded by the cracks of pistol fire and the sharp clangs of blades being struck against one another and the terrified cries of men losing their life's blood onto the spray-slicked planks of a rocking galleon—but the memory faded with a blink. Instead, new visions replaced the old. Dicing with Raphe on an upturned vegetable crate, singing shanties with the men of the *Mast*, the sun warming my face as rum did the same to my belly. And then, as quickly as the images of death and battle had been replaced by those of friendship and camaraderie, so too were the latter replaced by more recent memories. Memories of Gwen, her smiling face and tender caress, which warmed my heart in such a manner as the sun and rum could never hope to accomplish.

I sighed. "Our times together... They weren't all bad, were they Raphe?"

My old captain glanced at me. "You miss it, mate?"

I met his gaze. "Not at all, my friend. Not at all."

Raphe lifted an eyebrow.

I didn't elaborate, but I did respond. "It's good to see you, Raphe."

"Likewise, mate," he said with an absent nod. "Likewise."

"And I feel I should apologize," I said, "for not making yet making your acquaintance with my wife, Gwen, which I'll be sure to do as soon as she wakes from her slumber—whenever that might be. She enjoys her beauty rest. But she's an amazing woman. Stunning, intelligent, caring. She's the light of my life, Raphe."

"No need for apologies," he said. "Our first two meetings were a mite...*stressed*, should we say, with gunfire and rain and arrows and the like. But I'm happy for you, mate. She seems like a lovely woman."

"And you'll have to get to know Tom, too," I said. "He's a good man. Not the most loquacious, and he has a few vices, but all in all a solid fellow."

Raphe hummed in acknowledgement and nodded. I wet my lips with my tongue as silence momentary filled the void between us.

"I, uh...think that's about the extent of the small talk I can conjure," I said.

"Again, likewise," said Raphe.

"So you wouldn't mind if we move on to a few more germane topics?"

Raphe shook his head. "Not at all, mate."

"Good."

I stood, dusted my hands on my pants, and joined Raphe at the bulwark. "Now, do you mind explaining to me what in God's name you hoped to accomplish by stealing a golden idol from a group of savage natives while at the same time betraying your own men in the search of said treasure, you bloody, lamb-brained fool!"

"What?" said Raphe. "You've got it all wrong, mate. I didn't steal so much as a bean from those blasted Taíno! They're the ones who're thieves and ruffians all, taking advantage of my precarious situation. And I've no idea what you're referring to with regards to my men."

"The crew of the *Mast*," I said. "Didn't you cheat them of their fair share of your haul?"

A measure of that wild look I'd seen in Raphe's eyes now crept back in, and he cast his gaze back out to sea, toward the setting sun.

"The *Mast*... I thought I saw it, you know. Not long before you came up, out there on the horizon."

"Really?" I recalled my time on the *Mejillón*, when I'd sworn to Gwen I'd seen the same. I'd been sure the *Mast* had been tracking us, a supposition that had proven itself true when we'd encountered Nicolas and Chinue in Tortuga, but at the time we'd yet to find Raphe or his treasure. I glanced down at Raphe's belt loop and the sagging canvas satchel that hung there. Now that we'd presumably found both, what would happen?

"Let me ask you something," said Raphe. "On Tortuga. When you found me in the church. Did you...see them? Nicolas and Chinue and the others, I mean?"

"What?" I said. "Of course I did. Why wouldn't I?"

"So it really happened, then," he said, his eyes unfocused. "I'd held out hope that perhaps it was a dream. Perhaps I'd imagined it all."

"Raphe, what are you talking about?" I asked. "Are you feeling well?"

He ignored me. "I thought surely I'd seen the last of them. What manner of deviltry could've brought them back to my side?"

He cocked his head to one side, as if he'd heard a noise, his brows furrowed in thought.

"Are you even listening to me?" I asked. "I already told you. They're angry you cheated them out of their fair share of your treasure."

My words finally sunk in. Raphe straightened and surveyed me with narrowed eyes. "And how is it you know that?"

"Because they told me as much," I said, "when they came to my doorstep at the foothills of the Isla de Perdición. Now admittedly, they could've been lying, but—"

"*Wait*," said Raphe. "They came to you?"

"Yes."

Raphe stroked his chin, and his face seemed stressed to the point of breaking. "It can't be..."

"What?" I said. "Why not?"

Raphe lifted his head. "John... I saw them die, mate."

31

"Excuse me?" I said.

"My men. The crew of the *Mast*," said Raphe. "I saw them die. Every last one. I witnessed it with my own eyes."

I blinked, and while the sun set on the horizon, a new day dawned in my own mind. The crew of the *Black Mast*...were *dead*? Such a thing seemed impossible, and yet... Gwen had accompanied me to the *Mast* when she'd first dropped anchor in Soledad's bay. She'd been at my side when we'd encountered Raphe at the church in Tortuga, and she'd stayed there as we doggedly pursued him through the streets to the harbor.

I pictured Gwen's father, Paul, as I'd seen him in the graveyard when Gwen and I visited his tomb. His form always seemed so solid, so tangible, until one tried to make contact with the flesh of his body. I'd always assumed that even if I couldn't, Gwen could distinguish between the bodies of the living and of the departed, but what if that wasn't the case? We'd encountered those two pirates, Mandrake and Fat Porter, aboard the decks of this very same sloop, and during our conversation with them, Gwen hadn't mentioned anything to suggest a deficiency in their mortal character.

Of course, there was the issue of confusion. The longer removed from death one was, the greater the divide between the realm of the living and the dead— or so Gwen hypothesized—leading to bewilderment and a decided lack of chattiness in the ghosts of decades past. But the ghost of Gwen's own father, at least immediately after his death, had been quite lucid, if unwilling to believe or even recollect his own passing. Did all ghosts behave in such a fashion? If so, and if the crew of the *Mast* had only just perished...

As I mulled them over, Raphe's words rang strangely true. But even if genuine, they didn't come close to explaining the situation, including why a crew of ghosts would demand Raphe return their treasure, a treasure I'd seen him steal from the Taíno days after Nicolas and Chinue delivered me their threats.

My thoughts escaped me in an incomprehensible blurt. "But...the golden idol..."

"Pardon?" said Raphe.

"The Indian one," I said. "The one in your satchel."

Raphe bit his lip and regarded me with a tortured look, as if trying to decide how much to tell me. Eventually, he loosened his satchel's drawstrings and inserted a hand into the pouch. As he drew out its contents, I heard the mestiza's words resonate in my mind.

Raphe held in his hand a conch.

I blinked, first once, then twice. "I'm confused. I thought you recovered the fabled Taíno treasure. The one Lugger Slim constantly harped on about. The one whose map to which was rumored to be, and in fact was, in the possession of Governor Morgan."

"Really, mate?" said Raphe. "Lugger Slim was a kook. I thought if anyone, you would've been immune to his tall tales. That treasure doesn't exist, or if it ever did, it was recovered by the Spanish over a century ago."

"So why in the world did you travel to that Taíno village?"

"To ask them about this." Raphe hefted the conch. "Specifically, to ask their shaman about it. But apparently the man died of a pox some months back."

I shook my head and pressed a hand to my temple. "I think we should start at the beginning. Tell me what, exactly, has happened in the time since I've last seen you, and then, perhaps, I can shed some light on the remainder of this tale."

Raphe carefully replaced the conch in his satchel and tightened the drawstrings. "Have you ever heard of a place by the name of the Ilha dos Ventos?"

"The legendary isle whose winds always blow away from its shores so no sailor can ever approach it, no matter the direction he takes?"

Raphe nodded. "What if I told you such a place was more than mere legend?"

I wanted to tell Raphe such a place would be a physical impossibility, and that if he believed in such fictions, he should stop sampling random mushrooms he found growing in the forest, but I stilled my tongue. After all, there was a time not too far in the past where I didn't believe in the presence of ghosts either—at least not ones who spoke and looked as solid as the living—or in the ability of a storm cloud to blast a hole as large as a man in a foot-thick stone wall with the same ease as a shot from a forty-two pound gun.

"I'm listening," I said.

"I thought it was a myth, same as you," said Raphe. "Until we chanced upon it one day in the *Mast* while sailing west of the Caicos. I swear to you, John, it was just as the tales told. No matter which way we approached it, the winds shifted to push us back. And trust me, we tried. We were in dire straits at the time, in need of water and a safe haven to patch our hull, but despite the combined skill and knowledge of me and the rest of the men, we couldn't pull to less than a half mile of the island's shores.

"Luckily, we were able to make safe harbor elsewhere, but that discovery stuck with me. I had to know—what caused such shifts in the winds? Could there be a natural explanation? Or was it something more? Was it a power that could be harnessed? Think about it, mate. Imagine having control over the winds. As a pirate, there'd be no greater prize. We could sail wherever we wanted, whenever we wanted. Outpace our enemies and bear down on our prey with alarming speed. With that sort of power, no ship could match the *Black Mast*.

"So I asked about it, to everyone I could, everywhere we dropped anchor. Englishmen and Spaniards and Frenchmen. The Dutch and the Portuguese. I asked blacks and mulattos, free men and slaves. All thought I was crazy, and none had an explanation to satisfy my curiosity. And so I thought, if anyone might know the root of the legend of the Ilha dos Ventos, surely it would be the natives of these West Indies.

"Problem was, no one I knew had seen a Taíno in ages. Rumor was most of them died following the occupation by the Spanish. So I had to abandon that idea—until we chanced upon a whole village of them while in search of Lugger Slim's famed treasure."

"Hold on," I said. "Didn't you tell me Slim was a kook, and I a fool for believing there might've been some truth to his words?"

"Well, of course," said Raphe. "And I know that for a certainty because I tried to find said treasure and failed. Try to keep up, mate. Anyway, though I found no traces of golden idols among those Indians, I did find among them an old shaman, and while partaking with him in a bit of potent weed smoked from a ceremonial pipe, I asked him about the legend of the Ilha."

I lifted a brow. "You speak Taíno?"

"Not in the *strictest* sense, no," said Raphe. "But I'm highly effective with hand gestures. As was the old shaman, it turned out. As we smoked that weed, he told me the story of the Ilha, and while a fair bit of it went over my head, I did catch a few pieces here and there. Something about gods and death and curses. You know, typical mumbo jumbo. But what I did understand quite clearly was his response to my chief question: how could one reach the island? And you'll never guess his answer. To this day, I don't know if he meant it in truth or in jest, but it was quite brilliant in its simplicity."

"Being?" I asked.

Raphe drew his arms, hand over hand, in front of him. "To swim. And swim I did, after we navigated the *Black Mast* back to that isle. At least half a mile, in choppy waters, with a strong headwind the whole way. But eventually I made it. And what an isle it was, mate! Grand trees, beautiful birds, crystal clear pools. And a cavern system like you wouldn't believe! Why—"

I held my hands before me. "Slow down, Raphe. You're getting a bit animated. And quite honestly, I don't see how this has anything to do with that conch of yours."

Raphe blinked and spread his arms wide. "But, don't you see, mate? The conch is the key. The conch commands the winds!"

"*Excuse me?*" I said. "Do you mean to tell me, not only did you manage to make your way to a mythical isle that's impossible to reach, but that once there, you found a *conch* that controls the weather?"

"Among other things, yes," said Raphe.

"And how in God's name do you figure that?"

"Well, because—" Raphe pointedly glanced at his satchel, then up at me, his tongue wetting his lips. "Look, you'll just have to trust me on it."

"And how did you find this conch?"

Raphe glanced at his satchel again, and then shrugged, almost apologetically.

I crossed my arms and set my jaw.

"You don't believe me?" said Raphe. "Consider this then. As soon as I *liberated* this conch, shall we say, my world turned upside down, and it's yet to right itself. As I left the Ilha and began to swim back to my ship, the fiercest storm I've ever encountered materialized above me out of thin air, and I don't mean that figuratively. From a spotless sky, a hole tore through the heavens, and out of it poured clouds as dark as night, crackling with lightning and swollen with rains. They churned and swirled with tremendous force, and within minutes—minutes, I tell you!—a cyclone of epic proportions engulfed us. As I battled the waves, fighting for my life, a wave the size of a towering colossus rose out of the depths of the sea and capsized the *Black Mast*, sending it down to the sandy depths of the Caribbean. Such was its force that in seconds it was gone."

"And if such a thing is true, how did you survive?" I asked.

"Only by the grace of a god, ours or otherwise," said Raphe. "By some stroke of luck, one of the *Mast's* boats withstood the tempest—the skiff you saw me pilot—and drifted my way in the aftermath of our ship's demise. Tired and nearly drowned, I pulled myself into her belly, and though the winds blew as hard as ever I'd felt them, the rains and lightning and waves soon died."

Despite my skepticism, I found myself drawn into Raphe's tale. "What happened next?"

"Not much," said Raphe. "Or, at least, I think you know much of the rest of the tale. I drifted at sea for several days, caught in infuriating bouts of swirling winds followed by periods of complete and utter stillness. I had no food or water with me, and soon I fell into a dull stupor, where I dreamed of rum and wenches and the sweet release of death. The next thing I remember, I'd washed up at the foot of Tortuga."

"Really?" I asked.

"Truly," said Raphe. "I'd swear it upon whatever cross or talisman gives you faith."

I swept my tongue across my teeth as I absorbed my old friend's words, casting a glance at his satchel. "So you say the conch controls the weather. How does it work, then?"

"I've no idea," said Raphe, throwing his hands in the air. "I can't make heads or tails of it, mate. I tried to do some research on the matter in Tortuga while I recovered from my voyage at sea—"

"Whoring is now equivalent to recovery?" I asked.

"Just because you're married doesn't mean you have the right to ruin it for the rest of us," said Raphe. "Anyway, I didn't get very far in my studies before you and Nicolas and Chinue appeared—beyond all reason, I might add. Not that I would've made much progress, even with unlimited time. My Spanish is rusty, and most of the tomes in that church library were written in that infernal language."

Raphe's words pricked me in the side. "Oh, yes. Right. About that, Raphe..."

"About what?" he said. "You share my hatred of the romance languages?"

I shook my head. "Actually, I've been telling myself I should learn Spanish. It would make my current duties in life much easier. Rather, I meant about Nicolas and Chinue."

"Baffling, isn't it?" Raphe's brows furrowed as he adopted another vacant stare. "I can't even fathom how they survived..."

"They didn't," I said.

"Pardon?"

I explained Gwen's powers to the best of my ability, and noted her presence in all of our encounters with the *Mast's* crew.

Raphe stared at me, his jaw hanging open wide enough to allow a seagull to lay eggs in it. "So..."

"So they're all dead," I said. "Or at least, they could be. I really don't know. Though between what you've told me and what I've witnessed myself, it makes sense."

"But...the pistol fire. The cutlasses. Their ship..."

I shrugged. "I've seen ghosts manipulate objects. They're perfectly capable of such actions. And with an entire crew of the dead? It's possible they could man a ship."

Raphe blinked, and then his eyes widened, as if my words had finally wormed their way into the meat of his brain. "I... I need to get off this ship. Distance myself from you and that bedeviled bride of yours!"

"Careful, now," I said.

The wild look returned, and Raphe began looking about him frantically. "I'll take one of the cockboats. I've been adrift at sea before. I'll take my chances there rather than in her presence..."

"It might not do you any good," I said. "The veil between worlds is thinned around Gwen, allowing her, and those around her, to *communicate* with the dead. But that veil exists everywhere. Ghosts walk among us, even outside her presence. Trust me, she's made enough house calls to deal with mischievous spirits for me to know that—and that's without taking into account the dozens of tales of apparitions you and I both grew up listening to."

Raphe's breath became rapid, and sweat beaded at his brow as he tried to locate the ship's boats.

I grasped the man by the arms and set him down on the weathered planks of the deck. "Listen, Raphe. You need to relax. Breathe. We'll figure this out together. Why don't you tell me the rest of your story, to refocus your mind?"

Raphe blinked and looked at me, confused. My tactic had worked.

"The rest of my story?" he said. "What else is there to tell?"

"When we chased you through Tortuga, how did you escape? The winds took your ship like a lead shot out of a musket barrel."

"I told you," Raphe said. "I've no idea how the conch works. That's why I hoped to talk to that Taíno shaman again. I'd hoped he'd have some additional knowledge to impart to me, but unfortunately he died—and based on the reception the Indians gave me upon my return, I gather they think *I'm* the one who gave the old man the pox that killed him. But that's neither here nor there. I'm telling you, the conch has a mind of its own." He glanced at his satchel again. "Err...so to speak."

"Think man," I said. "If it works the way you say, you must have some control over it. What were you doing when we found you, stuck in those doldrums?"

"I don't know," said Raphe. "I was upset. Frustrated. I'd already faced that same weather after escaping the Ilha dos Ventos."

"Through the Captain's spyglass, I saw you yelling," I said. "At something, I thought. The conch?"

"Yes. Probably," said Raphe. "I mean, no. We were... Look it doesn't matter. I didn't ask it to produce those winds that took us to Jamaica, if that's what you're thinking."

"What about when you broke us out of prison?" I asked. "You can't expect to tell me the storm's lightning struck our cell by chance?"

"Well, of course not," said Raphe. "But that doesn't mean I commanded the action."

"So what happened?"

Raphe threw up his hands. "I don't know! Look, we needed to break you out of prison. It was only fair, given how you'd freed me from captivity at the hands of the Taíno. And besides, that Captain Handy of yours—who's quite a spitfire, but we can discuss her later—insisted we do it. Something about getting the money you owe her. But none of us had any bright ideas about how to spring you. So we sat there, thinking, and as time passed and our need became greater and greater...suddenly the storm was there."

I drew my thumb and forefinger across my beard, letting them settle on my chin. In all three cases where the weather had responded in abnormal fashion—as Raphe left Tortuga, as we closed on him in the *Pink*, and during our incarceration—he'd been driven not by desire or fancy, but by necessity. If Raphe was right that the conch controlled the weather—and that it, in turn, could be controlled—did it simply come down to a case of need?

"Look, mate," said Raphe. "While I understand your interest in the conch—and I've obsessed over the power it holds for months now—you haven't lived with it as I have. I thought I'd become a god amongst men with its power, but instead it's left me tired and half-mad, nearly dead on more than one occasion, and without a ship and crew to call my own anymore. Rather, the ghosts of the aforementioned now seek me out and wish my death—which, by the way, I'm still concerned about, despite your best efforts to distract me. Honestly, at this point, I'd love for nothing so much as to be done with it, once and for all."

"Then be done with it," I said. "Give the conch to Nicolas and Chinue and the rest. They asked for your treasure, so give it to them. And perhaps then they'll let you be." *As well as me and Gwen,* I thought.

Raphe paused to consider my words, but then he glanced down at his satchel. When he turned his face back to me, a snarl contorted it. "You say they came to you, telling you they wished me to return to them their treasure? Well, perhaps that's true. But never once did they make that same demand to me as they filled the air with lead shot while I fled them on the roofs of Tortuga."

I pursed my lips. I'd thought the same thing myself. If Raphe's stolen treasure was the true object of their desire, why act so violently toward the man? And without even offering parlay or quarter?

"Death." Raphe snorted. "Death, indeed." The man sat there, shaking his head as he stared at his boots.

"Excuse me?" I said.

"Death, mate," he said. "It's just as the shaman said. First him. Then the entirety of my crew. And now they aim to drag me down to the depths of Hell with them. Maybe there *is* a curse..."

"Curse?" The thought had crossed my mind, but I hadn't broached the topic with Raphe yet. "Well, I suppose—"

"What's that?" asked Raphe.

"You didn't let me finish," I replied. "I said I suppose—"

Raphe's eyes flicked to his satchel again. "Yes. You're right. That's the only way."

"What are you talking about, man?" I said. "What's the only way?"

Raphe looked at me and blinked. "Sorry...did you say something?"

"Are you sure you're feeling all right?" I asked.

"What? Of course I am," he said. "And I finally understand what I need to do to end this nightmare."

It could've been simple chance that the wind chose that moment to fill our sails and push our ship onto a northeasterly bearing, but I'd momentarily suspended my own belief in coincidences.

32

"So this is the famed Ilha dos Ventos, is it?" I asked.

"This is it," said Raphe, spreading his arms before him. "Pristine, isn't it?"

It was. We observed the peaceful isle from the decks of the *Pink*, which rocked gently, anchored as she was roughly a hundred yards from the shore. Densely populated with thick, dark green vegetation and surrounded by pale blue waters teeming with manta rays and cuttlefish and turtles, not to mention iridescent fish whose scales reflected every color under the sun, I had to imagine the island had never even felt the weight of a man on its sandy beaches—at least until Raphe defiled it with his worn boots.

"Truly the isle's worthy of all your accolades," I told Raphe. "Although I have to admit, I thought it would be...*windier*."

After Raphe's revelation—which he refused to expound upon—the winds had held steady, carrying us north by northeast, back through the windward passage and in the direction of the French Keys. They hadn't blown as violently as during our chase of Raphe and his skiff, but nonetheless they filled the *Pink's* sails, resolutely and without the slightest crosswind of hesitation.

Captain Handy thought she could bend the gusts to her will, and though she wouldn't go so far as to boast she could carry us back to Jamaica, she did think she could pilot her ship to anywhere from Cuba back to our own Isla de Perdición under such conditions. Raphe, however, was insistent we follow the will of the breeze, and I was of a like mindset, at least for the time being. Call me superstitious, but I had a feeling should we try to change course, the winds would shift to carry us to their chosen destination, despite our best efforts. Besides, having finally reunited with Raphe—and his supposed treasure—I wasn't entirely sure what path to take next. Nicolas and Chinue had demanded I find the man, but they hadn't told me when or where we would meet after the fact.

For a day and a half the winds held steady, though at the end they'd pushed more east than northeast, eventually bringing us to the shallows of the legendary Ilha, though at that point—much to the chagrin of the island, I'm sure—the winds simply died. Even now as we sat at anchor, not even the slightest zephyr tickled the *Pink's* sails—which given her name, I'm sure she would've loved.

Raphe seemed unconcerned by the change in the winds. He patted the brown canvas satchel hanging at his side. "It's to be expected, mate. We follow the will of the conch. And it demands we return it to its rightful throne."

I eyed my old friend warily. Now that we'd arrived at the island, his spirits seemed buoyed, but throughout the voyage, ever since the onset of the winds, he'd acted quite strangely—even more so than before. He became detached, refusing to speak, which for a man of Raphe's garrulousness was as good as a sign of illness. The few times my ears did catch a hint of his voice, they'd failed to catch wind of any other, and when I'd tracked him down, I'd found him alone, as if he'd been talking to himself. Each time I caught him he sported that same wild look in his eyes, though it faded quickly as he retreated into solitude. Even Captain Handy's presence failed to excite the man, and given her looks and feisty attitude, I was sure he'd be all over her like a capuchin monkey on a bowl of grapes.

"So what are your intentions, now that we've arrived?" I asked.

"Simple," said Raphe. "We'll travel to the heart of the isle. I'll retrace my steps, heading into the caverns, and replace the conch. Once I do that, all will be as it should again. Yes. *All will be as it should.*"

Part of me wanted to argue with him—for one thing, I didn't see how returning the treasure would appease the ghosts of Nicolas and Chinue—but Raphe's eyes had started to develop that same milky quality again, and I didn't think the man would register my arguments even if I made them. Regardless, if the conch really *was* responsible for everything Raphe gave it credit for—the vicious storms we'd encountered near Tortuga and Jamaica, the maddening winds, and the death of the entire crew of the *Mast*—I wanted nothing to do with it. Better to return it. And as for Nicolas and Chinue's threats? Well...I'd do whatever I needed to assure Gwen's and my own safety. Should matters go south, I'd started to develop a backup plan—one that was becoming more and more palatable to me the further Raphe descended into madness.

"I'll get the cockboats ready," said Raphe with a slap of his knee. "Make sure we're properly supplied. Not that we'll need much. Should be back before sunset. What's that? Torches?"

"I didn't—"

"No, no. Shouldn't need any," he continued. "Plenty of natural fissures in the caverns..."

The man walked off, and I frowned to myself. As much faith as I put in my old friend, I couldn't ignore his growing dementia, which of course threw all his suppositions and indeed his entire story regarding the Ilha dos Ventos into a state of suspicion. If not for the unexplainable tendencies of the weather, I would've thought him completely mad.

I caught sight of Captain Handy, glaring at me from near the helm. Like Raphe, she'd barely uttered a word to me over the past day and a half—choosing instead to express herself with her scowls—but for different reasons. I think the woman had about had her fill of the supernatural and was eager for her coin.

I couldn't blame her. I, too, itched for a return to normalcy. A return to solid ground and promises of dry clothes. A return to days spent lazing in the shade of the bobwoods that ringed my bungalow outside Soledad. And a return to sleeping in my own bed, in the privacy of my own quarters, with Gwen's warm, barely clothed form at my side.

Gwen must've read my mind. She appeared and sidled up next to me, though instead of making an amorous advance, she propped her back against the *Pink's* railing, crossed her arms, and stared at Raphe with furrowed brows.

"You know," she said. "Despite every obstacle we've encountered and every dangerous situation we've found ourselves in over the past week—pistol fights, violent storms, Indian attacks, imprisonment—I've never suffered a real sense of foreboding until now."

"Related to your abilities, do you think?" I asked.

Gwen shook her head. "Just an unfounded sensation, I'm afraid. I'm not sure if it's because I don't know the man as well as you do, but I fear perhaps the Badger has contracted rabies."

I gave my wife a sidelong glance. "Jokes? Now?"

She shrugged. "What can I say? I'm trying to lighten the mood. Perhaps banish my own eerie presentiment."

I snorted as I watched Handy's men hoist one of the cockboats with a pulley system set at the ship's side. "So have you given any more thought to our discussion last night?"

"Regarding the degree of deadness of the *Mast's* crew?" asked Gwen.

I chuckled. "That's one way to put it."

She shrugged. "I'm a firm believer in the idea that anything is possible, however improbable. So why couldn't they all be apparitions? Although it does throw their motives into question."

"Because ghosts are inherently deceitful?"

"Because the dead crave different things than the living," said Gwen.

"So you think Raphe is right to return the conch, then?" I asked.

My wife shrugged. "I'm not sure I believe he's of sound enough mind to know right from wrong, at the moment. And *why* he isn't should be of concern to us."

The cockboat splashed into the shallow waters below, and Handy's men called for the next boat.

"So," I said. "Am I to assume you'll be joining us on this expedition as well?"

Gwen snorted. "Do you have to ask?"

"Just checking," I said. "But on the bright side, I don't see what pitfalls could await us on an island such as this. Unless we succumb to the sun's heat or get attacked a herd of ravenous lizards."

Gwen sniffed in response, and I could understand her apprehension. Especially since, despite the brilliant, clear blue skies, in the far distance, I thought I could make out a hint of gray floating above the horizon.

33

I followed Raphe as he chopped his way through the underbrush, machete in hand. Sweat dripped from my brow. Above me, macaws screeched in sharp grating yells, and in the distance, I heard the high-pitched shrieks of the spider monkeys, no doubt frightened by our presence. Leaves and rotted wood squelched underfoot as we walked, releasing their earthy scents of decay into the air.

Beside me, Gwen's thin dress clung to her frame like a limp rag. She'd pinned her hair up, but the portions that had extricated themselves from her bun stuck to the side of her neck, plastered with sweat. She flicked a damp strand away from her face with her hand, only for it to fall right back into place.

"How much farther do we have to go, Raphe?" she asked.

The Badger's machete cut through a low-hanging bough with a hearty thwack. "Not far. Not far at all..."

I swatted at a winged insect roughly the size of my fist as it buzzed in front of me. "You know Raphe, you've never explained how you found your way to these caverns in the first place. The ones where you found that conch of yours."

"Simple," he said. "The caverns are at the center of the isle. From there, I merely followed... I followed..."

His voice trailed off, swallowed by the whack of his machete as it dismembered another leafy limb.

I frowned and glanced at Tom, who brought up the rear alongside Handy and a quartet of her men, all of them heavily armed with muskets, pistols, and blunderbusses, including the scarred, bearded fellow who'd I'd finally learned was named Pyeter. Tom shrugged in response to my glance, as if to say he didn't know what to make of Raphe's mutterings. Handy, however, shook her head and glared at me—*again*.

I'd started to find her sour routine wearing. "Don't give me that," I said. "You didn't have to come."

"And let you die out here on your own?" she said. "Then who'd pay my debt? You don't have any wealthy next of kin, do you?"

I snorted. I'd grown weary of that particular explanation, as well. While I certainly believed in her wealth-driven motivations—the woman was a pirate, for God's sake—I felt there was more to her constant hovering. Perhaps, as charges of her vessel, she felt a responsibility to keep us safe, as she would with any of her men. Certainly, she berated us as frequently as she did them. But perhaps there was more to it. She'd only grudgingly joined us on the expedition into the Ilha dos

Ventos, and only at the last minute, as Tom had settled himself into the second cockboat...

The screech of the macaws set my jaw on edge, and I swore under my breath.

An ear-splitting blast cleaved the air. I jumped a vertical foot as the shot rattled the leaves overhead, scattering the birds.

I turned to find Pyeter lowering his blunderbuss.

"What in the world is wrong with you?" I asked.

"Damn macaws," he said. "They're grim portents, they are. Scatter 'em all to Hell, I say."

I very much doubted the man's superstitions, but I didn't get a chance to dispute them, as Raphe's machete sliced through another branch. "Ah. Here we are."

I stepped forth through the gap in the foliage created by Raphe's handiwork and gazed on a small clearing. A hole yawned in the earth like the mouth of a giant beast, ringed by stone teeth worn smooth by millennia of winds and rain and covered with moss and lichens and the light green leaves of eager young trees. It progressed into the earth at a shallow angle, and at its center ran a rivulet, carrying barely enough water to fill a man's canteen.

"Yes. *Yes,* this is it," said Raphe. "Come on, now! Don't dawdle."

The man took off into the caverns at a jog, forcing the rest of us to follow. For a while the path stretched forward as straight as a musket ball's flight, but eventually it curved as it followed the whims of the tiny rivulet, first to the left, then to the right. The cavern stretched higher and higher above us the further we traveled, but after the distance between my head and the cave's ceiling reached the height of a flag flown at half mast, the slope's incline flattened.

True to Raphe's word, we found ourselves without need of torches, as narrow fissures in the rock above allowed light to filter in and bring life to the cave's interior. Long clubs of rock, shaped like icicles, hung from the surface above, occasionally depositing drops onto our heads or into pools of standing water. Deep blue light shimmered across the walls and floor, giving them the illusion of movement where there was none, except for the scurrying of blind, white geckos as they fled our path.

"Beautiful, no?"

"That it is," I agreed over my shoulder. "In a chilling sort of way."

"Pardon?" said Gwen.

"Just agreeing," I said. "Regarding the beauty of the caves."

Gwen glanced at me curiously, and I in turn glanced at the pirates. Which of them had spoken? The burly one on the far left?

Raphe increased his pace, stomping in puddles as he pushed his way through the sand and silt. "We're nearly there. Very close now. We've almost reached the end."

"Ah, but the end of what?"

"Excuse me?" I said.

I glanced at the pirates again. The voice had been the same as before, but now that I heard it again, I realized I didn't recognize it. In fact, while I grasped what the voice had said, I wasn't sure I comprehended the individual words—almost as if they'd been spoken in a different language, albeit one I intrinsically understood.

I caught Tom glancing over his shoulder. I opened my mouth to ask if he'd heard the same comment as me, but Raphe interrupted me.

"Here we are!"

He rushed forth to a small rise—no more than a foot high in elevation—that was bathed in the glow of a filtered stream of green and yellow sunshine from above. On top of the rise was a pile of rocks, shaped like a cairn, with large, oval-shaped ones set at the bottom and smaller, rounder ones near the top.

With fumbling hands, Raphe drew open his satchel, removed the conch, and set it upon the top of the heap. Then he stepped back, put his hands at the sides of his head, and held his breath.

We all did, though in anticipation of what, I wasn't sure. Silence filled the air, punctuated only by the rhythmic *plunk plunk* of water droplets cascading from the stalactites above.

Of course it was Captain Handy who broke the reverie. "Well? Is that it? Are we done here?"

Raphe blinked, then laughed—a full-bellied, joyous laugh I realized I hadn't heard from him in all the time since we'd chanced upon him in Tortuga. He grasped me by my shoulders, his eyes clear and a smile on his face. "Haha! Yes! We're done. We must be, for I feel wonderful! Oh, what a weight to be lifted from my shoulders! What a relief to have that infernal voice gone."

"Voice?" I asked.

I heard a clack of wood on stone, one I knew to be real because every man and woman in our party turned to face it. Out of the shadows, beyond the far side of the stone pile, emerged an old man, bent over and grasping a smooth staff made of a dark hardwood. He wore a tattered set of rags over his loins, and clusters of wrinkles crowded his forehead, cheeks, and mouth. His skin was dusky like that of the Taíno, but there was crusty, chalky quality to it—not the spotted skin of the elderly, but more as if he'd fought a losing battle with a fixture of acorn barnacles.

He moved slowly, dragging himself forward step by step with the aid of his staff, and I noticed he left behind him a trail. Footprints, but slimy, like mucous. With his free hand, he reached out and lifted the conch, and when he spoke, he did so in a now familiar yet still somehow foreign voice, one stronger than I would've guessed possible for a man his age.

"Done? No, not done, I think. Just beginning, once more."

We all stood there, entranced, and I was certain every once of us had processed his strange words. The pirates had leveled their weapons but otherwise stood transfixed.

"You..." Raphe's face twitched. "You're a man? I thought...the conch..."

"Not a man, no. But thankful. For your thoughts. So easily influenced."

In a moment of clarity, I understood Raphe's growing madness. The skittishness, the wild, confused glances, the moments spent talking to himself in secluded corners—or rather, not to himself. To the conch. To this man, whoever he was.

I glanced at Gwen, and based on the look of dismay upon her face, I could tell we were in agreement about the old codger. Though we'd both been fooled before, what were the chances such a man, at his advanced years, would live on his own, in the depths of a damp cave, on an uninhabited island, and next to a stone cairn, of all places?

"John," she whispered, her voice halting.

"Who are you?" asked Raphe. "What do you want?"

The hunched man drew his thumb across the surface of the conch. "I? I am called by many names. Zemí to some. Yocajú to most."

Yocajú? That name seemed familiar. Where had I heard it? Was it the Taíno girl perhaps, the mestiza? Hadn't she used that name in appeal, as if to a...*deity?*

The man closed his eyes, a crusty, white powder falling from his eyelids as he did so, and took a deep breath. When he released it, the breath came not from his lips, but as a gust of wind, pushing free from the mouth of the conch.

"*John...*" said Gwen again.

"What do you want?" said Raphe. "I did as you asked. I brought back the conch. Now leave me alone!"

"Brought it, yes," said the old man, his eyes still closed. "And I am thankful. But there is...*more.* I feel strong. Full. Not since the spiteful blow dealt to me from the treacherous hand of Guabancex have I felt so complete. Could it be? Did you bring me—" He opened his eyes and stared right at Gwen. "—an *opia ahiyaka?*"

The last of the spirit's words didn't translate in my mind as did the rest, but they didn't need to. The hunger and desire in the man's—creature's? god's?—eyes as he gazed upon my beloved spoke volumes.

"Run!" I yelled.

I intended the command for my bride, but everyone except Raphe obeyed me. I grabbed Gwen's arm and turned, racing past the white-faced pirates whose feet obeyed them slower than my own. Captain Handy led the retreat, leading Tom as I led Gwen, but barely had we taken a half-dozen steps in the opposite direction of the god spirit before the very fabric of reality around us *shifted*.

The air thickened around us, congealing in invisible form, so that it felt as if instead of running we swam. I fought against it, step by painful step, but with every foot gained against the god's form the air grew denser, until it felt as if I tried to push through molasses. It even stuck in my throat, and I gagged.

The spirit's laughter boomed in my mind, and I felt a tug at my legs.

I turned. Wind whipped around Yocajú's form, surrounding him with particles of sand and salt water from nearby pools. The gusts swirled around him, forming a cyclone that gyrated through the air before diving into the mouth of the conch he held above his head.

The wind currents grew stronger, grabbing me and pulling me toward him. The pirates shouted and cursed as the airy quagmire grabbed them and pulled them in, and Gwen screamed in pure terror. I dug my hands and feet into the sandy bottom of the cavern to slow my progress, but to no avail.

"Damn you to Hell!" yelled Raphe.

As the only man who'd not fled, Raphe threw himself at the spirit, but he passed straight through its deceptive form. Failing to grab him, he reached for the staff, but the winds surrounding Yocajú caught him and tossed him aside like a piece of chaff.

The spirit's laughter grew, filling my head to capacity with its evil mirth. Though the air thinned as we approached Yocajú, the strength of the winds increased, pulling us with unnatural force towards the sea snail's shell.

I stared at the mouth of the conch. Its wide pink ruffled edges looked like inviting lips, lips that stretched and pulled until they gaped so wide they filled my field of vision and threatened to swallow not only me but the entire cavern.

Gwen screamed, and a chill ran through my heart, momentarily breaking the conch's spell over me. Once again it appeared at normal size, though the winds still screamed toward it with greater and greater force. Next to me, Pyeter dug his hands further into the sandy floor, his blunderbuss slipping from his grip.

Yocajú's laughter dug into me like the cries of ten thousand angry macaws, but it was the look of terror and fear on Gwen's face that drove me to action.

I grit my teeth and ripped the blunderbuss from Pyeter's hands. I planted my feet, and with as much strength as I could muster, I launched myself toward the god spirit, giving in fully to the pull of the winds. I leveled the blunderbuss at his head.

"You cannot kill the dead, fool," I heard around his laughter.

I sailed through the air, nearing Yocajú.

"I know," I said.

I shifted the tip of the blunderbuss and fired into the conch.

34

Lead shot tore through the conch. Glistening pink shards flew into the air, a thousand tiny fragments. Again the air thickened, immeasurably so, arresting each and every fragment and catching me in mid air as solidly as if I'd been encased in stone. The winds around Yocajú froze, and for a fleeting instant, I feared we'd all be stuck there, immobile, doomed to an eternity caught in a moment in time.

Yocajú's form flickered and disappeared, and the point in space that had held the conch exploded.

A blast of wind threw me against the cavern floor, knocking the breath from my lungs, and a terrible, ear-splitting howl rushed by, carried along by the might of the explosion.

I blinked, dazed. A groan escaped my lips as I tried and failed to fill my lungs with air. The howl faded as it raced along the length of the cavern, but its departure gave my tired ears no respite, as a new sound—a fierce, grating rumble—rose up through the earth to greet me.

The ground began to shake, slowly at first but growing in strength. The sand at my back shifted, and droplets of water danced in previously still ponds. Bit of rock and dirt rained down on me from above. I heard a loud crack, and a stalactite as long as my arm splashed into a pool on the other side of the stone cairn.

Gwen cried out in fear, and I swiveled my head in her direction. I spotted her, struggling to regain her footing on the shifting sands. Not far from her, Tom knelt on all fours, his face ashen, though not as pale as those of the pirates who'd come along for the trip. Of our crew, only Captain Handy seemed to have kept a level head, channeling rage instead of fear.

"Get up you louts," she called. "It's an earthquake! We have to get above ground before this place caves in."

I stumbled to my feet. Though years of sailing had accustomed me to the rolling motion of decks underneath my feet, I'd never imagined having to use those same skills while on solid ground—not that there was anything solid about the sand underfoot. Slipping and swaying, I made my way to Gwen and helped her up, all while sharp cracks ricocheted overhead—the sounds of ten foot thick stone snapping like twigs under the quake's heel.

Gwen clutched my sleeve as she stood. "John...the conch... How did you know destroying it would banish the spirit?"

"I didn't," I said. "When I'm terrified, I get trigger happy. Apparently, as far as fear responses go, that's not such a bad one. Now, come on!"

Tom, Handy, and her crew had already begun to break for the exit—as best they could, given the continued shaking—so I grabbed Gwen by the arm and pulled her in that same direction.

She resisted. "But John... Raphe!"

I swore. "Damn! You're right. Where is he?"

I lurched in the direction I'd last seen him tossed by the god's winds, stumbling and splashing through pools of standing water that came to my knees, pools I swear hadn't been more than a few inches deep moments ago.

"Raphe? Raphe, where are you?" I called.

I spotted him on a mound of sand hidden in the cavern's gloom. He lay on his side, half submerged, but thankfully not his face.

I grabbed him by his shoulders and shook him. He didn't wake, which wasn't surprising once I gave it thought. How would my shaking rouse him if the earth's own convulsions couldn't do the same? Although, it seemed as if the ground's power had finally begun to expend itself, as the rattling in my bones had lessened to a mere jiggle.

I slapped my old friend. "Raphe! Wake up!"

His eyes snapped open, and he grabbed the front of my shirt in a death grip. "Driftwood? John? Is that you? My god, mate. Where are we? I've had the most horrible dream."

"Not a dream," I said. "Though I wish it were so. Can you walk? Or run? Running would be better, to be honest."

Gwen helped me drag the man to his feet, made possible only because the earth's rumbling had stopped. The gnashing of stone upon stone faded, leaving me with a lingering sense of dizziness and a headache, though the latter could've been due to the conch's explosion.

"Oh, thank God," said Gwen as the shaking finally ceased. "Let's get out of here!"

We ran after the rest of the crew, wading through water now thigh deep, but we'd only travelled a half-dozen paces before I heard the rushing. The sound was faint at first, but grew quickly before it was punctuated by a half-dozen cries.

"Johhhhhnnnnn!" Tom's voiced echoes across the cavern's walls toward us.

The waters at my feet churned.

Raphe realized what was happening about the same time I did. "Oh, for the love of Christ," he said. "I pass out for one minute..."

Waters surged out of the tunnel before us, knocking us from our feet and sweeping us back into the chamber where we'd found the ghost god. I vainly tried to grasp Gwen's hand before the waters swallowed me.

Darkness enveloped me as powerful currents spun me around and around. Something hard knocked me in the head—a branch, or perhaps the cavern wall—worsening my already limited sense of direction. I opened my eyes, ignoring the stinging of the salt water as I tried to orient myself. A faint hint of blue shone above me, so I kicked out with all my strength and reached for it.

My head burst above water, and I sucked in air.

"Gwen? Gwen!" I looked around frantically as I fought the currents to stay afloat.

A splash at my right. I turned to find Tom, gasping for breath.

"Gwen?" I asked "Where's Gwen?"

Tom shook his head.

Another couple splashes, Captain Handy and Pyeter, then another, Raphe, sputtering like a wet cat.

"Gwen!" I felt my heart constrict. I took another glance around the cave. She was nowhere to be seen.

I took a massive gulp of air and dove back underwater.

I could barely see in the gloom. Leaves and sand rushed by in the churning waters. Only in the rays of light could I see much of anything.

Then I spotted it. A flutter of cloth, near the cairn. I swam to it.

A branch almost large enough to qualify as its own tree pinned Gwen to the rocks. Gwen pushed at it vainly, a mask of fear and pain contorting her face.

I spun my body, pressed my feet against the rocks and my back against the trunk, and pushed.

It didn't move.

Gwen clawed my arm.

I pushed again. Still it didn't move.

Gwen's nails dug into me like knives, piercing through my flesh all the way into my heart.

I closed my eyes and pushed with every ounce of my being.

The tree gave—easily.

I opened my eyes to find Tom and Raphe both at my side, pushing alongside me. I wrapped my arms around Gwen, set my feet against the rocks, and launched myself toward the light.

We broke the surface, Gwen coughing and gasping and drawing ragged breaths. Her body hung limply in my arms, all her strength drained from trying to stay conscious. I held her—loosely, to allow her to breathe, fighting back the instincts that shouted at me to envelop her in a tight hug.

Tom and Raphe surfaced beside me. Raphe wiped his hair from his face, whereas Tom didn't suffer the same problem.

I blinked at the big man. "Tom...your hat? You lost it?"

"Bugger the hat," said Tom, rubbing a hand across his smooth crown. "How's Gwen?"

"I'm alive," she said, still gasping for breath. "Alive. And that's all that matters."

"Yes, but for how long?" Handy swam over to join us, along with three of her men. Where was the last one? I tried not to think about it.

I glanced around us. The waters in the chamber had risen precipitously, bringing us about two-thirds of the way to the cavern's ceiling—and submerging the tunnel through which we'd entered.

"The exit..." I said. "Can we still swim to it?"

Pyeter shook his head. "Not unless you can hold your breath as well as a seal. And even then, the current's too strong. Water's pouring in."

It was true. I'd felt it while freeing Gwen, even if the waters at the surface has started to calm.

"What in the world happened?" asked Tom.

"The earthquake must've split the rocks holding the ocean at bay," said Handy. "That or it lowered the elevation of the island somehow. Would've had to do it by several feet, though."

"So how do we get out?" asked Gwen, still breathing heavily.

No one spoke.

Eventually, Gwen answered her own question. "Oh... I see."

The waters continued to rise, bringing us with them toward the smooth, rocky ceiling. Sunlight streamed in through the gaps in the rock, some of which seemed wider than they'd been before the quake.

"No," I said, pointing up. "Those cracks. Specifically, that one over there. It might be big enough for some of us to get through."

"*Some* of us?" Gwen eyed the gap, perhaps three feet wide but only a foot across, at best. "But...what about Tom? He'd never fit through there. Or, anyone really, except maybe me and Handy."

The rock above approached as the waters still rose. I swallowed hard. "Gwen... It's the only way. Better two than none."

Even in the dim light and with hair drenched, I could see the tears sprout in her eyes. "John! Don't say that. There must be another way. There's always another way!"

"No," said Raphe. "Not always. Davy Jones awaits us all, and he'll only wait so long. Thought I'd outsmarted him for a while, but I guess not this time."

The gap in the stone was only about a body's length away now.

"Men, give me a boost," said Handy.

Pyeter and another man crossed their arms, and Handy used the makeshift bridge to launch herself up. With deft hands that spoke to her abilities as a sailor, she grasped a protruding edge of jagged stone and shimmied into the gap.

Tom swallowed, too, his face pale. "You're next, milady."

"What?" said Gwen. "No. No, I won't. Not without you, John. I'm not leaving you here!"

I tried to put on a brave face. "Come now, Gwen. Don't be silly. And think, it won't be so bad—not for you, of all people. Whatever happens to me, at least you'll be able to sail here on occasion to visit me. If you so desire, of course. I'll understand if you'd rather move on."

"No, John," said Gwen, tears streaming down her face. "Don't joke of that. I'm not losing someone else I care about. Not years before their time. Not you. Never you."

Handy slipped through the opening and hollered something at us I didn't catch.

"Go," I told Gwen. "Handy made it. Now's your chance."

"No," she said simply.

"Please," I said, hoping the strain in my heart wouldn't betray my voice.

"I refuse," she said. "If you die, then so shall I. At least I know we'll be together in death. Wherever it may take us."

Still the waters rose. I could've raised my hand and drawn it across the smooth rock, should I have wished it.

I sighed, my chest heavy and fear coursing through my veins, but at the same time with a sense of hope in my heart. "You're a fool, Gwen Malarkey."

"For following you here?" she said. "Undoubtedly."

She leaned forward and kissed me through her tears.

"You're both fools," said Raphe. "But at least you're fools in love."

I looked at Raphe, his eyes finally clear, and Tom, who sported a grim look on his face.

"Thank you," I said. "Both of you. For helping me save Gwen."

"You're welcome," said Tom. "Not that it matters, given the circumstances."

"It matters," I corrected him. "Every second spent with friends and loved ones matters, Tom."

He nodded, as did Raphe, and I grasped Gwen in my arms.

My head bumped against the rock. It wouldn't be long now. I held Gwen tighter.

Handy yelled something from above.

"What was that?" said Tom.

"I said get down!" cried Handy. "NOW!"

In my path toward resignation, I'd forgotten about the woman, but after my marriage to Gwen, I'd learned better than to argue against a lady's commands. I took a breath and dove, my hand clasped with Gwen's.

The chain shot ripped through the stone above with a deafening blast, sending rock shards spraying into the water. A dozen others pounded into the stone, shaking the cave and tearing new holes through the cavern walls.

I surfaced again, blinking in the bright light.

"Christ, Handy," called Raphe. "Some warning might've been nice. We could've been killed!"

She poked her head through the largest hole. "The irony of your complaint is astounding, given the alternative. Now quick, out! All of you. The whole island's going down."

Like sardines spilling out of a fisherman's net, we poured out of the cavern to solid ground—or so I expected, but Handy hadn't exaggerated. The entire Ilha had been reduced to a few sandy patches and a sea of trees submerged to the furthest reaches of their boughs.

Handy, grabbing a tree branch for support, helped us up. Not far in the distance, the *Tickled Pink* sailed through the trees, crunching through branches as she showed us her port side.

"Hope you've got enough energy left to swim," said the Captain. "I'm not sure if the *Pink* can get all the way here, though if we wait long enough, perhaps she will—at least at the rate this island is sinking. Now, let's move. And watch out for those spider monkeys. I don't think they're keen on drowning."

With the sun sinking low in the horizon, I laughed, loudly and fully. I can honestly say it's the first and only time I've ever done so while being threatened with rabies-laden monkey bites, but given our escape from certain death, I felt it was warranted.

35

Rum flowed freely aboard the decks of the *Pink*, spreading laughter and cheer and song through its sweet, golden spirits. A man had found a fiddle in the ship's hold, and through he didn't wield the thing with any great skill, his music helped the men keep time as they chanted along to the bawdy shanties. Lanterns burned brightly afore and aft, pushing back the night's darkness as we sailed south on swift currents.

I sat on a tackle crate away from the thickest of the celebration, watching everyone sing and dance, including Captain Handy. She'd relaxed her nighttime rules about sleep and drink in the aftermath of our escape from the Ilha dos Ventos's bowels.

And why wouldn't she? A bit of celebration was in order. After all, it wasn't every day a crew survived an encounter with a dead god that resulted in an entire island being swallowed by the sea.

I still had a hard time believing it. The isle had continued to sink as we'd swam back to the ship. Barely had we hoisted everyone to safety aboard the *Pink* than the last of it went under, which in turn created a vortex that tried to take us with it to the depths of the sea. It was only thanks to some keen sailing on the parts of Günther and the other men aboard the *Pink* that we stayed afloat in the island's wake.

Of course, celebration likely wasn't the *only* reason Handy had her men up. Following the ghostly supernatural debacle, she'd wanted to get us as far away from the site of the cursed isle's last gasp as quickly as possible, and given the winds had finally returned to their normal state, our sloop needed hands to guide her through the night.

Captain Handy's laugh drew my attention. She had her arm draped around Tom's shoulders, or at least as close as she could get given his height. I reminded myself to keep an eye on the big man. With as much rum as was being passed around, chances were Tom might engage in some manner of activity he might regret— though if I was right about Handy's intentions, he might not regret it at all.

Raphe waltzed by and slapped me on the shoulder. "John, mate. There you are. Been looking all over for you. Where've you been?"

"Right here on this crate," I said. "You didn't notice me?"

Raphe wobbled, a mostly empty bottle of rum clutched in his right hand. "Well...to be fair, it's a rather well-shadowed crate. A stealthy crate. An *obfuscrate*, if you will."

I chuckled. "Clearly you haven't had enough rum if you're able to engage in such manner of word play."

"Or perhaps I've had just enough," he said. "Languages never were my strong suit. At least not until the tender touch of toddy tickles my tongue. Hoo. See? I'm now a master of alliteration."

I shook my head, but I couldn't help but smile. Though Raphe's eyes were clouded, they were so from the strength of his drink, not from the ghostly touch of a long dead god passed into the mortal realm through a shell talisman. Though we hadn't talked much thanks to the celebration, I could tell his mind had returned to him fully—or at least it would once he'd sobered.

"Go on," I said. "Take your garrulous drunk speech elsewhere. Preferably where there's people who've yet to be impressed with your tales of adventure and debauchery."

Raphe adopted a shocked expression. "*What?* You mean you don't want to hear of my battle with the nine-tongued beast of Guadalupe? I've enriched the story since I last told it to you, you know. Has more wenches now."

"Off with you," I said. "You're almost out of rum."

That did the trick. Raphe glanced at his bottle and stumbled off in the direction of the party at the prow.

As he wandered off, I heard soft steps next to me and felt Gwen's tender arm drape across my back. She rested her hand upon my shoulders and extended a finger, which she used to play with the hair that dangled from the nape of my neck.

"Look at you," she said in a low voice made silky by drink. "Such a loner. Are you sure you left the *Black*

Mast of your own volition, or did the other pirates kick you off because you were such a stick in the mud?"

"It's not that I don't enjoy festivities," I said. "I'd just rather spend my time with people I care about. People like you."

Gwen snorted. "Only if they drop by mysteriously in the night and drape their arms across you, it would appear."

I gave her the fisheye. "I knew you'd be back. Didn't you go to relieve yourself?"

She pressed a finger to my lips. "Shh. Don't talk of that. It's not ladylike."

"I'm not a lady."

"Well, I am," said Gwen.

"Not like any lady I've ever met," I said.

"Damned right," she said. "And don't you forget it. Now kiss me."

She didn't give me much of a choice. She drew me in with her arm and pressed her lips against mine. Lips that were soft and warm and wet. Lips full of desire. Desire that had gone unmet in *far* too long.

I pulled back, drawing Gwen's scent into my lungs with a deep breath. Then, I glanced toward the prow, seeking out Captain Handy. I caught sight of her, drinking and laughing as she leaned against Tom.

Gwen turned my face back to her own with hands none too gentle. She gazed at me, staring into my eyes, her brows drawing together. "You're joking. You desire her...*over me?* And now of all times..."

"What?" I said, baffled. "No. You mistake my glance, dear. I was checking to make sure the captain was outside her cabin. She does have a real bed, you know. Not just a hammock."

"*Oh.*" Gwen puckered her lips and lifted her brows. "An illicit, clandestine meeting in the captain's quarters, then? Quite a precarious situation, I imagine. It could be dangerous if we were caught. I find that...*exciting.*" She slipped her hand under my shirt.

"Well, to be fair," I said, "it's not behavior that's completely out of line. Since the captain of a pirate vessel is elected democratically, their quarters are considered common ground for those who need it. So—"

"Shut up," said Gwen. "You're ruining the mood."

Gwen drew her hand down into my trousers and began to fondle me between the legs. I moaned.

I may be a bit of a fool, but I do usually know when to listen to my wife. I drew my fingers across my lips. "Lead the way my love."

36

We sailed on southeasterly winds throughout the night and well into the next day—or, at least, I gathered as much after talking to the ship's navigator upon waking. I missed the majority of the journey to a lengthy stretch of well deserved sleep.

As I broke my fast on another of the ship cook's pork and hot pepper dishes—apparently his specialty—I reflected on the perks of being a mere passenger of the *Tickled Pink* rather than a crewman, which allowed me to sleep off the effects of my rum instead of sweating it out toiling under a bosun's commands in the wee hours of the morning. And all thanks to the riches I'd acquired while pirating aboard the *Mast*. Though the gains might've been ill-gotten, they'd afforded me opportunities I'd never previously thought possible, even during my most optimistic days as a privateer. They'd allowed me to settle down to a life of modest luxury, and provide for Gwen, as well. Dear, sweet, *ravenous*

Gwen. I licked my spoon as I recalled our previous night's amorous activities.

Given what potentially awaited him on the other side, I wondered why Raphe hadn't given up the life long ago as I had. Was it because, as captain, he couldn't? Admittedly, the other members of the *Mast* had never approved of my departure, to put it mildly. Or was there another reason? Did the man simply love the thrill of piracy too much to leave it behind? Or had he blown the majority of his treasure on wenches and gambling and drink?

Regardless of the reason, it would be interesting to see what Raphe would do now that the *Black Mast* was no longer his to command. Assuming, of course, he survived the remainder of our journey.

And despite my relief at escaping the clutches of a long dead Taíno god and surviving the collapse of an entire Caribbean island, I had no delusions that our journey was, in fact, over.

I recalled very clearly Nicolas's instructions—to find Raphe, and bring him to them—accompanied by thinly veiled threats of violence and death should we fail to comply. Knowing the men involved, I knew such coercion wasn't idle chatter, and if anything, their deaths made the threats that much more terrifying, as though one might elude a mortal man in the furthest reaches of the earth, how could one possibly hope to escape the clutches of a ghost? For a few days or weeks, perhaps...but not forever.

I mulled over my options as the sun passed from one side of the *Pink's* mast to the other. Try as I might, I couldn't come up with a resolution to our problem that satisfied everyone involved, unless the crew of the *Mast* were willing to listen to reason, but I somehow doubted that. As the hours ticked by, I realized there was only one solution that would free Gwen and me from the burden of the ghosts' threats—and it wasn't one Raphe would be eager to partake in, to say the least.

I found Tom near the ship's prow and discussed my plans with him. Though he'd spent a few hours in Raphe's company over the last few days, and though I believed he tolerated him well enough, he didn't know the man as I did, and so he didn't share my emotional weaknesses. He'd put Gwen's and my safety above that of Raphe's and wouldn't be swayed by the man's pleas. If I told him to act, he would, and without question.

Though Tom wasn't happy with the situation, he agreed with me glumly, and should the situation unfold as I suspected it would, he'd do exactly as I'd asked.

So it was that with the sun heading toward the horizon, I found myself at the *Pink's* prow, on the starboard side, staring into the waves when I heard the lookout's cry.

"Land! Land!" he called.

As it always did, the cry brought a number of the crew to the ship's side, including Captain Handy.

She clapped me on the back as she approached. "Well, Driftwood, that'll be your home *isla*. Perdición. Which sounds like a horrible place to spend the rest of your days, if truth be told."

"It's a misnomer," I said. "The place is quite tranquil."

"I'll take your word for it," she said.

I rose an eyebrow. "So you won't be staying then?"

"Only as long as it takes you to unearth that hidden treasure of yours and pay me my debt," she said.

I snorted. "And here I thought you'd started to care about me and my friends. Or some of them, anyway."

"It's not that I don't care. It's that I'm a pirate. And gold *always* comes first. You, of all people, should understand that."

"I did, once upon a time," I said. "But priorities, like everything in life, have a way of changing."

Handy smiled. "You know, Driftwood. Don't take this the wrong way, but once I've taken my leave of you, I'll be glad if I never again see you until the end of my days."

"Given all that's happened in the week we've known each other," I said, "I don't blame you in the slightest."

Raphe stumbled up next to me and leaned against my side. "What's all this I hear about land?"

I glanced at him. Red cross-hatched marks stood out on his cheeks, and his hair stuck up on the side of his head at an awkward angle. He reeked of rum.

"Did you just wake up?" I asked.

"I had a bit to drink last night, mate," he said.

"*A bit?*" I lifted an eyebrow.

"Very well," he said. "A lot. And some early this morning as well. So where are we?"

"Almost home," I said. "For me, anyway. I'm not sure where you intend to go."

Raphe adopted a puzzled look, as if he hadn't thought of it, though to be fair I doubt he'd fully woken up yet.

Handy swore as she stared at the island through her spyglass. "God damn it, Driftwood. Trouble follows you like a bad stench, doesn't it?"

I took the spyglass from her hands and held it up to my eye. In Soledad's harbor sat a ship, and though I couldn't quite discern the color of her mast, I knew her profile like the back of my own hand. *The Black Mast.* Just as I'd expected.

"What is it?" said Raphe, taking the telescope from me in turn. He squawked and bobbled the thing, nearly dropping it. "God's breath! They're back!"

"You expected them to forget about you?" I asked.

"What?" said Raphe. "Well, no, mate. I mean, not exactly. It's that, well...when you destroyed the conch and banished that thing's spirit to the netherworld, I thought it might take the ghosts of the men of the *Black Mast* with it. Assuming you're right about them being dead and all."

I narrowed my eyes. Had Raphe forgotten everything I'd told him on our trip to the Ilha dos Ventos? Or had whatever spell the conch had cast upon him prevented him from fully coming to grips with the situation?

"No, Raphe," I said. "Whatever power that conch possessed, it doesn't control the veil between worlds. Don't your recall our conversation? The one I had with you about Gwen?"

He blinked, and his eyes widened. "Yes. Yes, I do remember. It's all your wife's fault, isn't it? We need to get away from here, as quickly as possible—or, I need to rather. Handy, go man the helm. John—sorry, mate, but we'll have to put you down in a cockboat. You and Gwen should be able to make it to shore from here, with the winds as they are."

Handy lifted an eyebrow. "Excuse me?"

I shook my head. "No, Raphe. It doesn't work like that. The veil thins in Gwen's presence, allowing her to speak to the dead and perhaps strengthening their aura in other ways, but ghosts roam among us even without her influence. Think about it, man. Gwen's been with us the whole time, and yet there sits the *Black Mast* at anchor. I've stood on her decks, and I can tell you she's as solid as ever. Her ghost crew sailed her there, just as they did when they sought me out the first time. If they can man a jib boom and draw rope across a block, then they can swing a cutlass or fire a pistol, even outside her presence. And they can find you, no matter where you go."

Raphe brought a hand up and drew it across his chin slowly, ending at his long, braided beard. "What are you saying, mate?"

I took a deep breath. "I'm saying you can't run from this problem, just as I can't. We have to face it, head on."

"And how do you propose we do that?" asked Raphe. "Do you have a clever plan hidden up your sleeves?"

I spotted Tom approaching Raphe from behind. He gave me a curt nod, and I acknowledged him. He knew what to do.

"Well, I don't know how clever it is," I said, biting my lip. "Actually, it's quite straightforward. Almost...obvious."

Raphe peered at me curiously. "John...what aren't you telling me?"

I looked him in the eye. "Raphe. I'm sorry, old friend. But there's really only one way."

I gave Tom the nod.

37

Captain Handy and her men swung the *Pink* around, to the east, then to the south, and finally back to the northwest, so we might approach Perdición in the shadow of the isle's mountains. As we approached the town of Soledad, I called for her to drop anchor. Once still, we lowered one of the ship's cockboats. One of Handy's men dropped into it to man the oars, followed by Gwen, who planted a long, slow kiss upon my lips before boarding. After our goodbye, the man set his shoulders to the oars, sending the vessel skimming along the waves toward town.

Gwen had fought me on the idea, of course, but I'd insisted that joining Raphe, Tom, and me aboard the *Black Mast* was far, far too dangerous. Not that it mattered to her. She'd raged, tossing insults and punches at me with equal amounts of enthusiasm, but as I'd explained the situation to her, she'd finally acquiesced, and not, I think, because of the danger involved. She knew what role she'd have to play, and that role couldn't be accomplished from the gently rocking decks of the *Mast*.

We waited in the shadow of the cliffs as night fell—for a full hour, as we'd agreed upon. Up in the mountains of Perdición, I spotted fog gathering among the dense green jungle foliage, at it had the night before we'd left, though it had yet to descend toward the level of the sea. If it was an omen, I prayed it was a good one—not that mysterious fog ever was.

Once we'd deemed enough time had passed, we sailed around Perdición's arms, into view of Soledad, and into her harbor, dropping anchor a few hundred yards from the still form of the *Black Mast*. As before, I saw no signs of men upon her, nor heard shouts or raucous laughter that might indicate their presence, but I knew they'd be there once we approached.

Under the light of the waning moon, Handy's men readied another cockboat. Tom boarded it first, leading Raphe, who was tightly bound in rope, by the arm. I followed. Handy nodded her head at me and gave me a perfunctory 'Good luck,' but that was the extent of her encouragement—though she did give Tom a more longing glance. They lowered us into the bay's still waters with a quiet splash, and Tom put his muscles to work manning the oars.

We traversed nearly a hundred yards of open water before Raphe spoke. "You're a bastard, mate."

"I learned from the best," I said, trying not to meet his eyes.

"A bastard and a liar, then," he said. "Admit it. You never thought that highly of me. Not when I was your captain, and not now. As if to think you could pull this off without me knowing. Without me catching wind of it."

"Should I gag him, John?" asked Tom, the oars splashing as he rowed.

"I don't know, Tom," I said, eyeing Raphe. "Should he?"

My once friend snorted in response, but he held his tongue.

We passed the rest of the distance to the *Mast* in uneasy silence. At least this time, with the fog holding in the mountains, we could see where we were going. Tom smoothly drew us against the *Mast's* hull, and I called up for a ladder. I heard the familiar coarse slip of rope on rope, and I ducked as a heavy set of rungs slapped against the ship's side. With me in front and Tom in the rear, we hoisted Raphe between us and set hands to the ladder, eventually managing to conquer it, though only through the aid of Raphe's unbound feet on the rungs.

Barely had we flopped onto the slick planks of the deck when I heard the familiar voice. "Ah, Driftwood. Zo good to zee you again."

I shivered and looked up. Nicolas loomed over me, wearing the exact same dark green coat and felt cavalier hat I'd seen him in before. Chinue stood at his side, bare-chested and arms crossed, flashing a sinister smile. Behind them, a good three score men fanned out across the *Mast's* main deck.

Raphe rolled into a sitting position and flipped his hair back. "Ah, Nicolas. Chinue. So good to see you, mates. You're looking hale and hearty as ever, I see. Pardon me for not shaking your hands, but my current condition makes that a bit of an impossibility—as does your own condition, I imagine."

"Evah da jokester," said Chinue in his thick pidgin. "Even when facin' death in da eye."

"Well, it's better than the alternative, isn't it, mate?" asked Raphe. "And that's not a rhetorical question. I assume you know. Except for the fact that you've never cracked a joke in your life."

Nicolas gestured with his fingers, and Tom and I stood, dragging Raphe to his feet alongside us.

"Zo," said Nicolas, drawing his thumb and index finger along his moustache. "I zee you have brought me ze one, ze only, Raphe Bartholomew. I have to admits, I did not zink you would be zis successful, Driftwood. Alzough, ze question remains: does ze *capitaine* bring wiz him zat which we discussed?" Nicolas's eyes twinkled hungrily.

"That wasn't part of our deal," I said. "You asked me only to return Raphe to you. This business of his stolen treasure is between you and him."

"Not true," said Raphe. "John's the one who destroyed the conch. He shot it with a blunderbuss. It's his fault I don't have it any more."

"Please," I said. "You're the one who insisted we return that thing to the Ilha dos Ventos in the first place."

"Something you clearly should've talked me out of," said Raphe, "as I was addled by that cursed god spirit's earthly influence at the time."

Nicolas narrowed his eyes and looked at Chinue. "Conch?"

"One of dose shells wit da pointy end," said the lean black.

"Yes, I know what eet iz," said Nicolas, turning back to us. "Ze question iz what zat has to do wiz our request?"

"The conch," said Raphe. "It controlled the winds— at least in theory. Isn't that the treasure you desired?"

Nicolas and Chinue looked at each other, puzzled. After a pause, they smiled and guffawed, which in turn drew a peal of laughter from the men.

"No, Raphe," said Nicolas as his mirth died. "Zat was always ze object of your *amour*, not ours."

"So what is it you wish, then?" I asked. "You said you desired his treasure."

"Not *his* treasah," said Chinue, "but da treasah dat he done strip from us by da action he take. His rash behavyah dat take someting very special from all of us. Da treasah...*of ouah lives*."

Raphe blinked. "You...want me to bring you back from the dead?"

Nicolas shrugged. "It would be nice, *non?*"

"I... But..." Raphe sputtered.

"Nice, perhaps," I interjected. "But such a thing's simply not possible. Trust me, my marital situation affords me more knowledge in that matter than most. Never in all my travels have I heard even an inkling that such a thing might be feasible, and if the fallen form of a Taíno god cannot even resurrect himself, I don't know how a mortal man could do the same for all of you."

A wicked grin split Nicolas's lips. "Ah, well. We did not really zink zat such a thing was *possible*, which is why we never demanded it of you, Driftwood. We only wanted Raphe, who you brought to us. Zo, as far as I am concerned, our *accord*, should we zay, is complete. But—" He eyed Raphe. "—zat is not true of you, Raphe Bartholomew. You must bear ze judgment of ze men for your actions zat led us to ze Ilha. And we have already cast a vote, have we not?"

The men erupted in a chorus of 'Aye's and 'Yea's.

Raphe swallowed, his face drawn. "Yes?"

Nicolas's smile widened. "Ze vote was *unanime*. You must remain as *capitaine* of ze *Mast*."

"Oh, good," said Raphe. "For a moment, I was concerned you might wish to inflict harm upon me of some sort."

"No moah jokes," said Chinue.

The black snapped his fingers, and a large, barrel-chested man with golden hoop earrings stepped forth. In his hands he held a piece of chain shot that had been attached to a set of thick, iron shackles.

"Would you care to do ze honors, Driftwood?" asked Nicolas.

I nodded to Tom, who took the heavy set of leg irons and began to attach them to Raphe's ankles.

Raphe looked at me, a mixture of anger, contempt, and even sadness in his eyes. "Really, mate? After all we've been through? After all our adventures? After I broke you out of prison? After I helped save your wife from certain death just yesterday? This is what it comes to?"

I averted my eyes. "What would you have me do, Raphe? You think I can fight off an entire crew of undead on my own? Or that you could, if we released you from your bonds? This needs to end. I need it to. For me, and for Gwen. I'm sorry. But it's the only way."

Tom finished with the shackles and stood, nodding at Nicolas.

Raphe twisted his lips, and I feared he might spit at me. "You're a coward, mate. A gutless scoundrel! I've met adulterers with more honor than you, war criminals with more compassion, and...and...latrines with a less foul stench!"

Nicolas waved his hand, and the burly pirate unhooked a rope from across a gangway. Tom pushed Raphe toward the gap in the bulwark.

"Come now, Raphe," said Nicolas. "Do not blame Driftwood. You brought zis upon yourself. Zis iz but *justice* for your own actions zat led to ze demise of ze *Mast*."

"Justice?" said Raphe as he approached the ship's edge. "You call this *justice*? I had no idea traveling to the Ilha dos Ventos would result in all of your deaths. That was never my intention. No. This isn't justice. This is murder, plain and simple. Murder on the *Black Mast*."

Tom set Raphe's feet at the edge of the planks.

"Zo, zen?" said Nicolas. "Will you meet your fate of your own free will, or must we coerce you?"

Raphe glanced at the dark waters at his back, his face pale in the moonlight. His breathing quickened. He turned his head back to us, his eyes wide.

"Please," he said, in a voice finally free from anger and jocularity. "I beg you. Let's talk this through. You can have a revote. There must be some other solution."

"*Non*," said Nicolas. "Ze will of ze crew iz what eet iz."

Raphe turned his eyes on me, and I made the mistake of looking into them. Fear filled them, as well as horror and pain, likely from the loss of one he considered a friend, even if the fates had conspired to draw us apart over the past few years. They begged me for mercy, for forgiveness...*for action.*

I spun and swiped at Nicolas. My fingers passed through his ghostly form, but they closed upon the solid wooden hilt that hung at the side of his belt. In one smooth motion, I drew his pistol and fired.

Raphe flew back into the bay's waters with a cry and a splash, pushed back by the force of the pistol shot.

"Now why in ze world would you do zat?" asked Nicolas.

The pistol thumped to the ground as I released it from my grip. "I couldn't stand to stare into his eyes any longer. And perhaps the shot will lessen his misery. Kill him a little faster than the waters alone would."

I approached the gangway and stared at the sea. The ripples from Raphe's entrance into the water were quickly swallowed by the waves.

The skin on my arms prickled as I felt Nicolas and Chinue approach me from behind. They, too, looked down into the ocean. After a moment, a few bubbles surfaced, but then nothing. The wind creaked the *Mast's* timbers, and waves lapped at her hull, as if eager for more blood. Not a man said a word. We watched, and waited.

"You bastard."

I turned at the sound of the voice. The men of the *Mast* parted, and through them, on the other side of the ship, stood a familiar figure with a bright red bandana, blonde and black hair that framed his face, and a long braided beard. He stood with his hands on his hips and his feet spread wide—no longer shackled by the thick irons. And his clothes and hair alike were bone dry.

"You bastard," Raphe repeated. "You know, I really didn't think you'd do it. I thought for sure you'd have some plan to save me hidden up those billowing sleeves of yours. Goes to show they don't make friends the way they used to."

He walked forth, and I stepped forward to meet him. "Raphe? Are you truly...?"

I stretched out my hand, pausing as it approached him. Then I reached further, and his chest dissipated as my hand passed right through him.

"Yes, I'm dead, you fool," he said. "Now stop trying to touch me, mate. That's bloody disconcerting."

I blinked, knowing what would happen, but still not fully believing of it. "How...how was it?"

"Well, the transition is no fun, let me tell you," he said, waltzing over to the gangway. "But now that I've passed...well, it's not quite as bad as I thought it might be. I feel strangely...*at home*." He turned and flourished his hands. "I have to be honest, it feels good to be back on the *Black Mast*. And a captain, again, of a real ship. No offense, but that dinghy simply wasn't cutting it, and as irresistible as that Handy woman undoubtedly found me, I don't think she'd have been willing to hand her ship over to me. Not that I fancied captaining a ship by the name of the *Pink* anyway, but she could've been re-christened."

I took a deep breath and let it out though my mouth. So that was it. It was all finally over.

"Look, Raphe," I said. "I just wanted to say—"

He held up a hand. "Don't. I've no desire to hear your lies couched as apologies. The only thing I desire of you is to never see your treasonous, back-stabbing face again until the end of my days. And for you to get the Hell off my ship."

I glanced at Tom. He shrugged.

"NOW," said Raphe.

I took that for what it meant and dove over the side of the *Mast*.

38

Tom and I trudged up the shaded mountain path toward my bungalow, both of us still dripping wet from our impromptu swim to shore.

"They could've at least let us retrieve the rowboat," said Tom. "Bad form kicking us overboard."

"To be honest," I said, "I was just happy to get off that ship in one piece. I can live with a bit of seawater in my ears. And it's a fitting end to this mad quest, seeing as I've spent at least half of it sopping wet from either rains or rivers or the sea."

Tom grunted in response. "Still, if I'd had my hat..."

"Which you don't," I said.

"I know." Tom passed a hand over his short hair. "I'll have to see if I can find a suitable replacement in town. Otherwise I might have to take a day trip to Anguilla in search of one."

I snorted. "Well don't expect me to join you. I've had quite enough adventures to last me a few months, thank you very much."

We turned a corner, and up the path a ways, I spotted my home. Moonlight filtered through the trees, illuminating it, while yellowy-orange light of a decidedly more man-made origin shone through the windows. I breathed a sigh of relief.

I clapped Tom on the back. "Come on, big fellow. We're almost there."

I traversed up the rest of the path with a bit of pep in my step. Once I arrived, I pressed my hand against the front door and pushed.

Inside our living room, I spotted Gwen in all her resplendent glory, seated by a roaring fire. On the other side of the hearth, with his boots off and drying his feet by the flames, sat a decidedly damp-looking Raphe.

"Hey, old chum," I said. "How's it feel to be dead?"

"Feels a lot like getting half-drowned and almost shot," he said with an unmistakable amount of sarcasm. "Honestly, do you see this on my cheek? That's powder burn, mate."

"Oh, come off it," I said. "I wasn't that close, with either the shot or the pistol's barrel. And I thought you'd like that piece of flair. I thought it added credibility to the show."

Raphe ignored me. "And my feet are killing me, mate. Why you let this lout with hands the size of skillets manhandle my ankles when you could've done it is beyond me."

Tom snorted. "Don't be a baby. I didn't even lock the manacles, and I sure as...well, sure as something that rhymes with 'hit' didn't scrape you or your precious boots."

"And don't even think to complain about how far you had to swim," I said. "Certainly not considering what Tom and I just went through. Given that we were able to speak with Nicolas and Chinue without issue, I'm guessing Gwen wasn't more than, what? A couple hundred yards away in the cockboat?"

Gwen nodded and shrugged. "Thereabouts."

Raphe frowned. He removed his bandana and hung it up next to the mantle to dry. "Well, I can see I won't be getting any sympathy from you lot. You're like a pack of wolves, banding against me as you are."

"Well, we're not badgers, certainly." I crossed the room and sat beside my wife.

She tousled my hair and gave me a kiss. "You're drenched."

"I know," I said.

She shook her head, lips pursed, but I could tell she wasn't in a mood to be angry with me. "You know, most people would take that as an opportunity to explain what happened."

"We went for a swim," I said. "Apparently your father makes for a ruthless captain."

"Only because the situation demanded it, I'm sure," she said.

"So I take it he was amenable to your proposal?" I asked.

"Are you kidding?" said Gwen. "You know how much he idolized the pirate lifestyle. When I offered him the chance to continue his career as a thespian by taking on the role of the most infamous pirate in the Caribbean, he jumped at the notion."

"I think the word you were searching for was *famous*, not infamous," said Raphe.

"You know, he was actually quite familiar with you," said Gwen. "Had heard almost all your stories, and because of his fascination with the brethren, he claimed to remember them all, as well—which I'm sure will help strengthen his ruse. All I had to was explain to him your mannerisms and speech and he was ready to dive into the greatest performance of his life—or afterlife, as the case may be."

"Mannerisms?" said Raphe with a flick of his hand. "What mannerisms?"

Gwen glanced at me. "I don't think he sees it. Do you?"

I laughed as I saw the confused expression on Raphe's face. "No, not at all."

Raphe frowned again. "Seriously. No sympathy. No sympathy at all."

I put my arm around Gwen and caressed the portion of her back below her neck. "You know, I have to admit it's an extremely fortuitous coincidence your father was roughly the same height and build as Raphe, not to mention only a half-decade his senior at the time of his death. But I have to ask—how is it he was able to obtain a headpiece and cosmetics to make him look so convincing? I have a hard time believing they have wigmakers in the afterlife."

Gwen waggled a finger. "Not necessary. According to father, one's form in the netherworld is indistinct at best. Most ghosts appear to us in the form they took at their death because it's the most familiar, the most readily accessible. But form can be modified. It's purely a question of will, and I suppose my father, given his experience in the dramatics, found it rather simple."

Tom had seated himself across from us. "So...do you think he'll be able to keep up the ruse? In perpetuity, I mean."

"I don't see why not," said Gwen, "given his passion for the subject matter. I just hope he doesn't completely lose himself in it. That he doesn't forget...who he really is."

I stroked Gwen's hair. "He won't, Gwen. Forget you? How could he?"

Gwen's eyes glistened. "That's sweet of you to say, John."

"I say it because it's true," I said. "No one could forget you, not even in death. I couldn't if I tried."

Raphe stuck his tongue out to the side. "Ugh. Perhaps death *would've* been preferable to this. Now, enough with the syrupy sweet sentiments. Let's celebrate! Tom, can you show me where these two insufferable lovers keep the rum?"

Tom rose and took Raphe with him to the pantry. I took the opportunity to give Gwen another kiss.

"So," I said, after releasing her lips. "You're more experienced than I am with the duties of a graceful host. How long do we have to wait before tossing the two of them out the front door?"

Gwen ran her hand up my leg. "We'll give them an hour, or however long it takes them to drink themselves into a stupor. Whichever comes first. Then? You're all mine."

39

The hot Caribbean sun shone on my neck, lambasting me with its harsh tongue, and even the best efforts of the light-hungry *jabillos* and *manzanillas* that surrounded Perdición's graveyard couldn't save me from the blazing rays.

Gwen knelt a half-dozen paces in front of me at the foot of her father's gravestone. I'd expected her to open her heart to it, as she always did when we arrived at the site, but today she spoke not a word. I'd always thought it was her way of dealing with the loss of her father, but perhaps she'd only voiced her thoughts as a way to draw the man across the veil into the world of the living. Now there wasn't any need for that—not with her father sailing the seas in the company of the *Mast* and her crew.

A week had passed since we'd returned to the isle. I couldn't vouch to it myself, as I'd been busy sleeping— as well as engaging in certain *other* activities—but the villagers in Soledad claimed the *Black Mast* had sailed out of the harbor the same night we'd arrived, disappearing past the curve of the island's northwesternmost point.

Captain Handy and her crew came ashore the next morning, and although the people of Soledad were initially concerned by their presence, they soon welcomed them. Perhaps it was because I vouched for them or perhaps it was because they were captained by a woman, although I suspect the real reason the townsfolk ultimately embraced the pirates was because they freely spent the coin I provided them with.

Handy's first words to me that morning had been spent asking me for her payment, which I delivered—after trekking an hour into the jungle outside my home with a spade over my shoulder, digging up my treasure, taking what I needed, replacing the rest, and then stumbling, sweat-stained, back to town.

After a day and a night of drunken revelry, the crew of the *Pink* had set sail the following morning, taking Raphe with them. I'd thought the man might miss the ship's departure, sleeping through it in a drunken, rum-induced stupor, but Gwen put it upon herself to make *sure* he left aboard the ship. She even slipped Handy a few extra pieces of eight to ensure she'd take him. Gwen insisted she didn't dislike the man, but that didn't prevent her from treating him like the uncle no one ever wants to entertain for dinner.

I almost thought I'd lose Tom to the *Pink*, too, given what I'd observed between him and Handy, but when I pressed the man about it afterwards, he claimed their relationship wasn't what I thought. That Handy wasn't that sort of woman, and that their passions had burned too bright to be sustainable—which to me sounded as if Handy had decided Tom wasn't as good of a lover as she'd thought—but either way, I was glad to have Tom stay. I needed his companionship and his axe at my side—the latter of which he still hadn't replaced following our escape from prison.

He'd left for Anguilla this morning in search of a new one, as well as a new hat. I wondered if he'd come back with a facsimile of his old one or if he'd buck convention and try something new. Perhaps buy a bicorn hat, instead.

Gwen stood and brushed the dirt from her dress. When she turned to me, I noted a wet trail traversing her face from the corner of one eye to her cheek.

"Are you all right, my love?" I asked, extending my hands toward her.

She wiped the trail from her face with her thumb before taking my hands. "Yes. I'm fine."

"You miss him, don't you?" I asked.

She nodded. "Of course I do. I always will. But at the same time, I'm also finally, strangely, *at peace*. Knowing he's out there, sailing the warm Caribbean seas, creating mischief and reinventing himself in a role he only could've dreamed of? That plague of the lungs that killed him robbed him of so much, but in the end, it also afforded him a second chance. An opportunity he never would've otherwise gained."

"And with luck," I said, "he'll even be able to temper the crew of the *Mast* a bit. No offense to Raphe, but your father was a better man than he's ever been."

"No offense, taken," said Gwen with a smile.

"Who knows?" I said. "Perhaps he'll even forge a new legacy for the *Black Mast,* one that strikes a little less fear into people's hearts, and take part in his own adventures that get told around mugs of ale at firesides and tavern tables. His version of the Badger might become more famous than the real one, which would have the added benefit of driving Raphe absolutely crazy."

Gwen glanced back at her father's tomb, and when she turned back to me, her smile had widened. She almost glowed.

"What is it?" I asked.

"I don't know," said Gwen. "I feel as if...oh, how do I explain it? As if a small hole, one I've carried around inside me for quite some time, has finally been filled. It's glorious."

I stepped back and glanced at her warily. "Truly? A *hole*? As in the sort that can act as a conduit between worlds? Could it be your acceptance of your father's death has finally closed the veil that your childhood accident opened?"

Gwen punched me in the shoulder. "Don't be an idiot. I'm just getting emotional, that's all. Now let's get out of here before those other ghosts appear. You know they always make me uneasy."

I turned, and with Gwen's hand held in my own, headed for the graveyard's exit.

"You know," I said. "I'm glad we came here, despite my earlier misgivings. You found closure, even if it did result in a few tears along the way. See? Sometimes it's good to express one's emotions."

Gwen raised an eyebrow. "Are these sage words of advice really coming out of *your* mouth?"

"What?" I said. "Admittedly, I'm not the best at laying my heart bare for all to see, but it seems to work for you."

"Is this your way of telling me I should act more womanly?"

"Now, now," I said. "Don't distort my words. I'm more than glad you came with me on our journey, despite the impropriety of it all. I doubt I would've gotten through it without you, to be honest."

Gwen leaned in and kissed me, then I jumped as she pinched my bottom.

"Of course you wouldn't have gotten through it," said Gwen. "Because you're a fool, John Malarkey. Now why don't we get back to our bungalow so I can show you how womanly I can be?"

"Honestly, woman?" I said. "This is what you think about? When in a cemetery? And after mulling thoughts of your own father? I've said it before, but sometimes I think there's an aspect of you that's deeply disturbed."

"Too disturbed for you to want to make love to me?" asked Gwen.

I waggled a finger. "Again, stop putting words in my mouth. Now, let's go. Before one of us says anything else to kill the mood."

"You, most likely," said Gwen.

I nodded in agreement, and with Gwen's hand grasped tightly in my own, we headed down the hill toward our home.

ABOUT THE AUTHOR

Alex P. Berg is a mystery, fantasy, and science fiction author, a scientist, and a heavy metal aficionado. Connect with him at www.alexpberg.com. If you'd like to be notified when new books are released, please sign up for his mailing list on his website. You will only be contacted when new books come out, your address will never be shared, and you can unsubscribe at any time.

Word of mouth is critical to author success. If you enjoyed this novel, please consider leaving a positive review on Amazon. Even if it's only a line or two, it would be a *huge* help. Thanks!